ALL HER LIFE

ALL HER LIFE

Louise Pakeman

CHIVERS

British Library Cataloguing in Publication Data available

This Large Print edition published by AudioGo Ltd, Bath, 2011.
Published by arrangement with Robert Hale Ltd.

U.K. Hardcover ISBN 978 1 445 83686 7
U.K. Softcover ISBN 978 1 445 83687 4

Printed and bound in Great Britain by
MPG Books Group Limited

CHAPTER ONE

'No, Papa, I will not apologize.'

'I am afraid I insist, Eleanor.' At the use of her full name, Ella knew her father was seriously displeased, but she didn't care; she didn't consider she had done anything wrong. She tilted her chin defiantly. As father and daughter glared at each other, they looked remarkably alike though neither of them would be pleased to hear that. 'I have done nothing to apologize to Walter for.'

'You did not behave as a young lady of good breeding, an affianced young lady, should.'

'I did nothing wrong . . .' Stubbornly, Ella reiterated her innocence. 'I was at a ball and a gentleman asked me for a waltz. As Walter appeared to be otherwise engaged, I could see no harm in accepting. Surely one goes to a ball to dance?'

'When you are betrothed, you dance only with your fiancé, or gentlemen in your own circle, certainly not with unknown "persons" who have the effrontery to accost you and ask for a dance.'

Ella sighed. 'Papa, it is ridiculous to make such a fuss over one short dance. Walter, my betrothed fiancé, as you keep reminding me, is an indifferent dancer far more interested in speaking with you and his business friends than stepping out with me. And I do not need reminding that we are engaged. We have been now for four years which seems to me a long time to live in this nothing state.'

'What on earth are you talking about—nothing state?' Richard Wagstaff demanded testily. 'You can hardly describe being promised in marriage to one of—no, *the* most eligible bachelor in the district as a "nothing state".'

'I can and I do. As Walter's fiancée, I am no longer an unattached young woman, nor am I a married woman. What is more, I have been in this unenviable state for nearly four years which is a great deal too long. I am getting bored with both my situation and with Walter, which does not bode well for a happy union.' Until she said the words out loud, Ella had not realized just how bored she was with the estimable Walter Crutchley and, as if to remind her, she saw again the laughing brown eyes of the man who had, however briefly, rescued her from her boredom. 'To tell you the truth, Papa, I am not at all sure that I will marry Walter after all.'

For the briefest of moments, Richard looked truly shocked at his daughter's words, but of course she didn't mean it.

'Your betrothal is not a matter for levity.' His voice was curt. 'I am afraid you are a little overwrought, my dear. Get to bed and we will say no more on the matter.'

2

Eleanor sighed. She had not been joking—well, not completely—but she did wish her father would accept that she was no longer a child to be told what and when to do every little thing. 'Goodnight, Papa.' Her kiss on his cheek was feather light and with a whisk of the long skirt of her ball gown, she turned and made her way to her room.

As she prepared for bed, she wondered what demon had made her answer her father back as she had. The same one she supposed that had urged her to her dance with William Weston. She slid further down the bed and pulled the sheet higher as if by so doing she could delete the memory. But she could not forget that startling moment when she had looked across the ballroom and her eyes had met that hard, brilliant stare. Their glance had held and she had known in that instant not just that he would ask her to dance with him and that she would accept, but that he would in some way change her destiny. It was one of those startling moments of knowing that had come to her just a few times in her life; knowing that had always proved correct. By the time she was twelve years old, she had learned to keep her own counsel at such times; talking about her premonitions even when, or especially when, they were proved correct only brought ridicule, or worse, anger.

She could not see why the fact that she was usually right annoyed people. Instead of being

3

grateful for the warning, they looked on her as weird and seemed to think that because she had predicted an event, she had also made it happen. She certainly did not regret dancing with William (already she thought of him in this familiar way in her mind), but she was sorry that she had probably caused her gentle mother distress. Her father, she knew, would heap coals of fire on her defenceless head for allowing her daughter to behave in such an inappropriate manner. Sorry as she was, she had no real regrets, for dancing with William had been the most exciting thing to happen to her since Walter had proposed. After a few moments' reflection, she decided that it had eclipsed that proposal.

*   *   *

'Good morning, Papa,' Ella said to her father's back as she moved to the sideboard. She poured herself coffee, selected toast, butter and marmalade and took her place at the table.

Richard glanced up from his bacon and eggs as he grunted a barely audible 'Morning.' Ella would have assumed that he was still annoyed with her for the previous evening except that this was his normal morning greeting. Her mother was not at the table, but this was not unusual.

Richard finished his breakfast in silence,

4

snatched the white linen napkin away from his neck and flung it down on the table without bothering to fold it. He glared at Ella down the table as he pushed his chair back.

'When you have finished your breakfast, you had better go and attend to your mother. She is "indisposed" this morning. Your behaviour last night was upsetting.'

Ella thought that it was likely to be her father's reaction rather than her behaviour that had upset her mother. But she kept her thoughts strictly to herself, merely murmuring a meek, 'Yes, Papa,' as, without another word, he left the room.

'Ah, it is you, dear.' Lillian Wagstaff smiled at her daughter, her voice much stronger than the one she had used to say, 'Come in,' now that she could see who had tapped on her door.

'I thought it might be your father,' she explained hesitantly.

'No, Mama. He has already left for his office.'

The smile that passed between mother and daughter was one of understanding, almost conspiratorial. Lillian patted the bed. 'Tell me about the ball,' she invited.

Ella sat down, smiled at her mother and tilted her chin. 'I danced with someone other than Walter,' there was a ring of defiance in her voice, 'but of course Papa will already have told you that.'

5

'Indeed he has. I am afraid you have really annoyed him, Ella.' Lillian raised her eyes and smiled again at her daughter, and Ella knew that her mother had weathered the storm of her father's indignation and anger and that he had not won her sympathy. 'Especially as, according to him, you dared to be impertinent and argued with him.'

Oh, Mama, I didn't intend to be impertinent. I just pointed out to him that one went to a ball to dance and that as Walter quite obviously preferred talking business to taking the floor, I accepted an invitation to waltz from . . . someone else. Besides,' she added defiantly, 'poor Walter is really such a bad dancer and Will . . . Mr Weston is excellent.'

'I do not see that was such a terrible crime,' Lillian murmured, 'however, your father also told me that you spoke of your fiancé in a very disrespectful manner. That you even . . .' Here she lowered her voice until it was barely audible. 'That you even intimated that you were not sure you really wanted to marry Walter. Is that so, Ella?'

Ella looked down and missed the glint of humour in the grey eyes regarding her so closely. 'Well, yes, I did,' she admitted grudgingly. 'It is not that I dislike him, Mama. It's just that he is so very dull.'

'There are many worse vices in a husband, Ella, than mere dullness,' Lillian sighed. She

6

feared at times for this somewhat rebellious daughter of hers. It had been her own experience in life that a woman could often achieve more by quiescence than rebellion. Walter may not be the most exciting of suitors, but he was, she felt, safe. Probably a kind man, even a good man, but—yes—indubitably dull. She could not understand why he was dragging out this engagement; it was small wonder that Ella, never famed for patience, was getting restless. Maybe a change of scene would be a good thing; it might also prod Walter into action.

'Perhaps you would like a change, my dear?' she suggested gently.

'A change, mother?' Surely her mother could not mean that she change Walter for—well, someone else. William, for instance?

'A change of scene, a change of air, a little holiday.' Lillian smiled gently. She had watched the hope flit across Ella's pretty face and guessed the thought that had prompted it. 'Perhaps you would like to spend a short while with your Aunt May. You could,' she added pointedly, 'buy things for your trousseau. Your aunt has excellent taste and would so enjoy shopping with you. I am afraid it might be too tiring for me.'

Lillian determined that while Ella was away, it must be made clear to Walter that his affianced bride was getting restless—it behoved him to do something about it. The

7

wedding date must be fixed and if Richard would not speak to him then she would have to, well, hint at it at least.

'Do you really mean that, Mother, that I may stay with Aunt May and shop for . . . for my trousseau?' Ella clasped her hands together and gazed at her mother with shining eyes. May was her mother's much younger sister. She was married to a wealthy businessman and lived in London. Although she had three young children, she also had a house full of servants. Ella adored her and the visits she paid her were highlights in her existence.

Lillian nodded. 'I will write to her at once and arrange it,' she promised.

The affection between Ella and her young aunt was a two-way thing. In spite of Gordon's money and the servants it paid for to make her life easier, in spite of—or maybe because of—her three lively young children, May often found life restricting, almost boring. Her husband was a good deal older than herself and his friends, if possible, were even more staid than he was. Her mother had also recently sold up her own home and moved in with her younger daughter. May sometimes wished Gordon were not quite so kind and obliging, but it had actually been he who had made the suggestion that his mother-in-law make her home with them. May sometimes suspected that his motive was as a minder for

8

herself. It would be good for her to have Ella staying; she always enjoyed her visits. Not so very distant in age and very akin in spirit, they were more like sisters than aunt and niece. To be entrusted with the purchase of things for the younger woman's trousseau was likely to be an enormous pleasure as well as an honour.

Most of this she conveyed to her niece as she escorted her to the guest bedroom upon arrival. Ella looked round at the spacious, comfortably appointed room with delight. She clapped her hands lightly together and beamed at her aunt. 'Oh, Aunt May, this room is quite lovely. I am sure I shall never want to go home.'

May looked pleased. 'It has been decorated since you were here last, I am glad you like it. You must be tired after the journey. I will send a maid up with some hot water for you to refresh yourself and she can unpack for you. Would you like a rest, or would you prefer to come downstairs for afternoon tea?'

'Oh, come down, please. I am not at all tired, just a bit dusty from the journey.' Ella did not want to waste a moment of this precious visit in unnecessary resting. She almost protested that she could unpack for herself then thought better of it. May had so many servants she probably had difficulty finding enough for them to do. Thus, with her conscience salved, she left the young maid who brought her hot water, putting her clothes away in the huge oak wardrobe and tripped lightly downstairs to seek out her aunt.

Her spirits were only slightly dampened by the sight of her grandmother, dressed as always in black, sitting bolt upright in a straight-backed chair, her wrinkled and jewelled hand resting on the head of the silver-topped cane that she used more to attract attention, by banging it briskly on the floor, than to help her walk.

'Good afternoon, Eleanor.' Her eyes raked her granddaughter from head to toe and back again and she tilted her head in such a way that suggested, correctly, that she expected a dutiful peck on the cheek. 'So, your mother has sent you to us to get your trousseau, has she?'

Ella threw a glance at her aunt after dutifully performing the required salutation. At the thought of her grandmother helping purchase her trousseau, she had a wild vision of herself appearing at the altar in black, beneath which she wore depressingly plain and serviceable underclothes. May's warm smile was reassuring. In actual fact, Ella did not dislike her grandmother and was certainly not afraid of her as most of the family appeared to be. On the contrary, she rather enjoyed the old lady's acerbic tongue, especially when it was directed at someone else. Ella alone, of all the family, dared to answer her back, something her grandmother liked. She thought Ella had

10

spirit, a quality she felt sadly lacking in her daughters.

'Yes, Grandma. At least that is the reason she gave for allowing me to visit.'

The old lady gave a snort of appreciation, approval or merely agreement. Ella was not entirely sure which. 'And what other reason could she have, pray?'

'I don't know, Grandma,' Ella replied demurely, but when her eyes, too wide for total ignorance or innocence, met those of the old lady, a spark of mutual understanding flashed between them.

'Well, my girl, if you ask me, it is high time you were safely married.'

'Yes, Grandma,' Ella replied meekly to this enigmatic remark. Unconsciously she made a slight moue at the prospect of being safely married to the worthy Walter. Even shopping for a trousseau could not make it seem in the least exciting.

'Let us hope your parents will convince him that your engagement has lasted quite long enough.' She banged her stick on the floor so hard to lend emphasis that Ella actually jumped.

'Yes, quite long enough,' the old lady repeated. 'I can see that your nerves are playing up.'

'Yes, Grandma,' Ella answered absently only to jump again as once more the end of the stick hit the floor, even harder this time.

'Haven't you anything else to say but "Yes, Grandma"?'

As of course she had intended, this threw Ella into a quandary. Whether she said 'yes' or 'no' in reply, it was bound to be wrong. She kept silent but looked her grandmother squarely in the eye and smiled, she hoped beguilingly.

The old lady looked her up and down; Ella looked back. 'Your mother says you have annoyed your father by your behaviour at some ball or other. She did not think you had done anything so terrible and neither did I when she told me, but she did think that maybe it was time you were married. And so it is—that is, if you really want to marry that good but extremely dull man you have been engaged to for so long.'

Ella murmured another meek 'Yes, Grandma' while wondering whether she really did want to marry Walter. But of course she did; wasn't she here to buy her trousseau? That would be fun anyway.

'Oh, go away with you, girl!' The old lady's voice was tart, but there was a surprising look of concern on her face as she watched her favourite grandchild. For some reason, she was worried about her.

Ella and May set out the very next day on their buying spree. May instructed the children's nurse to meet them later on in the morning in Regent's Park and it was there that

Ella came face to face with William once more.

Her three young cousins were playing with a rather large, red ball and Jonathon, the eldest, brought it to Ella with a request that she play with him. She jumped up and for a few moments, they threw the ball happily to one another, then May called out something and Ella, distracted, threw the ball to the little boy rather too vigorously and somewhat wide of the mark.

'Oh!' she gasped in horror as she saw it fly over the head of a man sitting on a bench with his back to her, engrossed in his open paper. The ball landed fair and square in his lap and the paper flew out of his hand. He jumped to his feet and looked around to find the source of this missile.

Ella, afraid that Jonathon might be blamed, hurried forward to apologize. 'Oh!' she repeated. 'I am so sorry, I—I didn't mean . . .' her voice trailed away as she recognized the man staring at her. His angry stance had now changed to one of delighted surprise.

'Miss Wagstaff!' he exclaimed. 'What an extraordinary—what a very pleasant surprise!'

'Mr Weston!'

For a moment, they stared at one another in mutual astonishment. Ella dropped her gaze in a belated attempt to behave in a seemly fashion. She was all too aware of the warm colour flooding her throat and cheeks and was

13

sure that the frantic beating of her heart must be visible through her clothes. For a wild moment, she thought she might swoon in the finest tradition of fictitious heroines. But swooning was not Ella's style so she breathed deeply and slowly raised her eyes. He was still staring at her, his deep brown eyes almost as soulful as those of a spaniel, but their expression belied by the smile teasing the corners of his mouth.

'Miss Wagstaff,' he repeated, 'this is a truly delightful surprise. I heard you were staying with your aunt in London, but I did not expect, or even dare to hope, that I might have the pleasure of meeting up with you. May I . . .' His voice was hesitant. 'Would you allow me to walk with you?'

'But certainly, Mr Weston. I do apologize for—for the ball landing on you like that. It must have given you quite a shock.' She dimpled up at him, barely attempting to hide her amusement. 'I would be delighted to walk with you, just a little way, here in the park. I am with my aunt. It was my nephew who sent the ball flying into your lap.'

'As you say, quite a shock. But well worth it when I saw you.' He looked around for the aunt she mentioned and was surprised when a stylish and very young-looking woman approached them.

Ella introduced her. 'And this, Aunt May, is Mr Weston.'

14

May didn't need the meaningful look that Ella bestowed on her to know at once that this was the young man whom all the fuss was about. Meeting his warm smile and looking directly into those melting eyes, she understood her niece. Who in their right mind would want to marry the good and worthy Walter Crutchley when this man was expressing an interest.

'I am charmed to meet you, Mr Weston.' She half turned to Ella. 'I have to get back home with the children, but there is no need for you to hurry if—that is, if Mr Weston would be kind enough to escort you back to the house.'

And so Ella found herself alone with William Weston, walking first in the gardens and then demurely back to her brother-in-law's residence. By the time they arrived there, he had suggested another meeting and Ella had joyfully agreed.

That was how it began; innocently enough with a gentle walk in the park. But within a few weeks, Ella had returned Walter's ring and her father had come storming to London intent on bringing his daughter home. However, Walter, although he generously returned the ring to Ella, refused to renew the engagement and William found himself in honour bound, taking his place.

So the wedding plans went on, the trousseau was bought, albeit less extensive and splendid than originally planned as Richard drastically reduced the amount he was prepared to spend. In spite of this, William had high hopes that his father-in-law might see fit to set him up in some way. He did, but not quite as the young couple had envisioned. He paid their passage to Australia and settled enough money on his new son-in-law to set up in business.

Lillian wept copiously at the wedding then retired to her room. Aunt May put a good face on things though in truth she was more than a little dismayed at the turn of events and vowed never to meddle in other people's affairs again. Grandma told Ella sternly that now she had made her bed, she must lie on it, thinking even as she said it that maybe she should not have used that particular phrase under the circumstances. Ella floated through the wedding ceremony on a romantic cloud, only wishing as she and William headed for Southampton that someone had explained a little more about marriage to her; she knew she would be expected to share a bed with William from now on but had only the very haziest notion of what happened there.

CHAPTER TWO

Ella's romantic ideas of a long honeymoon cruising at sea were rudely dispelled by the time the ship left port. Their quarters, even though her father had generously paid for a cabin for them, were cramped and far from luxurious. She could not imagine how appalling it would have been if they had been forced to travel as so many emigrants did, the women in separate quarters to the men. Even so, she did wonder at times if it might be so much worse than being cooped up in such a small space with William who, truth to tell, by the time they had been at sea for a few weeks, she was finding almost as dull as the worthy Walter.

The trouble was that he took a great deal longer than she did to find his sea legs and, as ministering angel had never been her forte, she spent less and less time in the cabin, finding his moans and groans extremely tedious. Most of the other women had brought a lady's maid along with them and on making inquiries, she discovered that if she approached the woman in charge of the female emigrants, she might be able to find a young girl to help her in this capacity. She was lucky; a fifteen-year-old was travelling on her own and Rosie Malone was more than willing to spend her days in Ella's company and only have to return to the cramped women's quarters at night.

'Well, now that I am more accustomed to the motion of the ship and can keep you company, you can send that wench back,'

17

William told her some weeks into the voyage.

'But William, I need her,' Ella protested. 'She is a such a help to me.'

'Doing what?'

'Well . . .' Ella searched her mind to find words to convince him that Rosie was indispensable to her comfort. 'She fetches me things, helps me keep my clothes in order . . .' She had grown fond of the girl and would miss her company more than anything.

'Hrrumph,' William grunted; however, a glance at his pretty young wife who looked little older than her maid softened him. He reminded himself that it was thanks to her that he was on this ship at all with a new life ahead and his ever mounting debts behind him. Once he had recovered from the seasickness that had plagued him, and Ella from her hysterical reaction to his advances as a husband, they had settled down together well enough and he could, he knew, have done a great deal worse. If having a maid was what she wanted then have a maid she should. He smiled at Ella and patted her arm in a way that to her seemed more paternal than lover-like. 'Very well, my dear, the arrangement can stand for the time being.' It did, after all, give him more freedom to follow his own inclinations.

William had found a convivial group of young men around his own age who were heading for the diggings and it did not take them long to convince him that prospecting for

18

gold was by far the surest and swiftest way to come by wealth in the land they were heading for.

'But William,' Ella protested, 'the money Father settled on you was specifically to enable you to start up in business, not speculate.'

'Exactly, my dear, that is just what I plan to do—in the goldmining business.'

Ella was doubtful, but did not feel strong enough to argue. Curiously, now the voyage was nearly over, the tables seemed to have turned and William strode about the ship as if he had been at sea all his life while Ella was prostrate with nausea.

Curiosity prompted Ella to ask her young maid what was going to happen to her when the ship landed them at Melbourne.

'Me dad's meeting me. When my mam died, he sent the money for me to come, said he had been saving it to pay for her passage. Said now she was gone, I might as well come instead.'

It all sounded somewhat casual to Ella. 'I see,' she said thoughtfully, 'so you will have somewhere to go then?'

'Oh, yes. Dad will meet me off the ship, I'm sure.' Rosie's voice trailed away. Truthfully, she was not at all sure. From what she remembered of her father, he was more likely to break promises than keep them.

Ella considered her thoughtfully. 'Well, if anything happens and he doesn't turn up or you are left stranded . . . well, if anything like

19

that happens, you had better come to me.'

'Thank you, Ma'am, I will do so. Only thing is, how will I know how to find you?'

Ella found a scrap of paper in her reticule and quickly wrote out an address. 'This is a connection of my father,' she told the girl. 'We have to go to his offices. He promised my father he would find temporary accommodation for us and help my husband to set up in business. He will know where we are.' She gazed at the younger girl. 'Do you know, Rosie, I have become quite attached to you on this journey. In fact, I don't quite know how I shall manage without you. You couldn't . . . you wouldn't be able to . . . ?'

Rosie shook her head. 'I have to meet my dad. But don't you worry. You'll be all right, you've got a man to look after you.' She spoke with determined cheerfulness, wishing she had more than the hazy memory of the man she had last seen nearly ten years ago.

'All the same . . .' Ella's voice trailed away. What was she doing almost begging this young servant girl to stay with her? She tried to tell herself that it was concern for the girl's welfare. Well, so it was—just a little—but in all truth, it was herself she was thinking of. As the voyage had progressed, it seemed she had seen less and less of her husband and come to rely more and more on Rosie for companionship. Now, as the ship finally docked after a long and tedious journey, it struck her that she was

20

going to miss the girl's company as well as her help. She looked at her now, slight to the point of being scrawny, dressed in one of Ella's own gowns that she had decided was too warm for a hot climate; Rosie had spent painstaking hours with needle and thread making it fit. Ella, who had been brought up to take servants and what they did for her totally for granted, was surprised, almost dismayed, to find that she had come to rely on Rosie, even to be grateful to her. She had made the voyage bearable, if not exactly enjoyable.

As they said goodbye, Ella pressed five sovereigns into the girl's hand. 'Keep them safe until you really need them,' she urged. 'Remember, if your father—well, if anything goes wrong, go to the address I gave you and you will be able to find me.'

Ella turned away quickly to hide the sudden tears in her eyes, ashamed at this rush of emotion, and went in search of her husband, for in a very short time they would be disembarking. She wished she felt more enthusiasm, but all that filled her was a nameless terror of this new, strange land that already felt so different even before she descended the gangplank. Repressing such gloomy thoughts, she gathered up her hand luggage and followed William who was striding ahead of her with a confidence she could only envy.

CHAPTER THREE

'Go out?' Ella could barely open her eyes let alone lift her head from the pillow. Just getting off and away from the ship had been utterly exhausting, not to mention finding the office of the connection that her father had given them. Edwin Sanders had turned out to be a lawyer, to her surprise nearer William's age than that of her father.

'I have arranged accommodation for you in a lodging house . . .'

'A lodging house!' Ella had interrupted. 'Surely you mean a hotel. I am sure my father . . .'

'Your father specifically directed me to arrange accommodation for you in a lodging house,' Edwin in turn had cut her short. 'I can promise you it is both clean and comfortable.'

Now, lying on the bed in their room which was only slightly less cramped than their cabin on the ship, Ella conceded it was clean although not exactly what she would describe as comfortable. With an effort, she forced her eyes open and stared at William. 'I seriously doubt whether I have strength enough to get off this bed, let alone go out. What time do they serve dinner?'

'They don't. That is why we need to go out. I, for one, am extremely hungry.'

Ella sat up, shocked to discover that there was to be no meal laid on here and aware that she too was hungry, positively ravenous in fact. Breakfast, which she had skimped, seemed a lifetime ago and lunch had simply not existed as they had been struggling with all the hassles and formalities of getting themselves and their baggage off the ship. Faced with the alternatives of staying here and starving or getting up and accompanying William, Ella swung her feet off the bed and, with a muffled groan, stood up.

They walked in silence. The day was still warm and the air clung round them in a manner that Ella found both oppressive and enervating; however, it did nothing to lift her spirits and the crowded café William led her into, with a noisy fan moving air which seemed to her quite fetid, plummeted them even further. As she slumped down on a hard wooden chair, Ella decided she did not like Australia and resolved to return to England as soon as possible. William, to her surprise, seemed quite cheerful.

'Well, Ella, we are here in Australia—the promised land, land of opportunity.'

'Yes, we're here,' she responded in a dull voice, 'and I wish we weren't. I can't see much "promised land" about it.' She looked around the café. She had only seen such places from the outside before, but she supposed they did exist in England too.

By the time they had both downed a simple but more than welcome meal of fish and chips, Ella was feeling marginally more optimistic. 'What about opportunities, William? Did that lawyer fellow have something good lined up for you?'

William's face darkened. 'I'm not really sure. The money your father promised me to set up in business is with him. I can't say I am too happy about that. He will let me have it when I have a need for it—so he says.'

'That's all right, then. I am sure Father would not have put him in charge of our funds if he was not to be trusted.'

William glowered. He saw no reason why his father-in-law had not simply handed the funds over to him.

Overcome with a sudden lassitude, Ella yawned. William was all solicitude. 'You are tired, my dear. I will escort you back to our lodging.'

'Are you not coming to bed?' Ella was surprised to see her husband carefully combing his hair and adjusting his necktie.

'Not at this moment. I do not feel in the least tired. I think I shall go out and . . . explore the area.'

'But William!' Ella protested, wanting to tell him that she would appreciate his company in bed with her but unable to express her wish for lovemaking, feeling that well brought up young ladies, even married ones, did not admit even

24

to liking this side of marriage, let alone actually wanting it.

'I shall not be long, my dear.' Perfunctorily he bent down and kissed her on the forehead. He was already finding marriage restricting, but consoled himself with the thought that it was the means, the only means it had seemed at the time, to financial independence and an unloading of his debts.

Ella pouted. 'I shall try and stay awake for you.'

But of course she didn't. Within half an hour of William closing the door behind him, she was dead to the world. Not even his blundering about the room on his return roused her.

When she opened her eyes the next morning, he was still sleeping noisily, flat on his back, stentorian snores emitting at regular intervals. She raised herself on one elbow and looked at him with a newly critical eye. The well-dressed debonaire suitor who had won her heart surely could not have melted into this somewhat uncouth person sharing her bed, his outer clothes flung on the floor and him sleeping in his underwear. She sat up swiftly and almost immediately flopped back on the pillow as the room began to swim and she was engulfed in a wave of nausea. Surely seasickness was not going to continue plaguing her now she was on dry land?

After a few moments she tried again, much

more cautiously this time, and managed to reach the carafe of water on the stand on the other side of the room. She sipped it gratefully before sinking down into a chair, the only one in the room. She tipped water from the jug into the basin and splashed it over her face and, feeling somewhat revived, carefully and slowly began to dress herself. Breakfast, she remembered the landlady informing them, was served between seven and eight o'clock, and that was the only meal provided. It was already seven forty-five. She glanced at her husband, wondering which would annoy him most: being wakened or missing breakfast. Tentatively she shook his shoulder.

They reached the dreary dining room a few minutes before closure.

'You are late,' they were told sternly. 'However, as it is your first morning, I will overlook it.'

Ella refused the porridge; the mere sight of it caused a swift return of her nausea, but she drank two cups of strong tea with appreciation. It revived her enough to tackle a thick slice of bread and jam.

William ate a good breakfast, including a lavish helping of the nauseating porridge. Both were preoccupied with their own thoughts.

'You will be quite comfortable here.' William broke the silence between them.

'Yes, we will—for a short while until we find somewhere of our own to live.'

'Not "we". You, Ella. I am going to try my luck on the goldfields; it would not be suitable for you.'

'William!' Ella was aghast. 'You cannot just go and leave me here, alone in this strange place.'

'I have been talking to people and it seems there is money aplenty to be made at the diggings. But it is a rough life; I could not expect you to accompany me. I shall need to persuade that lawyer friend of your father to advance me the funds.' He spoke quite calmly, as if it were all settled.

'I am not staying here on my own. Either I come with you, or I shall talk to that Edwin Sanders myself and persuade him not to let you have the money you need.' Ella was aghast at the prospect of being left alone in this awful place while William went off goodness knows where for goodness knew how long.

William glanced at his wife, almost with distaste. He could imagine what a drag Ella would be. Adventure and fortune beckoned, and he intended to grab them with both hands. With Ella tagging along, he was sure he would miss out on both. 'We will go together and see him, my dear.' He was convinced the lawyer fellow would persuade Ella to remain in Melbourne. After all, he was, in a way, answerable to her father for her well-being.

By the time they set out for the lawyer's office, Ella was feeling much more like herself.

27

She had regained her land legs, a night's sleep and breakfast had restored her considerably and she had taken the trouble to dress herself in a becoming outfit.

William looked at her approvingly.

'You look very nice, my dear.'

Ella smiled, accepting the compliment as her due, suppressing her irritation at the faintly proprietary tone in his voice.

*　　*　　*

The quick flash of appreciation that crossed Edwin Sanders's features as he greeted them had no such undertones. Ella accepted his proffered hand and returned his smile. 'Good day, Mr Sanders.' Fleetingly, as their hands touched, she looked into his eyes, noting they were as blue as these antipodean skies. Her breath caught in a barely audible gasp, she freed her hand and turned away to the chair he was indicating to her. As she sat down, she was overcome by the sense of timelessness that usually accompanied her flashes of inner knowing, for in that brief moment when she had met his eyes, she knew with absolute certainty that she was going to see a lot more of Edwin Sanders. Uneasily she recalled feeling much the same the first time she met William. Well, she had been correct then, so why not now?

Determinedly, Ella focused her attention on

the conversation. William was leaning slightly forward, almost touching the desk between them in his anxiety to persuade Edwin Sanders to release sufficient money for him to journey to the goldfields and stake a claim.

The young lawyer frowned slightly, rolling his pen between his fingers, his thoughts busy as he listened. William had not made a good impression on him; he detected truculence beneath the surface charm. Richard Wagstaff and his father, George Sanders, had been close friends in their youth; they had even managed to keep in touch after George opted to try his luck in the colonies. Richard had been newly married and his bride did not want to leave her family and everything she knew. George married in Australia and decided to settle there. Though parted, the two men had kept up with each other as much as possible over the years. Richard had written to George that his headstrong daughter would not listen to his advice and he did not entirely trust his son-in-law which was why the money had not been handed over to him directly.

Unfortunately, a heart attack had carried George off while William and Ella were still on the high seas and Edwin had taken over

the responsibility of discharging his father's promise to his old friend.

Edwin sighed, wishing with all his heart he had not had this responsibility thrust upon him

29

as William expounded at length his need to get hold of at least some of the money held in trust. Edwin cast a covert glance at the lovely young woman opposite him; he hoped she would not have to pay too high a price for her defiance of her father.

'I do not think you fully understand, Mr Weston. Your father-in-law lodged sufficient funds with me to start you up in—er—some enterprise. I think he had farming in mind; land is cheap here—very cheap compared to England—and anyone prepared to work can do well.' He paused, trying to imagine William engaged in hard physical labour and wondered if he had the faintest idea what mining entailed. He imagined he would see looking for gold as just another form of gambling. Guessing that young Mrs Weston was unaware of her husband's gambling and the debts that had been paid off by her father, he said no more.

'That is what I told my husband,' Ella interjected. 'The money my father made available for us was to help us establish ourselves here in Australia.'

'Indeed it was,' Edwin Sanders agreed, smiling approval at her. 'You are, I hope, comfortable in the lodgings I arranged for you, Mrs Weston.'

Ella shrugged. 'Tolerably so. They are not, of course, quite what I am accustomed to and I am anxious to be settled in my own home as soon as is practically possible.'

'Quite so . . . quite so . . .' Edwin Sanders murmured, shooting a glance at William as he spoke. He observed the sullen look on his face with some satisfaction. 'If farming does not appeal to you then there are plenty of opportunities in trade. This is a developing country still.'

'Trade!' William spat the word as if it was an expletive. 'I think not. No, if I am to be denied the goldfields then farming it must be.' After all, he thought he would be a landowner and thus a gentleman.

Edwin ignored this outburst. 'Do you plan to stay in Melbourne? If you intend to farm then you would be better to move out of the city.' His voice was dry as he made this statement. Contact with William was rapidly confirming his opinion that the man was a fool. The sooner he discharged his obligations to him the better. He felt sorry for his young wife. If the fellow had been on his own, he might have suggested he would be better off in some far-flung place, a different state perhaps, but after all, it was because of her father's concern for her that he was in charge of the arrogant young fool's finances. 'The Bendigo area is fast developing and Bendigo itself is a pleasant and growing city; there has been a rail line from Melbourne for over forty years.'

William's interest was aroused, remembering things he had heard on the ship

31

from those returning to Australia after a trip home. 'Wine . . .' he reflected aloud. 'Yes, maybe I will take up winemaking. That would be a gentlemanly occupation and I understand there is profit there.'

Edwin smiled thinly and told him with some satisfaction, 'You are too late for that, I am afraid, by about ten years. You are correct in thinking that part of the country was renowned for its fine wines, but unfortunately the phylloxera virus hit the district around 1893 and decimated the industry. You would do better in sheep. That is, if you insist on trying your hand at farming. Why don't you find work on a sheep station for a while and learn the ropes?'

William would have none of this. 'I have not come out here to be another man's servant,' he said haughtily. 'I will travel up to this Bendigo place and have a look around and see how the area appeals to me.'

Both men turned to look at Ella as she interposed firmly.

'*We* will go, William.'

'Surely, my dear, it would be better for you to stay here in Melbourne and leave me to attend to this.'

'Certainly not. I too have to live there. And I think you have forgotten that the money you will be using comes from my father.' Her tone was cool, but a bright spot of colour burned in each cheek. Edwin noticed that she sat up a little straighter and there was a glint in her eye that suggested she might, after all, be able to make something of what he personally considered an unfortunate marriage.

'If you insist, my dear, but you may find the long journey tiring.'

'Indeed you might have done, Mrs Weston, had you been one of the early arrivals, but, as I have just pointed out, not today. The train line has been open since 1862 and changed a journey of many days to a few hours. You might even enjoy it.'

Ella smiled and inclined her head. 'I am sure I shall, Mr Sanders. It will be interesting to see some of the country.'

Edwin Sanders furnished them with recommendations to agents and also advised that they read *The Bendigo Advertiser*, established in 1853. 'The first newspaper on the Australian goldfields,' he told them with some pride.

It struck Ella that when young Mr Sanders spoke of Bendigo, there was a note in his voice that spoke of more than merely suggesting a good place to settle.

'Do you know Bendigo well?' she asked.

'Indeed I do. I was born there so it is my home town.' He smiled directly at Ella. 'I visit whenever I can.'

Ella smiled back, feeling that in him they had found a friend. 'Then I hope that we will see you when we are settled. Don't you,

William?'

'Eh—what's that?' William, studying a map of Bendigo and its environs, had missed this exchange.

Once again the briefest of smiles flashed between Ella and Edwin Sanders. 'Mr Sanders was born in Bendigo, William. So, I think we can be sure any advice he gives us will be of value.'

'Yes, yes indeed,' William agreed. Taking advice from anyone was not his strong suit. On the other hand, the fellow may have some useful connections.

CHAPTER FOUR

Three days later, Ella and William stepped down from the train at Bendigo. It was a hot day and Ella was indeed tired but already full of enthusiasm for the city. Small by English standards, it had been proclaimed a city in 1871 and already boasted some fine buildings thanks to the gold beneath and around it. Ella noticed there were plenty of shops; trams serviced the town and its immediate environs so it was easy to get about. William, ever the gambler, expressed his delight to find there was a long established racecourse. All in all, as they told each other, it seemed a very civilized place.

They had been in Bendigo just over a week and Ella was on her own. William had gone to look at a property north of the city, but Ella had opted to stay in bed. Having woken with a headache and nausea, she felt unequal to the trip in the summer heat which she was finding far more fierce than anything she had experienced before. Perhaps if she stayed in her bed for a while, the nausea that had assailed her would abate as the day wore on.

She was hurrying to the bathroom still in her nightclothes, a handkerchief pressed to her mouth, when she met the landlady who flattened herself against the wall as if afraid that Ella might throw up on her before she reached her destination. She was in their room looking severely at the disarray when Ella returned, whey-faced and thinking only of returning to her bed.

'I have come to inform you, Mrs Weston, that there is a person downstairs, a female person, asking to see you. I told her I must check with you first as she did not look the sort of young woman I would expect you to know.'

'Did she give her name?' Ella asked, suppressing a moan.

'She said it was Rosie Malone,' the woman answered with a sniff that suggested this to be an unlikely name, and if it was correct then it was certainly Irish and she, a staunch Calvinist, had no use for the Irish, their religion or their blarney.

35

Ella sat up only to subside again instantly with her damp handkerchief pressed to her head. 'Send her up to me—at once, please.'

Martha Thompson turned to the door where she paused, one hand on the knob, and gave another derogatory sniff. 'As you please. I must say she is not quite—well, not quite the sort of person I like to admit.' She paused long enough to let this sink in then added, 'I hope you find somewhere suitable soon, Mrs Weston. I am sure you understand that I do not usually accept ladies in your condition, but as you obviously have some time to go, I will say no more at the moment.' With a final sniff she was gone, leaving Ella wondering what on earth the woman was talking about.

'Rosie, how good to see you.' Ella's voice trailed off as she took in the girl's bedraggled appearance. 'Oh, Rosie, it is so good to see you,' she repeated, realizing how much she had missed her, 'but whatever has happened to you?'

'Oh ma'am, I am glad I've found you. When the gentleman you told me to go to if I didn't find my dad told me you had left Melbourne and come up here and were looking for a property to settle here I was that upset. But he was real good to me when I explained how I helped you on the ship and that you told me to go to him. He told me where to find you and gave me the money for the train, so that's how I got here.'

Her words fell over one another so fast that Ella had to ask her to repeat it all. 'Much slower this time, please, Rosie,' she begged, dropping back on her pillow and wiping her forehead with her damp hanky.

Rosie was all contrition. 'Oh, I'm sorry, miss, ma'am, I shouldn't have thrown it all at you like that. I can see you aren't feeling up to much. It's your condition, I expect.'

Ella was so startled to have her condition referred to twice in this oblique manner in so short a space of time that she sat up and demanded: 'What do you mean, my condition? I admit I am not feeling too well this morning. Just a slight indisposition, something I ate maybe—or just this appalling heat. I shall feel better directly. I usually do later in the day.' It did not cross her mind that if it really was the heat causing her malaise then it would not improve as the day got warmer.

Rosie found it hard to believe that young Mrs Weston was really so ignorant of her own condition. But then she had already discovered that her knowledge of such matters was woefully thin compared with what she, several years younger, knew. Maybe she just didn't want anybody to know, though goodness knows why not; she was married, after all.

Feeling that the best way to ensure she was not put back on the train to Melbourne was to make herself useful, Rosie offered, 'Shall I help you dress, ma'am?' When she received no answer, she added, 'That is, of course, if you feel up to it.'

Ella opened her eyes and looked round the untidy room, suddenly hating it. She sat up carefully and was relieved to find that it didn't spin around her. 'Yes please, Rosie. I would be very grateful.' Cautiously she moved sideways and let her feet touch the floor. When she still felt fine, she stood up.

Rosie was sorting out the clothes Ella had flung over the only chair in the room the night before. 'I think it is going to be hot today.' She looked doubtfully at the rather heavy fabric of the dress and even more so at the fearsome looking corset. For once in her life, she was truly thankful for her status; women of her class were not expected to have an hourglass figure. 'Have you a cooler dress, and do you think you need your stays?'

'Of course I do. Whoever heard of a lady going out without her corset? Come along, help me into it. What are you doing fiddling with those laces?'

'I was just letting them out a wee bit,' Rosie admitted.

'Well, don't—just do them up for me.' Ella took a tight hold on the bedrail and breathed in. It had suddenly seemed vitally important that she did not give in to this absurd physical weakness that had taken hold of her.

Rosie took one look at the white knuckles gripping the bed and even whiter hue to her face and threw the corset back on the chair. 'No, I won't do it. Not in your condition and in this heat, and what's more, I'm finding you something more sensible to wear.' She turned to the cupboard and rummaged through Ella's gowns, finally selecting a light muslin. 'This will do.'

Ella was about to say it would not, remembering that William had said she looked like a servant in it. But he was not here to see her. 'It will do fine,' she told Rosie, holding up her arms for it to be slipped over her head. Emerging from the soft folds, she asked, 'What do you mean, "my condition"?'

Rosie looked at her in surprise; surely she must know that she was pregnant? Even allowing for the extraordinary way in which well-brought-up young ladies were kept in total ignorance of such matters.

'That disagreeable landlady said much the same thing. I told her I had a slight stomach upset and I have felt very tired, quite exhausted in fact since we left the ship. I thought I would feel better when we were on dry land again . . .' she babbled on as if trying to reassure herself. 'It is not my monthlies because I haven't had one for a while . . .' Her voice trailed away and she stared at Rosie, momentary delight flitting across her features quickly followed by stark terror. 'Oh, no! You don't think . . . do you?'

Rosie nodded. 'Yes, ma'am, I do. You are

expecting.'

Ella dropped down on the bed. She stared at the younger girl. 'But I can't. Not here, on my own.' She covered her face with her hands and burst into tears. 'Oh, Rosie, I don't want it—not yet, I'm not ready. I'm too young and this is a strange country, and it's so hot. Oh . . . I wish I had never left England.'

In that moment when she accepted the truth she had been fighting, she longed more than anything for cool air, soft English rain, her family round her, especially her mother. She didn't want this . . . thing that had taken over her body, and she knew with a dreadful clarity that marrying William was the most foolish thing she had ever done. The dream of a new life in a new country was rapidly turning into a nightmare. Here she was, alone in a strange city on the other side of the world, married to a man she felt she barely knew and who wasn't even here with her. God only knew what sort of place he would make her live in.

She looked up through her tears and saw Rosie staring at her with anxious sympathy. She reached out a hand to her. 'Will you stay with me, Rosie?' she pleaded.

'Course I will, ma'am. That's why I came looking for you, to see if you would have me.'

CHAPTER FIVE

It was two weeks before William returned to Bendigo. Ella had no word from him in his absence, but thanks to Rosie did not miss him as much as she might have done. Although Ella was a married woman, she was very much on a par with Rosie; in fact, as far as knowledge of the world went, she was probably behind, yet they became firm friends in that time with the line between mistress and servant blurring to the point where it became almost non-existent.

They enjoyed exploring the city together discovering not only a new world in their surroundings, but a new way of looking at life as they saw it through the other's eyes. Ella was forced to agree with Rosie that most of the expensive clothes she had brought with her were unsuitable for a person in her condition living in a hot climate. As Rosie's wardrobe was quite sparse, they spent many hours altering dresses to fit her and letting out others to be comfortable on Ella.

Living as she was, almost entirely in the moment, Ella almost forgot William's existence until he arrived back at the lodging house late one evening. As Rosie had nowhere to go and no money, Ella had simply shared the lumpy double bed with her, an arrangement she secretly found a great improvement on having William in the other half. Rosie made no demands and, moreover, took up a great deal less room.

The night he returned followed a stifling day and it felt too hot to climb into bed. Both girls had taken off their outer garments and were sitting in front of the window, opened in the hope that the air outside might by this time of the evening be cooler than that inside. They were fanning themselves and each other with whatever came to hand when Ella stiffened.

'We must put our dresses on,' she told Rosie. 'Quickly. My husband is coming back tonight.' She snatched up her own garment and tossed Rosie's over to her. 'Hurry! We do not want to be caught like this.'

'How do you know?' Rosie willed Ella to be mistaken, knowing that when Mr Weston returned, he might very well order her immediate dismissal.

'Oh, I just do, I just feel it in my bones. Hurry, get dressed!' Ella was agitated; it had crossed her mind that William might well send Rosie on her way. In his absence, she had come to rely on her so much she felt she could not bear the thought of that happening.

Tidying her hair in the mirror, Ella could see Rosie standing behind her, a strange expression on her face, a mixture of awe and fear. How did Ella know things like she did without any aids, not even a deck of tarot cards?

'Don't look like that, Rosie. I am sure there is no need to worry. When I explain to William what a help you are and tell him about the baby, I am sure he will want you to stay.'

Rosie looked doubtful. She looked round the room with its one bed. 'But where, Ma'am?'

Ella shrugged, but before she could answer there were footsteps outside and William flung open the door. He looked pleased with himself and, both girls noted, the worse for liquor. He strode into the room, grabbed Ella and swung her round without noticing Rosie who was partly hidden by the door.

'I've found it!' he exclaimed. 'The perfect place. We must celebrate!' As he swirled Ella round with her feet swinging off the ground, he saw Rosie and put Ella down so suddenly she almost lost her balance.

'Who is this?' he demanded, then, answering his own question almost before he finished asking it said, 'It's that Irish chit who helped you on the boat. What on earth is she doing here?' He loosed his hold on Ella and stepped towards Rosie. 'I thought you were joining up with your father. So, what are you doing here?'

He sounded so put out that Rosie was bereft of speech and merely stared at him.

'Well, what are you?' he repeated impatiently, turning to Ella before she

43

answered. 'Is she struck dumb or what?'

'She—she's been helping me, William.'

'Helping you with what?' He glared suspiciously from one to the other. 'Well, now I am back, she can go to her father.'

Ella shook her head. 'She can't find him, William. Please, can she stay? I . . . I could do with her help.'

William looked round the room. 'Stay . . . where?' It was obvious Rosie had been sharing the double bed with Ella. 'If you mean in my bed, no she damn well cannot.'

'I think I had better go.' Rosie was gathering up her few belongings and already heading for the door. Ella grabbed her by the arm.

'No, you can't go—not now. We'll work something out.' The thought of all that confronted her in the future without this girl she had come to rely on was too much for Ella. She hadn't planned to blurt it out to William, but reaching out her other hand, she grabbed his arm so that the three of them stood like a human chain. 'No, William, please don't send her away. I need her, I really do. I . . . I'm with child!'

For a moment they stood frozen like statues, then William shook his arm free from Ella's grip and turned to face her.

'You are *what*? What did you say?' he demanded. This was not in his scheme of things at all. He needed Ella able-bodied to help him settle in on the property he was

44

purchasing. The last thing he wanted was a limp and sickly wife. From what he remembered of his sisters and the wives of friends back in England, when they were in this condition they were not much use for hard work yet expected to be treated with kid gloves and waited on. He turned his eyes to the girl. He hadn't taken a great deal of notice of her on the ship, but now he saw she looked strong and healthy, if a bit on the scrawny side. No doubt plenty of work in her, desperate for somewhere to live by all accounts and quite comely too, now he looked at her properly.

'I won't send her away,' he said grudgingly. 'She can come with us, just so long as she makes herself useful.'

'Oh, William, thank you so much! And the baby—you are pleased about that, aren't you?'

'Of course I am.' And he was, now he thought about it. With a grandchild in the offing, no doubt Ella's father would be even more willing to see that things went right for them. Yes, he rather liked the idea of a son.

Somewhat ungraciously, the landlady found a place for Rosie to sleep. A tiny, hot, stuffy bedroom in the roof of the house. Although she was grateful to have found a roof and work, Rosie determined to spend as little time in it as possible.

The next few weeks were occupied in getting ready for their move to the property. William had to complete the paperwork and of course pay for it, and for this he needed Edwin Sanders's approval.

Mindful of his responsibility to Ella's father, Edwin had insisted on viewing the property himself before he released the money he held. Grudgingly he conceded that the sheep run was good buying, especially as it was a walk-in walk-out deal and William could take it over ready stocked. Privately he worried that neither he nor Ella knew anything about farming on either side of the world and had no conception of the work and hardship that could lie ahead. The only bright spot was the girl, Rosie. As far as he could see, she had her head screwed on and was willing to work hard. He urged William to ask the two farmhands already employed on the property to stay on.

Edwin managed to get Ella alone for a few minutes before he left to take the train back to Melbourne. He thought she looked pale and tired and wondered how she would cope on a lonely sheep property. Had he known of her condition, he would have been even more concerned. As it was, he held both her hands in his for a second and searched her face anxiously.

'You are happy about this?' He felt a slight tremor in her hands, but her expression did not waver when she looked up at him.

'But of course, Mr Sanders. It is what my husband wants, therefore . . .' She shrugged slightly, implying that she only wanted what

46

would make him happy.

'Of course.' Edwin smiled thinly. 'But I wish you had seen the place before he settled on it. I am glad you are taking the girl with you. I shall be in touch with your father. I may tell him that all is well and that you are both satisfied with your husband's choice?'

'I shall be writing to my parents directly to give them our new address.' Ella's voice was cool. While she liked Edwin rather more than she cared to admit, she didn't like the way he had been appointed their minder by her father.

Reluctantly, Edwin let her hands drop. He wished he felt more confident and that he had not had the responsibility of handling William Weston's affairs foisted on him.

'I will say goodbye then, but please remember I am always available to help you should you need it. Your father and mine were good friends; I want to be sure that you look on me as a friend. Please do not hesitate to call on me—in any capacity—should you need to . . .' Edwin's voice trailed; he was afraid he sounded foolish and wondered why he cared what happened to this girl who had, according to her father, behaved in a very foolish and headstrong way. All the same, he smiled at her and hoped her feisty spirit would bear her up in this new life she had chosen for herself.

Ella was unprepared for the feeling of abandonment as she watched Edwin leave. It was as if her last link with civilization was being abruptly severed. She told herself she was giving in to the worries and fantasies induced by her condition and, gathering up her writing materials, started a letter to her parents. For some reason, she felt it important that her news about William taking up farming reached her parents before Edwin's correspondence. There was also the need to tell them they would soon be grandparents. She managed to sound both confident and happy about both events; pride would not let her express her fears and misgivings.

CHAPTER SIX

Ella found it was not quite so easy to be optimistic as they travelled up to the farm; the road leading to it was nothing more than a rough cart track. She could imagine that the ruts that bounced them uncomfortably now in the dry, hot months might well turn into a sea of mud in the winter.

What she would have done without Rosie did not bear thinking about. She thanked the providence that had disposed, in whatever way, of the girl's father so that their dependence on each other was mutual. Ella thought longingly of her childhood in her comfortable, middle-class family and bitterly regretted her defiance of her father who had provided so well for his family that she had seldom been asked to do anything more strenuous for herself than get dressed in the morning. Now, with no practical experience whatsoever, she was expected to run a household under what, to her, were primitive conditions.

The wood-burning stove she might have learned to cope with, the never-ending diet of mutton perhaps learn to tolerate, but the heat, the dust and multitudinous flies were altogether something else. Being pregnant made everything worse; she was desperately homesick for England and her family. She could not escape the realization that what she had imagined was love for her husband had been nothing more than an infatuation fuelled by the excitement of rebellion. What a fool she had been. She would give anything to be back in England safely married to good, solid Walter who, in retrospect, didn't seem dull at all.

She was determined, however, on one point: she would never admit any of this to her family. Her letters home were about the few things she found to praise in her new environment. Rosie was one, the kindness of neighbours on the rare occasions she met any of them another. She wrote about the colourful parrots, but did not mention the isolation. She told her parents that Mr Sanders had been very helpful in getting them installed on a farm and glossed over William's lack of expertise as a farmer. Letters from home made her unbearably homesick, but after writing one of her own rose-tinted missives, she often felt better as if she actually believed her own optimistic words.

As autumn turned to winter, the days cooled and the nights lengthened. She rejoiced in the crisp, frosty mornings and when the winter rains turned the dry, dusty earth a vivid emerald, she almost liked the place. She was standing at the open door marvelling at this transformation when the first pang of labour caused her to drop the bowl of scraps she was about to give the hens and scream for Rosie.

As unprepared for childbirth as she had been for marriage, Ella glared at the midwife fetched by William and informed her that she knew she was dying.

When the woman placed her daughter in her arms some hours later and congratulated her on an easy delivery, she stared at the woman in disbelief.

'If that was easy then I'm certainly not going to risk anything more prolonged and painful.' She announced, 'This will be an only child.' The midwife assured her that she had heard that before—many times.

Ella looked down at the bundle in her arms wondering how such a scrap could have caused her so much pain. She was not disposed to like her. But when she moved the all enveloping shawl away from the tiny face and a small, claw-like hand appeared, a wave of emotion gripped her and she conceded she might come to care for her in time.

It was William's reaction that roused her maternal feeling rather than the baby herself. Ella was propped against her pillows endeavouring to absorb the astonishing fact that she was now a mother when she heard William's heavy tread in his farm boots as he entered the kitchen.

'Well?' he demanded. 'Is it over yet? Is my son born?'

There was a short pause before the midwife, on her way from the house, replied. 'The baby is a girl. You have a daughter, Mr Weston.'

'Are you sure?' William demanded. 'It can't be. I wanted a son!'

Ella strained her ears to catch the midwife's answer. 'Do you think I can't tell the difference?' she demanded. 'You'd best go in and see for yourself!'

The door burst open and William stood there. 'Is it true? We have a daughter?' he demanded.

'I'm afraid so,' Ella admitted, glancing down at the baby in her arms. As she did so, the baby's eyes opened for a second and mother love was born belatedly in Ella's heart. *Poor mite. What a welcome to the world*. 'I am sorry,' she murmured, all the time knowing she wasn't

51

in the least sorry. She hadn't gone through the rigours of childbirth merely to boost William's ego. She held the baby closer as she experienced a deep longing for England, home and above all, her own mother. 'What do you want to call her?' she asked, knowing that William had only thought of boy's names.

'You can call her what you like,' he snarled, barely glancing at either of them before turning away.

'Violet . . .' Ella said, remembering the shy, purple flowers with the exquisite scent that grew in the hedgerows round her childhood home. 'Violet Lillian, after my mother.'

William grunted. 'Call her whatever fancy name you like. The next one will be a boy and I'll have the naming of that.'

Ella dropped her eyes; she had no wish for him to see the hurt and simmering anger she felt. She reiterated to herself her decision that there would not be a 'next one'. Unfortunately, the only way she knew to ensure this was to keep her husband away from her bed and that, she felt, would not be easy.

Indeed it was not. Less than a year later, Ella was brought to bed to be delivered of a stillborn son. There was no swift and easy labour this time as it was a breech presentation. William hit the whiskey bottle and drank himself senseless. Ella reflected bitterly that this ill-fated pregnancy had begun and ended with William angry and drunk.

Weak and in pain from her breasts bound tightly to prevent the milk coming in, she stayed in her bed long after the normal lying-in period and sank into a deep depression unhelped by her physical weakness.

William, grieved and disappointed at losing the son he longed for and denied even the companionship of his wife, let alone the comforts of the marriage bed, paid less and less attention to his farm and more and more to the whiskey bottle. Rosie struggled on caring for little Violet and doing her best to lift Ella from her unhappy lethargy. It was six weeks after Ella's confinement that Edwin, hearing a rumour that William was neglecting his farm and that his wife was sick, decided to visit them and see for himself.

He was not prepared for the general air of neglect about the property and was concerned to see little evidence of sheep. He hunted down one of the hired men and was told that numbers had indeed been reduced as the boss was selling them off steadily. He was shocked by Rosie's reaction when she opened the door to him. She stared at him for a moment then burst into noisy tears. There was no sign of Ella. Clinging to the sobbing girl's skirts was a toddler, and he could see that beneath the red jam covering most of her face, the little girl was very pretty.

Without a word, he pushed past Rosie and walked into the house, looking round for Ella.

There was no sign of her.

'Where is Mrs Weston?' he demanded. Surely both the Westons hadn't just left the property and the child? Anxiety sharpened his voice. 'Pull yourself together, girl!' he demanded, 'and explain to me just what has been happening here.'

Rosie sniffed, loudly and inelegantly, took a deep breath and swallowed her last sob on a great gulp. 'Oh, Mr Sanders, sir, I'm that glad to see you. I just don't know what to do . . .'

'What has been happening here? Where is Mrs Weston?' His voice was sharp with anxiety, his fists clenched to make sure he didn't grab hold of Rosie and shake some information from her. With an effort, he controlled himself. 'I am answerable to her parents for her welfare.' This was stretching the truth; his involvement came to an end when he released the money for William to purchase this property.

Rosie's eyes looked beyond him and he turned to see Ella Weston standing in the doorway behind him. He was appalled at the change in her. Thin to the point of emaciation, her hair looked as if it had not been combed in weeks, her garments as if she had slept in them, but worst of all were her eyes, or rather the expression in them. Bleak and lifeless, they stared at him blankly. But he was mistaken to think she did not recognize him.

'Why are you here?' she asked tonelessly. 'If

54

you have come to see if my husband is using the money my father invested in him wisely then I can tell you he is not. You may tell my father that if you wish; I really do not care. All I would like to do is leave all this behind me and go home. Unless you can help me do that then there is no point in you being here. There is nothing to say.' She turned away from him, but he stopped her with a sharp command:

'Wait! It is not the money I have come to check on, it is you. I heard rumours you were sick and came to see. I—I happened to be in the area.'

Ella swayed slightly and for a moment Edwin thought she might fall, but she seemed to make a supreme effort to pull herself together. She walked slowly across the kitchen to the nearest chair on which she then slumped down. 'Will you take a cup of tea with me, Mr Sanders?' she asked politely for all the world, he thought, as if she were entertaining in a civilized drawing-room.

'Thank you, yes.' The girl, he noted, had already pushed the kettle over to the hot spot on the stove.

Ella indicated the child. 'My daughter, Violet,' she told Edwin politely before frowning and saying to Rosie, 'Clean her up, please.' Beyond that, she took no more notice of the child—or anything else, it seemed to Edwin—but sat silently at the table while the girl wiped the jam off Violet's face and dumped her firmly in her high chair before turning her attention to the boiling kettle to make a pot of tea.

Edwin did his best to make conversation, but he had the impression that Ella was not actually there. He turned to Rosie when she sat down at the table and poured the tea into three cups. 'How long has she been like this?' If Ella noticed that she was being talked about, she gave no sign.

'Since . . .' Rosie began, then glanced across at Ella, noting that she still seemed immersed in her own dark world. She lowered her voice before continuing. 'She had a bad time with the last baby—it was born dead. She seemed to think it was all her fault. It was a boy, you see.'

Edwin didn't quite see what the sex of the baby had to do with it, but instinct told him that if she was blaming herself then more than likely that idea had been fed to her by someone, and who else but her husband? 'Did Mr Weston want a son?' he asked Rosie, following this hunch.

The girl nodded.

'He never takes any notice of this one here. Treats her as if she doesn't exist. When the next one was born dead, he was . . . upset.'

Edwin took that to mean he went on a blinder. He looked at Ella, her fingers, thin and claw-like, were curled round the mug of tea which she held to her lips and sipped from slowly, all the time gazing across the room with that blank look on her face. Remembering the lovely girl he had first seen when she arrived off the ship in Melbourne, his heart turned over. *What in God's name would her parents think if they saw her now*? A shaft of guilt shot through him; he had not been exactly in loco parentis, but he had been the link between them and their daughter. He should have been firmer and refused to release her father's money for William Weston to go into farming when he was totally ignorant of anything to do with the land—anywhere, let alone in Australia. He made a sudden decision.

'My mother and sister live in Bendigo. I will take her back there with me.'

Rosie gaped at him. 'But . . . what will Mr Weston say?' she finally stammered.

'Where is he? If you can tell me that, I will soon find out what he has to say. It is obvious to me that if something isn't done, the only way she will leave this place is in a box. Has she seen a doctor?'

Rosie shook her head. 'Mr Weston said she was to pull herself together.'

'Do you know where he is?' Edwin repeated. 'I suppose I should say something to her, not just take her away. On the other hand . . .'

Rosie shook her head once more. 'I think he is in New South Wales somewhere. He said something about going to buy sheep; a lot have died and he wanted to replace them. I don't think he will be back for several days.'

'In that case, pack her a case and I will take her to my mother.'

Rosie stared at him. 'And Violet?' she asked, leaving the words 'and me?' hanging between them.

Edwin hadn't taken the child or the girl into consideration. He wondered whether that would be too much of an imposition to put on his mother. On the other hand, the girl might be a help. From what he could see of Ella, she was in no fit state to do anything.

'Pack for the lot of you.' In for a penny, in for a pound, he told himself. 'Can you find me a pen and paper and I will write a note for Mr Weston to say where they are.'

*　　*　　*

Edwin felt he had never admired or loved his mother as much as when she took one look at Ella and simply held out her arms to her.

'I had to bring her; I couldn't leave her there and tell her parents she was all right. I didn't know what to do about Rosie and the child. William is away somewhere and it didn't seem right to leave them, so I brought them too,' he ended apologetically.

'You did right,' Alice approved. 'Beth, will you take care of them?' She turned to her daughter who murmured agreement. 'I am going to get this poor soul into bed—right now.' And with that she shepherded Ella from the room, leaving brother and sister looking at each other.

'You had better tell me their names for starters.' Beth's voice was brisk as she spoke to her brother.

'The child's name is Violet,' Rosie put in before he could answer, 'and I am Rosie. I have been with Mrs Weston helping her since we were on the ship. If you can just show me where I can put her to sleep, that is all the help I need.'

'Oh, yes, of course—Rosie.' Beth glanced at her brother. 'Do you think the sleep-out would do?' she asked uncertainly. 'I expect Mother has installed Mrs Weston in our only spare bedroom.'

'I should think it would be fine.' The 'sleep-out' was an enclosed veranda at the side of the house with louvered windows and furnished with a comfortable chair and a day bed. Over the years, it had been used to accommodate unexpected overnight guests, frequently his own friends before he had moved permanently to Melbourne. He sighed with relief as he watched Beth leave the room, leading Rosie with the child asleep in her arms.

CHAPTER SEVEN

With Ella, Violet and Rosie safely installed with his mother, Edwin returned to his Melbourne practice and his own wife. Appalled by Ella's total retreat into herself, Alice Sanders called in her own doctor. When the circumstances that had brought Ella to this state were explained to him, he prescribed rest and good food. This confirmed Alice in her belief that he was an excellent doctor, for she would have prescribed exactly the same.

Gradually the colour crept back into Ella's cheeks, her appetite returned and she began to take an interest in Violet. The subject of the farm, even of William, seemed taboo. Alice calmly awaited further instructions from her son.

Summer was already sliding into autumn. Because William was never mentioned, it was almost as if he did not exist. Then, one unusually quiet and peaceful afternoon, Rosie took Violet out for a walk while the three women sat on the patio outside, a tray of tea between them and sewing in their laps. Each was lost in her own thoughts; Beth wished she had gone with Rosie and Violet, Alice was planning just where to plant the lemon tree she had just purchased and Ella was simply relishing the peace of her surroundings.

'I think . . . about there.' Alice pointed vaguely across the lawn, but her quiet voice was lost by a hammering on the door at the front of the house. They all started and Beth got up to investigate. She was followed back by William.

'Oh!' Ella jumped to her feet, dropping her teacup. She stared at the broken pieces, burst into tears and fled into the house.

Alice Weston, after a slight nod to her daughter, interpreted correctly as instructions to follow, put down her cup, rose to her feet and extended her hand.

'Good afternoon, Mr Weston.' Her voice was as cool as if he had been expected. 'Do sit down and have a cup of tea.' She gestured to the vacant chairs, picked up the broken cup and fetched a fresh one from the house. William had obediently sat.

'You have come to see your wife, I expect?' Alice smiled as she poured his tea.

'Thank you.' William reached out and accepted it. 'Actually, I have come to take her home. I am sure she has prevailed on your kindness quite long enough. And, well, there are things to do. I am finding it very hard to manage on my own.'

'I am sure you are, Mr Weston, but your wife has been very sick. I do not think she is ready yet to return to her duties on the farm.'

William drank his tea thoughtfully then looked directly at Alice Weston. 'That is as may be, but she had a long lie in after . . . after my son died, and then several weeks of doing very little. The girl, Rosie, kept things going.'

'I can understand your difficulty, Mr Weston, but if she has a relapse, things will be worse for everyone—you particularly.'

William scowled into his teacup; he had the uncomfortable feeling that he was not in charge of this conversation. 'I have to say, Mrs Sanders, that while I am grateful, under an obligation to you, in fact, for the care you have given my wife, I do feel that your son behaved in a somewhat high-handed way when he removed her. I am sure you must realize how very difficult it is for me to manage without her.'

'I realize,' Alice returned dryly, 'but I am sure that you also understand that having a sick wife could be worse than no wife. In fact, you must know that from experience.'

'Will you allow me to talk to my wife, or do you intend to keep her away from me?' William asked, an undertone of belligerence roughening his voice.

'But of course you may speak to me, William.' Ella's voice behind them made them both swivel in their chairs. Alice was relieved to see that Ella had a firm grip on her emotions. Her face was white but composed and only the faint tremor in her voice betrayed the depth of her feeling. 'But Alice is right. I do not yet feel strong enough to return. In fact, it is questionable whether I ever will.'

'But . . . but . . . you are my wife!' William spluttered.

'Yes, I am. But I am not your slave or your chattel. Violet and I will stay here for a while longer. That is, if Mrs Sanders can continue to put up with us.'

'For a while longer' did not suggest she would never return, so William controlled his feelings and conceded: 'Very well, my dear, another couple of weeks if Mrs Sanders will be so kind as to keep you. Maybe I should take Rosie back with me—to get things ready for your return.'

Alice Weston bit her lip, determined not to get any more involved in this difficult marriage. She was wondering how to say that it was not quite proper for Rosie to return with him on her own when William got abruptly to his feet.

'I will return in two weeks' time, and take you all home.' He inclined his head slightly to Alice. 'It is extremely kind of you, Ma'am, to look after my wife. I can see she looks a great deal better. But in two weeks' time, she must come home.'

William realized that if he took Rosie and left Ella and her child, she would probably never return to him. He must think up a foolproof way to get his wife back, or he knew he could kiss goodbye to any further financial help from his father-in-law. He was fast coming to rue the day he had met Ella. Penury in England would be preferable to his present situation. Sheep farming, he had discovered, was a hard life and his debts were now just as great as they had been in England. He knew that if Ella did not return to him, he had little or no chance of her father releasing any more funds. In spite of his thoughts, he managed to smile and bow graciously over Alice's hand as he bade them goodbye, assuring them that he would return when Ella was fit enough to take up her position once more as his wife. Controlling his anger in front of the women, he left, not to return to his property but to take the train to Melbourne.

*　　*　　*

It was no surprise to Edwin when a truculent William Weston arrived at his office right at the end of the day. In fact, the working day had ended, but Edwin had stayed behind to finish some work and was about to leave.

'Ahh, Edwin, I'm glad I've caught you!'

'Mr Weston, what a surprise.' Edwin had no desire to enter into first name intimacy. 'As you can see, I am just leaving for the night.' He pulled his watch out of his pocket and consulted it. 'I was going for a meal. Maybe you would join me if you need to talk.' Edwin was hungry and tired and felt that unless he remedied this, he would not be able to cope with William. Fortunately, he had told his wife that he intended working late and would eat before he came home. He was sure she would not have been able to cope with an unexpected guest, especially one as truculent as this one might be.

'Well, yes, that's very kind of you.' William, surprised by the offer, did not stop to reflect that eating with Edwin might possibly put him at a disadvantage. But he lost no time in coming to the point when they were seated opposite each other in the dining-room of a nearby hotel.

'It's about my wife . . .' he began.

Edwin sighed. 'I rather thought it might be.'

'While I am grateful to you—of course I am—especially to your mother for looking after her so well, I feel it is high time she returned with me and, er, took up her duties as my wife.'

'I would agree with you—in theory—but in practice, I am not sure she is capable of doing that. My mother tells me she is still far from well. But if she is anxious to return and you understand she needs care, then of course . . .' Edwin shrugged as his voice trailed away. He could not stop the man taking his wife back home.

'That is the point; she does not wish to return. At one point, she said categorically that she would not—ever.'

'At one point?' Edwin left the query hanging

in the air.

'Yes, then she more or less agreed to reconsider in two weeks' time.'

'In that case, what are you worrying about? You know my mother will care for her. There is nothing to concern yourself about.' Edwin could not hide his pleasure that Ella had been reprieved for a while longer.

William itched to hit this bland, smug man who had virtually kidnapped his wife; however, he knew that if he had any hope of getting out of the mess he found himself in, Edwin held the key. He was wondering how to put it over in a reasonable and plausible manner that he needed money when Edwin continued.

'Things looked a bit . . . shall we say, run down when I was up there. Your men told me that sheep numbers were down. You not only had considerable losses but had reduced your stock by selling.'

'I thought selling sheep was one of the ways a sheep farmer made money.' William's voice was surly. 'I have been up in New South Wales hoping to restock. I heard prices were very low there due to the dry summer. Unfortunately, they weren't low enough for my limited means.'

Edwin ignored this. 'I suggest you get back up there and do something to pull things together rather than buy more stock.'

'I need cash for fencing, labour, etcetera.'

'I am sorry, Mr Weston. But my

responsibility is to my client in England, Richard Wagstaff, Ella's father. The money he forwarded was to set you up, not to keep you going. I do not intend to request more; that is something you must do yourself.' Edwin had no wish to be the go-between for William and his father-in-law forever.

'But surely he would not want to see his daughter suffering?' William was almost whining by now.

'No, he would not, so I hope you will not consider forcing her to return until you have done something to get things in order and ensure that she has a little more care and comfort in future. If you undertake to do that, I will see what can be done when she returns to you. Until then, well, it is up to you. It is a pity . . .' he could not resist adding, 'that you did not find out a little more about Australia and conditions here before you set out from England.'

With rare restraint, William managed to resist saying that it had not been his choice to come to Australia at all.

Feeling, as he usually did, disturbed by William, Edwin decided to visit his mother and see for himself just how Ella was. He arrived early the following afternoon to find her weeping hysterically and his mother and sister distraught. Rosie and Beth had taken Violet with them to do the weekly food shopping. They had got into the habit of doing this together so that there were more hands to carry home their purchases. It had been a shock to meet William whom they both believed to be back at the farm. He had seemed pleasant enough, had even made much of Violet to the extent of giving Beth a fistful of coins to get a bag of sweets at a shop they were passing. Beth was at the counter when she heard a commotion and her own name being called. When she reached the door, it was just in time to see Rosie climbing into a cab. The only sign of William was his hand grabbing the girl's arm as he helped, or hauled her in. As there was no sign of Violet, Beth assumed she was already inside. Frantic, Beth tried to push her way out of the shop, but new customers were blocking the doorway and by the time she had pushed past them and out into the street, the cab had disappeared.

'Didn't you follow?' Edwin demanded angrily.

'I was on foot; they were in a cab!' Beth retorted. 'By the time I had found out which direction they had taken, they had vanished. I had no hope of catching up with them.'

Edwin looked at the three distraught women. Ella pulled herself together first, to his surprise and admiration.

'This is my fault,' she told them, choking back her tears. 'I should have agreed to return. After all, I married him. It is my duty. He has taken Violet to force me back and Rosie to look after her. Will you escort me—home—please, Edwin?'

He stared at her. The very last thing he wanted to do was hand Ella over to her husband, yet he knew that in the circumstances, he had little choice. At least he could see she came to no harm on the journey and do his best to impress on William the need to take proper care of her.

CHAPTER EIGHT

In the short time it took Ella to throw some clothes into a case, she knew she ceased to be a girl, a rather spoilt and selfish one at that, and became a woman. When her child was snatched away from her so cruelly, she really knew what it meant to be a mother and discovered in herself an inner strength she did not know she had.

Edwin, watching her calmly kiss his mother and sister farewell, wondered if this calm was about to crack or whether in touching bottom, she had found resources in herself that she had been unaware of until that moment.

'I am ready.' Ella's voice was controlled. 'Shall we go?'

Edwin stared at her for a moment, shocked by the realization that he didn't want to lose her; didn't want her to go back to her life with that senseless oaf who totally failed to appreciate her. He bent and picked up her case. He could not afford to let his thoughts wander on those lines—he had nothing permanent to offer her.

'Goodbye, Mother,' he said curtly and without another word moved to the door, leaving Ella to follow in his wake.

Alice stood in the centre of the room, watching them leave. Then, heaving a sigh that seemed to come from the very depth of her being, she murmured, 'Poor Edwin.'

'Don't you mean, poor Ella?' Beth said in a dry tone. 'She recovered so well here with us. I hope this doesn't set her back again.' It was her turn to sigh now. 'I shall miss her, and little Violet. The place will seem quiet without them—Rosie too, I liked her.'

'We shall both miss them all. It will seem *very* quiet. I am surprised how much I enjoyed having a child in the house.' She had begun to think of the lively little girl as a surrogate grandchild, had even fantasized about Ella as a daughter-in-law. She repressed these thoughts, knowing that she must accept the fact that Edwin's wife was a permanent invalid and that she could not hope for any grandchildren from that quarter.

'I must say she,' Beth was saying, 'Ella is braver than I thought she would be. Not just for going back, but for travelling with Edwin in that new contraption of his.' There was a hint

70

of sour grapes in Beth's remark, for this was the first time they had seen Edwin's new pride and joy, his 'horseless carriage', and Beth would have dearly loved a trip in it.

*   *   *

Ella pulled the silk scarf tight under her chin. It belonged to Beth who had generously insisted she take it to keep her hat on her head. Although this was the first time she had been offered the chance to ride in one of these new vehicles, her mother had told her all about the one her father had bought nearly two years ago and of the necessity to tie one's headgear down well to avoid it blowing away. Rather surprisingly, her mother had extolled the virtues of this new form of transport, saying how much easier and quicker it was to get to wherever it was one wanted to go. Ella did, however, hope that Edwin was cognisant of the workings of the thing. Something of her thoughts must have shown on her face, for Edwin told her as he scrambled up on to his seat beside her after cranking the engine into life, 'I did drive it here from Melbourne, you know.'

Ella nodded and held on to her hat as they lurched forward. She wanted to ask him about the cost of what she considered his new toy, not because she cared what Edwin spent but because she felt reasonably sure that William

71

would soon be convinced he needed one too. She was sure of this when she realized that they had actually arrived at the property before William, in spite of his head start.

'Thank you, Edwin,' she said as he helped her down. 'I must confess that I enjoyed the journey. I think William will be somewhat surprised to see that I am here before him.'

Edwin had the feeling he was being dismissed, but he had no intention of leaving until he was sure that the child was safely reunited with Ella. He was also concerned for her as she seemed to him unnaturally calm, given the circumstances, and remembering her mental state when he took her to stay with his mother, he was afraid she might relapse. He followed her into the house.

'I shall be fine, Edwin. There is no need for you to waste any more time if you want to return. I am sure you need to get back to your office.'

'I do need to get back to my office, Ella, but not as much as I need to stay with you. I will go when I know that you are all right and only then,' he managed a thin smile, 'and only if you promise to let me know if you need help of any sort.'

She reached out and clasped his hand, 'Oh, Edwin, you have already done so much for me. I cannot imagine what life would have been like without you. Your mother too—and of course Beth—they were both so kind.'

72

Edwin's grip tightened on her hand and without thinking, he pulled her closer. 'Promise me this, Ella. If you are ever in any trouble, you will let me know.'

'I promise, Edwin.' She looked up into his face and as their eyes met and held, she was intensely aware of her hand still in his. Her voice shook and she tried to lighten the moment with a small joke: 'It is always good to have a lawyer as a friend.' But her voice faded along with her smile. She knew she should take her hand away from his, drop her eyes from that compelling gaze and move her body out of his orbit, but instead she leaned towards him and her sigh was a slight moan as he bent his head and kissed her. With that kiss came the searing revelation that she loved Edwin Sanders with every fibre of her being. She also knew of his own disastrous marriage. Beth, concerned for her brother and anxious that he should not get too deeply involved in what could only be a messy situation, had taken care to tell her. She stepped quickly away, shaking her head.

Edwin put his hands on her shoulders and spun her round to face him. 'Don't stay,' he begged. 'Let me take you and Violet back to my mother.'

'Oh, Edwin!' her voice shook. The temptation to walk out of her marriage, away from this place was strong. 'No . . . it—it wouldn't do. I married William, Violet is his child. I have to stay. My father would never forgive me if I brought such disgrace on him.'

'Ella!' Edwin's grip tightened on her shoulders and he gave her a slight shake, 'your father is in England, on the other side of the world. Surely he wouldn't want you to stay with a man you were so unhappy with? After all, he never wanted you to marry him in the first place, did he?'

'That's just it, Edwin. He tried his best to stop me and I defied him. I even broke off my engagement to the man he did want me to marry; that was scandal enough. When I insisted I wanted to marry William, he did the best he could for me and settled enough money on William to set us up—you know all that. Besides . . .' her voice trailed off.

'Besides . . . besides what, Ella?' Edwin probed.

'I have my pride. I couldn't admit that he was right all along and that I was headstrong and stupid.'

'You regret breaking off your engagement?'

'In some ways—yes. Then I remind myself that I would not have travelled to Australia, had Violet, or . . . or met you. But I would have had security, position and respect. I would also have had my family around me. I miss them so much. No, what really disturbs me is that I am not sure I trust myself. I thought at the time that I loved William enough to cause a scandal. How do I know

74

that I am right this time?'

'This time? Are you saying that you love me?'

'I am saying that I think I do, just as I thought I loved William.' Ella turned away from the pain in Edwin's eyes. 'Now there is a child, there is Violet to consider. This time it would not just be a scandal, it would be a breaking up of a marriage. I made vows, serious vows in church, before God and everyone I knew. I must at least make an effort to abide by them.'

Once more Edwin spun her round to face him and pulled her close to his heart. 'I think you are afraid, Ella. No—no, not of William,' as she began to protest, 'he is weak and stupid and could easily be managed by a woman with determination, such as you. No, you are afraid of your father and his reaction and most of all afraid of yourself and your own emotions.' His lips twisted into a bitter smile. 'Well, stay here, Ella Weston, and do your damndest this time to make your husband see sense before he goes under and sucks you down with him, and while you are doing it, remember me and the "might have been".' He broke off to pull her tight against him. Ella was aware of the full length of his body against hers, of his hardness, and when his lips met hers, she had no power of resistance and opened her mouth to receive his probing tongue while her arms, of their own volition, clung to him. Then as suddenly

75

as it had begun, it was over. He pushed her from him and spinning on his heel, made for the door. There he paused and, turning briefly to face her with the ghost of a smile on his lips, reminded her: 'I meant what I said. If you need a good lawyer, I'll be there.'

Choking with tears, Ella stood at the window and watched him crank up his car and disappear with a roar, a plume of dust rising behind him. He had not mentioned his wife and when she had intended to remind him, the words had died in her throat. Ella was still standing there when William returned, puce with fury about some idiot in one of those 'newfangled motors' that had roared past him and scared his horse.

'We are lucky to be here in one piece,' he complained, then as realization dawned, 'You must have come in the damn thing. That is how you managed to get here before I did. I suppose that lawyer fellow brought you.' It was a statement rather than a question and Ella did not bother to answer. Instead she picked up Violet who had run towards her, excited to see her, swept her up in her arms and held her close against her cheek for a moment. She caught Rosie's eye over the top of the child's head.

'I think we could all do with a good cup of tea, and maybe something to eat, if there is anything in the house.'

CHAPTER NINE

Ella was twenty-four years old when she returned to the farm—she felt at least fifty-four—and little Violet was two. She was a pretty child and good at amusing herself. Rosie adored her and, so Ella sometimes thought, spoiled her. Even William, although he had not yet forgiven her for failing to be the son he craved, could not entirely resist her. Ella, claiming to have not yet recovered from the birth of her stillborn son, kept William at arm's length.

Only the thought of the report that Edwin would send to Ella's father kept William there. His eyes strayed frequently to Rosie, just going on eighteen. She had developed generous curves over the last year or so, making him think of a ripe plum about to fall. He just wanted to be there when she did.

The opportunity came sooner than he expected.

A letter came in the mail from Alice Sanders addressed to both Ella and William. Ella opened it, something she would not have done if she had thought it was something to do with business, but she thought of Alice Sanders as her personal friend rather than a mutual one. She was surprised when a card dropped out of the envelope and even more surprised to see it was a wedding invitation. Beth Sanders was marrying.

Ella had met her fiancé when she stayed there. David Trembath was another lawyer, an old friend of Edwin's. The enclosed note from Alice explained that he would be starting up a branch of Sanders in Bendigo. Ella was glad for both Beth and her mother that she would not be going far away. She put the note in the pocket of her apron and the invitation on one side to show to William, hoping but not expecting that he would be prepared to accept.

She was not surprised when he refused, but was astonished when he urged her to go.

'Go for a couple of nights. Rosie can manage here.'

'What about Violet?'

'You can leave her here. She'll be fine with Rosie.'

William had no wish to go himself; Edwin would be sure to be playing a major role at his sister's wedding. William thoroughly disliked him and blamed him, unfairly, for most of his own troubles, but he had no wish to antagonize him. Farming was proving a far tougher game than he had imagined and he was hoping for some more financial assistance from his father-in-law.

So great was Ella's pleasure at this unexpected break in the dreary sameness of her days that she was even able to repress her guilt at leaving Violet and dismiss the thought that William might seize the chance to take advantage of Rosie.

Her niggling doubts and concerns evaporated when she saw Edwin waiting for her at the station. She glanced round anxiously, wondering if his wife was with him, but no; she would be waiting at the house in comfort. As if divining her thoughts, Edwin told her that he was alone as his wife was not up to the journey to Bendigo. Ella felt a prick of elation as he placed his hand under her elbow to steer her gently out of the station.

In the bustle and excitement of sending the newly married couple off after the wedding party at the Sanderses house, Ella thought of her own wedding and how things had turned out. With all her heart, she hoped things would be better for Beth. When Edwin materialized at her side, she turned and smiled a little shakily.

'I can relax now we've seen them on their way. I didn't realize how arduous it was being the father of the bride.' As Beth's older brother, it had fallen on Edwin to take on this role.

'She is lucky to have you—and to be starting her married life so close to you all,' Ella remarked, unable to keep the wistful note out of her voice as a wave of homesickness swept through her. She turned away from him to hide the tears in her eyes.

Later, when the party was still in full swing,

she stood by the window looking out on the moonlit garden and reflecting on her own folly.

'It's beautiful outside. Shall we go out?'

Ella turned and smiled rather shakily at Edwin, ashamed of her unhappy thoughts on such a happy occasion. 'That would be . . . nice.'

Instinctively they both moved away from the lamplight falling on the garden and into the shadows. Edwin told himself that he was thinking of the report he would make to her father when he asked Ella, 'How are things these days? The farm . . . William?'

Ella shrugged. 'We manage.' Her tone was dull; she had no wish to discuss or even think about William out here with Edwin.

'What a shame your wife couldn't be here,' she remarked, more as some sort of shield between her and Edwin than because she really cared.

'Yes, she never goes anywhere, she—' He reached out his hand and caught Ella's arm as her toe caught in a rough bit of paving on the path.

'Oh!' Involuntarily she turned in his arms. 'Oh, Edwin!' Her resistance, such as it was, melted as he kissed her and she responded with a passion she had not known she possessed. Only when he begged her to stay, murmuring endearments against her hair, did she remember Violet. She braced her arms against his chest and pushed back. 'I can't. I have to go back—there is Violet.'

'Bring her with you.'

'She is William's child.' Her voice was flat. 'And I am his wife, Edwin. I stood in church and made vows, for better or worse. You too. Well, it's turned out for worse, hasn't it, for both of us. But that is our bad luck—it doesn't alter anything.'

She broke away from him with something like a sob and dashed into the house where she did her best to put up a bright façade as she mingled with the still partying guests.

Alice threw her a keen glance and wondered where Edwin was.

In spite of the tiring day, Ella tossed in her bed, sleep quite elusive while her mind was in such turmoil. She knew she had done the right thing—her conscience and her upbringing told her that—but her heart was heavy and her body betrayed her with its memories and its yearnings.

She was still awake, still tingling from the feeling of Edwin's arms round her, his kisses on her mouth, still reminding herself that marriage vows were sacred when she became aware of a slight scratching, tapping sound at her door. She lay quite still and did not cry out when it opened very slowly.

'Shhh!' Edwin put his forefinger to his lips as he stepped inside. 'Don't be alarmed. I just want to talk.'

Very quietly he moved across the room and sat down on the bed.

'I don't think you should be here. What do you want to talk about, anyway?' Ella whispered.

'I couldn't let things end like that. I need you to know that I really care about you. I never want to hurt you in any way.' He reached out a hand but didn't quite touch her.

Ella caught her breath on a sob and with one hand on her mouth to stifle the sound, she reached out and touched him with the other. What happened then was inevitable, or so she told herself afterwards.

CHAPTER TEN

Ella reached out her hand as she woke, half expecting to find Edwin still there. As she surfaced to full consciousness, she realized this was absurd; he could not risk discovery—for both their sakes.

She had slept late and the sun was pouring into the room. She stretched, enjoying the unusual luxury of just lying in bed with no pressing chores demanding she get up and attend to them. For a few sweet moments, she savoured the pleasure of the previous night before reality, and what she tried to think of as sanity, took over. She tried to convince herself it had all been a dream; it simply was not feasible that she, who had never particularly enjoyed sex with William, should have found it so pleasurable. Even more impossible that she could have broken her marriage vows so easily and so eagerly. Of one thing she was certain: it had to be a once only occasion.

She dressed slowly and carefully, sure that everything about her would shout to the world, certainly to Alice Sanders, just what she had done. She wondered how she would face Edwin and how he would face her. But she need not have worried. When she made an appearance for breakfast at last, it was to discover he had left very early for Melbourne.

'In that motor of his, dear,' Alice told her. 'He said he had an early consultation and needed to be back at his office. I do hope he drives carefully. I would have felt happier if he had gone on the train.'

Ella murmured agreement and, surprised that she felt so hungry, enjoyed a good breakfast. She told Alice that she thought the wedding had been a great success; Beth had looked lovely, her new husband was very nice and appeared to be ideally suited to her, and the reception had been perfect. 'I envy her living so near you,' she added. 'I really miss my family, my mother particularly, and feel sad that Violet does not know her grandmother.'

Alice reached out across the table and lightly touched her hand. 'I know it is not the

83

same,' she said gently, 'but think of me as a sort of secondary mother and a grandmother to little Violet. You know how fond I am of the child. Beth too. She already thinks of you as a sister, I know, and Violet as a niece. We love you both and are more than happy that your father asked Edwin to keep an eye on your welfare.'

At her words, Ella found her toast was sticking in her throat and could feel a warm flush spreading up her neck. 'You are too kind,' she mumbled inadequately, suppressing the thought that if Beth thought of her as a sister then that was not how Edwin saw her.

'Not at all, my dear, just bring little Violet to see us sometimes and we will be rewarded.' Alice smiled before adding in a more serious tone, 'And don't forget I am here any time for you if ever you need . . . anything. Just as your mother would be.'

Ella's thanks were warm and genuine; knowing that she had such a good friend was indeed some slight compensation for having no family of her own in Australia.

When she returned home, Ella was immediately aware of what her mother would call 'an atmosphere' between William and Rosie. Her husband was gloomy and morose and Rosie appeared to be avoiding his company. This did not surprise Ella as she did not find a great deal of pleasure in it herself. It was not cheering to hear his constant moans

84

about the difficulties of farming, his complaints about the weather and the men who worked for him; one less, she discovered, than when she went to Beth's wedding.

'You should have come with me,' she told him, for he had been included in the invitation. 'It would have been a break and you would have enjoyed it.'

'I have never yet found the least pleasure in that toffee-nosed lawyer's company,' he snarled. 'Charming enough, he may be to you, and no doubt he smarms up to your father, but he treats me as if I am a convict in chains instead of a free settler. Not surprising as he has such a tight hold on the purse strings.'

Ella let that pass, even though she felt in her heart that maybe her father was being harsh on William. She supposed he was doing his best in a strange country and, after all, he had never had anything whatsoever to do with farming, even in England.

'Violet looks well. She is growing up, isn't she?' Ella deliberately changed the conversation and smiled at her daughter who came skipping in at this moment with an egg in each hand.

'Rosie and I have been getting the eggs. Look at these lovely brown ones.' She held them out to Ella. 'Rosie has got a lot more, but these two were the brownest.'

Ella took the eggs and looked up as Rosie came in with a bowl in her hands containing several more eggs. When Ella intercepted the girl's glance from William to herself, it struck her in an illuminating flash why there had been an uncomfortable feeling in the house since she had come home. Rosie did not want to be alone with William because he had made advances towards her while she, Ella, was away. The look she saw her husband throw at Rosie was one of sheer lust before he hastily resumed his normal, disgruntled expression.

Ella's immediate reaction was that she did not want to lose Rosie. This had to be stopped. 'William . . .' she smiled at him, 'I have noticed that Rosie's bedroom door does not latch too well; it has a tendency to blow open in a high wind. Do you think it would be possible to fix a bolt on the inside?'

As she placed the eggs she had taken from Violet into the bowl in Rosie's hand and took them to the larder, she noticed with some satisfaction the look of astonishment on both their faces; a shiver of relief also crossed the girl's features. Ella knew that her intuition had been correct but also that a bolt alone would not solve the problem. That was up to her.

Although Ella knew that her future lay with William and her marriage, it was a few weeks after her return that she faced the fact that this had become a necessity. She was with child again, and it had to be Edwin who was responsible. Feeling far more of a harlot than she had when she and Edwin became lovers,

86

she succumbed with as much grace as she could to William's advances, closing her eyes and praying that he would now keep his hands away from Rosie and, above all, that the girl would stay.

When she told William that she was expecting another child, he was delighted, appeared to put his back into the farm work and was more gentle and thoughtful towards her than she had ever known him to be. Overcome with guilt, she did her best to be a good wife in every way, and for the months of her pregnancy was content, if not happy.

*   *   *

Ella lay back on her pillows, exhausted. Like her last confinement, this one had been slow and difficult.

'I don't think you got your dates right, Mrs Weston,' the midwife insisted. 'Whatever you say, this is a very big baby for eight months. It doesn't look like an eight-month baby to me. See her nails? They are too long.'

Ella was looking not only at the baby's nails but at her features. To her guilty eyes, she looked incredibly like Edwin, so much so that she was sure it had to be obvious to everyone.

'I did not make a mistake in the dates,' Ella insisted, willing the woman to stop harping on about the baby's size. She tightened her arm slightly round the bundle as she heard William outside the door.

'There's your man now,' the midwife told her, then turning to Rosie added, 'You can let him in now.'

'Is everything over? Can I see him now?' William strode towards the bed, his eyes on the baby. 'My, but he looks bonny!' he exclaimed with pride.

'She is bonny, fine and strong for an eight-month baby.' Ella's arms again tightened their grip on the baby in her arms. She closed her eyes and sighed. If only the stupid woman would shut up. Her insistence on the advanced development and strength of the baby might start William thinking. But the baby's size was not concerning William any more than his wife's condition.

'What do you mean "she"? It's a boy—look at the size of him. That's not a girl.'

'I'm afraid it is, Mr Weston. It isn't size, you know, that determines sex. You are a farmer; you must know that.'

'Hold your tongue, woman,' William snarled. 'Let me look at my son,' he said to Ella.

Ella opened her eyes and looked up at him. 'You have no son. This baby is a girl,' she told him and could not quite hide her elation at the thought that Edwin's child would be wholly hers.

'Are you telling me that after letting my son die, you have produced another girl. I can't believe it.' He looked so shattered that Ella almost felt sorry for him. The midwife certainly did not.

'You are upsetting my patient. She needs to sleep.' She walked over to the door and pointedly held it open. 'You should be thanking God that this time you have a healthy baby and your wife has stood up to the birth so much better.' She turned to Rosie who had been standing silent through this exchange. 'Make a cup of tea, please, for Mrs Weston. For you and me as well,' she added. 'I still have some clearing up to do before I go.' She turned back to Ella. 'Don't let him upset you, my dear. Men do get so set on having sons. Now, what are you calling this one?'

Ella looked down at the baby. 'Marguerite.'

'Margaret. That's a nice name.'

'No, Marguerite. You know—like the daisy.'

The woman didn't know, and busy with her clearing up and hoping Rosie would appear soon with a good cup of hot, strong tea, she mumbled, 'Very nice . . . Margaret . . . Daisy.'

Ella smiled. 'Yes . . .' she murmured, 'my little Daisy.'

*   *   *

Ella resumed her household duties, but not her marital ones. Making the excuse that the baby would disturb William at night at a time when he was so busy on the farm with shearing, she moved into Violet's room with the baby. William protested.

'Why couldn't you just put the baby in there?' he asked, reasonably enough.

'She's too young; she needs to be with me.'

With a flash of insight, William thought it was the other way round; Ella needed to be with the baby. He regretted his words when she was born, but the disappointment had been so intense. He had been quite sure that Ella was carrying a son who would replace the one who had died. To add to his frustration, after a couple of nights Violet moved into Rosie's room. He told himself that he would never have taken advantage of the girl by going to her room uninvited, but it had given him a vague sort of comfort to know that she slept there alone. He did not know that Rosie had actually suggested the child move in with her.

'Let her move in with me. She's not getting enough sleep,' she had said to Ella when Violet was particularly tired and cranky after two nights of broken sleep.

'Yes, yes, I want to sleep with Rosie. I don't like sleeping with you and that horrid baby.'

Ella turned away to hide her hurt, yet she agreed.

On the surface, they appeared a normal family, but beneath there were deep divisions. Ella and Rosie worked side by side during the day doing the household chores and caring for the children. William grew more disgruntled and found more solace away from home and in drink. The crunch came when he came home one evening to find Rosie and the children in bed and Ella alone, warming a pan of milk on the stove.

William stood inside the door, watching her for a few moments.

'Ella . . .' His voice was thick with emotion. She looked young and vulnerable standing there in the lamplight in her nightgown with a wrap draped round her shoulders. 'Ella— please . . .' He moved forward with one hand outstretched. It was a pleading gesture, but Ella recoiled instinctively. If he had not taken her by surprise, she might have schooled herself to some other response—or so she told herself afterwards.

As it was her reaction inflamed him, he took another step and his outstretched hand grabbed her by the arm, the grip of his fingers on her bare skin causing her to cry out as she tried to pull away. William had not drunk enough to be unaware. He pulled her to him, his free arm encircled her and, cursing under his breath, he held her even closer and forced his lips down on hers.

Ella gasped and tried to turn away, but her resistance merely inflamed him more. As he pushed her back against the solid wooden table, she felt herself being bent backwards with his knee against the inside of her own leg.

Shocked by his violence and nauseated by the smell of beer on his breath, Ella fought to get away only to make him more determined to take what he felt he had a right to.

Just when Ella thought she might suffocate, he took his mouth away from hers to release the angry words tumbling over themselves. 'Are you coming to bed, or shall I take you here?' he snarled. 'You can take your pick, but you are my wife, and it is more than high time you behaved like it.'

With a superhuman effort, Ella got a hand free and, raising it to his face, she raked her nails down William's cheek. The pain was so unexpected that he released her and she fell back on the table with a scream. The pan of milk fell over with a clatter as his open hand hit her across the face.

'William!' The shocked and angry cry from the doorway made him spin round. Ella, looking past him, saw Rosie standing there, bridling with outrage. She pushed past William and flung herself, sobbing, into the younger woman's arms. It was a long time afterwards that she registered the fact that Rosie had called William by his Christian name, for the first time in her presence. She did not notice the quelling look she threw at William; only heard her voice taking charge.

'You had better wash your face,' Rosie told him. 'You don't want to get an infection, nails . . .' she trailed off and turned her attention to

Ella. 'I'll get a cold compress for you. Even so, you may get a black eye—certainly a bruise.' She pushed Ella down into a chair at the table. 'Sit there while I clear this mess and get you a cloth and some cold water.' She glanced across at William who was already at the sink splashing water on his face.

Rosie bustled about with rags and water, mopping up spilt milk and dabbing at Ella's face somewhat indiscriminately. There was, she thought, only so much a normal red-blooded man could stand. She wondered whether William had the same thoughts about baby Daisy that she herself harboured, or whether this outburst was just the result of normal frustration. She sighed, wondering what was going to become of them all.

'Hold this wet cloth against your face,' she almost snapped at Ella, adding before she could stop herself, 'and stop crying. You will have both the children awake and bawling too in a minute.'

Ella gulped. 'Oh—Rosie . . .' she gasped, watching William leave the room with one last furious glare at her, 'what shall I do? I can't—I won't stay here with that . . . that brute.'

Rosie, wringing out a cloth over a galvanized pail, looked at her and sighed. 'No, I don't suppose you can. But where will you go? Back to England?'

Ella shook her head vehemently. 'How could I? Even if I could bring myself to admit to my father what a terrible mistake I made in marrying William, I haven't the money for the passage. No, Alice Sanders said I could always go there if I was ever in trouble, so that is what we will do. We will go tomorrow.'

Rosie stared at her in dismay. She liked it here on the farm. Without either of them, she doubted whether the hens would be fed, the cow milked or a thousand and one chores dealt with. She had stuck by Ella steadfastly, but now—well, she didn't think all the blame could be laid at William's feet. And how could he cope at all without either of them? She opened her mouth to say something along these lines, but shut it again. To say anything now would only send Ella into another fit of hysterical weeping. Best to sleep on it anyway, and make her decision in the morning.

In the end, Rosie kept silent until the cab deposited them all at Alice Sanders's gate. Her heart thumping, she turned to Ella. 'You will be all right now,' she told her, 'Mrs Sanders will look after you. I am going back to hold the fort until you feel ready to come home.' She bent down and enveloped little Violet in a tight hug. 'Goodbye, Vi. Be a good girl for your mother now.' Rosie straightened up and, without a backward glance, walked away just as Alice opened the door to exclaim in surprise at the sight of Ella, already sporting a blue mark on her face and with her bags at her feet. One arm cradled a baby and the other hand firmly gripped Violet who was trying to pull away to run after Rosie. Alice stepped forward and snatched the sobbing child up in her arms, carrying her firmly inside and leaving Ella to follow with her baby and her explanations.

CHAPTER ELEVEN

Ella never returned to the farm. With Beth married, Alice was alone and was glad of the company and the help. Daisy grew up thinking of her as her grandmother and Ella never knew if Alice knew the truth, that Edwin was Daisy's biological father. Occasionally she caught Alice watching Daisy intently and she would sometimes compare her development with that of her own children, but she was quite impartial in her treatment of the two children despite Violet being prone to nightmares and tantrums in the first few months. Also, Violet had repeatedly asked for Rosie at first, but with time she seemed to forget her.

Edwin was a regular visitor; the children learned to call him 'Uncle'. William came to visit once and tried, rather half-heartedly, to persuade Ella to return home. The truth was that he was finding life better without her. Rosie was an efficient and hard worker, she ran the house well and once she was convinced that Ella was not coming back, she also shared his bed.

They both missed Violet, particularly Rosie who had done so much more for her than her own mother, but finding she was pregnant compensated somewhat and this was when she suggested to William that he should take the clothes and personal belongings that Ella had left behind to her. This, Rosie knew, would make it clear to Ella that no one expected her to return to the farm.

The two women never met again. Rosie persuaded William to sell up and move to New South Wales where they would not be reminded of the past.

Eventually Violet had stopped asking after Rosie, but she never forgot her and never quite forgave her mother for, as she thought, 'sending her away'. Gradually 'Grandma Alice' earned pride of place in the child's heart for, however hard she tried to be impartial, or at least to appear so, Violet always knew that Daisy was her mother's favourite.

Curiously, the relationship between Edwin and Ella did not blossom into a passionate love affair but settled into a solid, deep friendship. Ella knew that she could always rely on him should she need advice or help; he on his side was grateful to her for the help and companionship she gave his mother, thus relieving him of the responsibility. He organized her divorce from William and when her father died suddenly and unexpectedly, he arranged for the small inheritance he had left her to be carefully invested so that she received a quarterly sum. This made her financially independent although far from wealthy. When Edwin's wife died and he asked her to marry him, Ella prevaricated. He didn't press the matter.

The months slid into years. Daisy knew no other home and memories of life on the farm, even of Rosie and her father, faded for Violet. It was a happy, untrammelled childhood for both of them. Violet got engaged to her childhood sweetheart, Bill, almost as soon as she left school and was soon totally absorbed in wedding plans. Daisy, on the other hand, announced that she intended to go to England.

'I want to see where I came from,' she announced.

'But you didn't. You were born out here,' Violet pointed out.

'I may not have come personally, but Mum did. It's where we originated,' Daisy insisted.

It was Edwin who suggested that if she were so determined to go then it would be a good idea for Ella to go with her. But Violet was getting married and that would mean either postponing the wedding or that Alice, now ageing and rather frail, would be on her own. It was Alice who suggested that Violet and Bill live with her until Ella and Daisy returned.

Edwin held Ella close for a moment and

promised her, 'I shall ask you again when you come back.'

'Ask me?' Ella, her mind on the coming adventure, was puzzled.

'To marry me, of course. I know you have secretly yearned to go home for a long time and accompanying Daisy is a good chance; she wouldn't be safe on her own, and now Violet and Bill are going to stay with mother, we don't have any worries. So, enjoy yourself— and come back soon.'

Ella promised she would, but she was excited and terrified at the same time about this trip. Would she find everything and everyone very changed? More importantly, had she changed so much that she would no longer fit in? Daisy had no such qualms; she was fulfilling a childhood dream.

*   *   *

Ella and Daisy spent a good deal of time planning Daisy's future on the journey home in between the various social events that were so much a part of shipboard life. Oddly enough, neither of them had thought much beyond the fact of actually going to England. Ella was merely planning a visit to catch up with the family she had left behind. But Daisy, it seemed, had greater plans.

'I want to stay for at least a couple of years, Mum. I want to really live there, not just be a visitor.'

'You mean you want to work?'

'Yes, I do. Problem is, I don't really know what at.'

Ella suggested the two main career paths for women in those days: teaching and nursing. Daisy pulled a face.

'I don't want to do either of those. Teachers always seem to end up dried up old maids. Anyway, I have no qualifications. I should have to go to college for about three years. Besides which I don't think I like children nearly enough to dedicate my life to them.'

Ella smiled; she couldn't quite see Daisy in the role of dedicated schoolteacher either. 'Well, that only leaves nursing,' she pointed out, 'unless you just want to take some sort of unskilled job in a shop or office, or worse still, housework. Why don't you just do the rounds of the relatives and then come back to Australia with me?'

Daisy pulled a face again. 'Mum, you are missing the point. I want to live in England for a couple of years, find out what it is really like. I don't want to be taken round like a pet dog on a lead.'

'Well, if you are really serious then you have to train for something,' Ella insisted.

'How about doing a really good secretarial course?' She held up her hand as Daisy began to protest. 'I don't mean just a shorthand and typing course, I mean a *secretarial* course where you would learn other things.'

'Mmm . . .' Daisy could see that this idea had possibilities. So it was that she enrolled in a private secretarial school in Oxford that prided itself on turning out efficient personal secretaries who could get interesting jobs and command good salaries.

Daisy enjoyed both the life at the secretarial college and the life outside it. Oxford was an exciting place to be; there always seemed to be a party somewhere. Often she and her friends would go to two or even more on a Saturday night. She made many friends and found the work interesting and far from difficult with exciting possibilities always dangling in front of them in the job market. For both Daisy and her mother, Australia became if not exactly a dim then a rather dreamlike place somewhere in the back of their consciousness.

*   *   *

Ella found that her family—her mother, brother and sister-in-law—automatically assumed she was a widow. She supposed she must thank Edwin for that. They asked after Violet, but whether from tact or lack of interest (she was not sure), did not question her about William. Her mother obviously looked on her marriage as an unfortunate mistake in her past and therefore best forgotten. Ella was not altogether sorry that,

100

elderly and frail, her mother did not seem to have a very clear memory of the circumstances that had led to Ella's departure for Australia.

One of Ella's favourite relatives had always been her mother's younger sister, May. Actually closer to her niece in age than to her elder sister, she had married very young, and very well in all respects. Gordon was not only an extremely successful man of business but a loving and generous husband and father. Their family of three children had now grown to seven, but with the four eldest married and settled in their own homes, it almost seemed to Ella that time had stood still when she visited her. After her time with William struggling on the farm and even the years with Alice Sanders in her modest home, the opulence of her aunt's house made her feel she was living on a film set.

Daisy seemed so settled and happy in her new life that Ella was thinking rather vaguely of returning to Australia. Distance, she had found, had made Edwin fade into rather a dim figure. She had slipped into her old life and felt totally English again.

'Ooh!' May squeezed her arm as she walked with her up the wide, sweeping staircase, 'this is so lovely, Ella, having you staying here again. Now, promise me you will stay at least six weeks. You won't go racing back to your mother, or worse still, rushing back to Australia, will you?'

'Well . . .' Ella demurred, 'I am supposed to be going back in a month, you know. I thought I would spend two or three weeks with you—if you can have me that long.'

'Oh, Ella, you do talk nonsense. Six weeks at least is what I expect. I have no end of plans to give you a really great time to remember when you go back to that dull life of yours, starting with a little dinner party tonight.'

'Oh, anyone I remember?'

'Probably, dear, certainly people who will remember *you*.' May's smile was arch.

Ella told herself that she should have guessed her aunt was plotting something.

'Now,' May continued, 'I sent Carter up to unpack for you so you can have a little rest—a bath too, if you like—before you change for dinner. Drinks about seven in the drawing room.'

As promised, Ella found that her cases had been unpacked. Her clothes hung in the huge wardrobe with her nightdress placed on the pillow, the bed already turned back and her hair brush and make-up on the dressing table. She wandered into the adjoining bathroom and found large, fluffy towels, soap, bath crystals and talcum powder all ready. Unused to such luxury, she frowned slightly, filled with the odd sensation that she was somehow surplus to the scene.

Back in the bedroom, she opened the wardrobe door and surveyed her modest wardrobe. What on earth should she wear for dinner tonight? She finally selected a short shift evening number with a drop waistline she had bought in Oxford when she was settling Daisy in there. She had protested at the time that it was much too youthful for her but had finally succumbed to the urgings of both the saleslady and Daisy after trying it on and seeing, with some surprise, that it really did 'do' something for her. Looking at herself in the mirror, she thought that she and the dress had somehow met, agewise, so that it appeared exactly right for her. The colour, a wonderful shade of peacock blue, was what the dress relied on for impact. She pulled it out and hung it on the outside of the wardrobe and stripped off for a leisurely soak in the large tub.

It was just before seven when she walked into the drawing-room. Her brother-in-law was talking to another man at the other end of the room. Engrossed in their conversation and turned away from the door, they did not see her hesitate as she came in. May, however, swiftly detached herself from the group she was chatting with. 'Ella, darling, come and meet . . .' but Ella had stopped dead in the middle of the room, for the man talking to Gordon had turned to face her.

'Walter!' she thought she yelled, but in actual fact, her voice came out as a sort of strangled croak. She might have made a bolt for it if her way had not been blocked by the last couple of guests arriving and the fact that Walter was moving towards her, his hand outstretched.

'Ella, how good to see you again.'

He can't really mean it, she thought; he always was polite. Then she glanced at May, saw her visibly relax as Walter took her hand and knew this meeting had been carefully orchestrated.

By the time the guests moved into the dining-room some thirty minutes later, Ella was wondering how she could ever have been so crass as to throw over this kind and attentive man for the young William. The years had been kind to him; he had not changed a great deal. In fact, Ella felt that she had, in some way, caught up with him so that now they seemed like equals. In the days of their engagement, he had seemed so much older. She had thought of him then more as one of her father's contemporaries. Over dinner, she learned that he too had been married and was now widowed.

'My wife was actually a little older than I was,' he told her, and though his voice was serious, the slight twinkle in his eye made her say, 'You had probably had more than enough of young and flighty females.'

'She was quite different from you. A widow with a young son. I had known her for some time; we were excellent friends and I was

104

always very attached to James. I think of him now as my own son.'

Ella felt pleased that it had not been a great romance and immediately ashamed of the thought. When he asked if he could see her again, she agreed.

CHAPTER TWELVE

'Mother, please try—in front of Richard, anyway.'

'If he doesn't like "Daisy", what is wrong with "Marguerite"?' Ella demanded. 'And what's with this "Mother" business?' She held up her hand. 'Don't tell me; Richard doesn't like "Mum" . . . in every way,' she added to herself. She grumbled, 'Your given name is Marguerite. A marguerite is a daisy. You have been Daisy to me since the day you were born. All right, all right . . .' she said placatingly, seeing an ominous tremble to her daughter's lips. It seemed to her that the nearer they got to Daisy's wedding, the more fragile her emotional state. As she pointed out to Walter when he endeavoured to soothe her, Daisy had barely been out of college a year before she was planning to put her head in the noose of marriage to an older, dominating man.

'Everyone hasn't the spirit to kick over the traces and break free, like you did,' Walter

105

reminded her with a twinkle.

Remembering how she had broken her engagement off all those years before and the less than happy result of her marriage to William, Ella grunted. How good it was that she and Walter had eventually been reunited and that he could tease her about it and she could laugh with him.

'You have to let Daisy make her own mistakes, and bear in mind, this may not be one of them. It is the only way any of us can learn. If Richard wants to call her Margaret and her to call you Mother, then go along with it. What's in a name anyway? You are still the same people. You surely don't want to cause a rift over a little thing like a name?'

Ella grunted again. Of course she didn't, but she didn't like Richard and she had an uncomfortable feeling that Daisy was not going to find life easy as his wife. At least as his private secretary she had the option of giving in her notice—in theory anyway. It was disappointing enough that Violet would not be here for her sister's wedding, her second pregnancy the reason. Walter, she knew, was right. Ever the peacemaker, she thought, recalling how he had accepted their broken engagement all those years ago. Walter would never do anything to rock the boat.

She sighed, 'I know you are right. I can't help but feel she may well need me in the years to come, so I certainly don't want a permanent estrangement. But,' she added with a flash of defiance, 'I shall still call her Daisy when we are by ourselves.'

A week later, she fought the lump in her throat as she watched her daughter, through blurred vision, looking young and beautiful, bind her life irrevocably to Richard Dobbs, twelve years her senior. As Richard was good-looking and reasonably well-endowed with this world's goods, it was held by the family that she had made a good match. But he had always struck Ella as cold and lacking in humour. She wondered if it was her fault that Daisy had chosen him; she found it hard to believe she had fallen in love. Was she subconsciously searching for the father she had never really had? William, her legal father, had never wanted much to do with her and Edwin, her biological father, had never acknowledged she was his daughter, even if he had guessed. She wondered now why she had never told him. Was it because she did not want to break up his marriage? This belief had given her a sense of virtue over the years. Or was it because, deep down, she did not wish to share this precious second daughter?

Ella bowed her head as the bridal pair made their vows. She felt swamped by her own sense of guilt and the certainty that this was not a union made in heaven.

*   *   *

'What do you mean, you *think* he is dead? Is he, or isn't he?'

Daisy took a deep breath before answering in a voice she managed to keep steady with difficulty. 'My father-in-law has just died, Dr Wilson.'

'Oh, very well, I'll come. I'll be there shortly.' He sounded resigned now and though gruff, which was normal, not actually annoyed. Daisy guessed she had probably caught him in the middle of his evening meal. She should have pulled herself together before she dialled his number and not bleated out in a quavering voice, 'I think he is dead.' After all, she knew perfectly well the old man had just died; she had been there with him at the time, the only one actually in the room as it happened. Perhaps that was why she had been dispatched downstairs to the study to phone. She was only the daughter-in-law. Maybe his children felt the need for a few moments alone with him. Even as she thought this, she knew she was being sentimental. She may not have been related by blood, but she had loved him.

As she turned and made her way slowly back up the massive oak staircase dominating both the hall and the landing above, she sighed. Yes, she had loved him, and so had her children. If no one else did, at least they would miss him.

'He is on his way,' she told Richard as he

came out of the old man's room and met her at the top of the stairs. Daisy turned away from him and headed for the nursery.

Her spirits lifted as she closed the door behind her. This was another world, an island of light in The Grange, the sombre, Victorian pile that she called home.

'Go see Grandpa?' Giles looked up from his Lego building task and began to scramble to his feet in the confident expectancy that his mother would accede to this request, or command, as she did to most things.

Daisy caught him up in her arms and, dropping down on the Victorian nursing chair, held him so close that he struggled to free himself. She shook her head. 'No, darling, I am afraid you can't see Grandpa. He . . . he has gone.' How on earth, she wondered, did you explain to a two-and-a-half-year-old that he would never see his grandpa again? At least Hazel, sitting upright with her toys around her in the centre of the playpen, was too young at barely twelve months to ask such questions, or probably even to notice that the old man was no longer part of her social circle. But with this thought came the realization that she would not even remember him.

She gulped around the sudden lump in her throat and her arms tightened again round Giles's small body in search of comfort. This time he pushed himself away firmly and slid off her lap. Setting his lips in the stubborn

109

lines of a two-year-old determined not to be thwarted, he stamped to the door. 'Go see Grandpa!' he repeated pugnaciously. Fortunately, the door handle was beyond his reach or ability to open.

Sighing, Daisy got up, took him by the hand and led him back to the heap of Lego where she dropped down on the floor and began to grope among the pieces. 'Let's make a truck. Come on, help me find the right bits.'

'No. See Grandpa,' Giles retorted with the single-mindedness he was capable of displaying when he had set his mind on a course of action. The Lego had been something to do until he went to see his grandfather; he had no intention of being diverted.

'I've told you, Giles, you can't.' Daisy hadn't meant to speak so sharply and was shot into a paroxysm of guilt when his eyes filled with tears and he repeated through trembling lips, 'See Grandpa.'

Dear God, this was going to be worse than she had imagined. Daisy pushed herself to her feet and held out a hand to him. She forced her mouth to curve into some semblance of a smile. 'Come on, help me down the stairs with Hazel.' Bending over the playpen, she managed to pull her younger child close enough to the edge to hoist her out. 'You know I need you to hold my hand when I am carrying her downstairs.'

110

She was terrified every time she needed to get both children down the staircase. She positioned Giles on her right and, with Hazel hoisted up in her left arm, she instructed him to hold on to the banister with one hand and her with the other as they began what she always felt was a descent more akin to descending Everest than anything else. Going up was actually easier as Giles could climb on all fours, or at least he used to; now he had just reached the stage where he felt this was unnecessarily babyish.

As they made their slow and perilous way down, Daisy decided that whatever Richard said, she must organize a downstairs playroom for the children.

It had been disturbing to discover that he had such firm views on the place of children in the home and that that place was not with him. She supposed it was because he had been brought up in the era of live-in maids and nannies, nurseries both day and night for the children and drawing-rooms for the adults. By the time Giles had reached the crawling stage, Daisy had learned that if she wanted to maintain a harmonious relationship with her husband, it would be as well to keep the baby and his toys in his own quarters.

Safely down in the hall, Daisy made her way to the kitchen at the other end of the house. This was where she seemed to spend most of her time. Being large, other people usually

111

looked at it, aghast, and described it as huge, but Daisy liked it. An Aga stove dominated one end, ensuring that the room was warm on even the most chill of winter days. At the opposite end, a large window over a wide sill bright with geraniums and busy lizzies dispelled the gloom that permeated so much of the house. In between, there was room for a vast table surrounded by seven chairs; six plain wooden ones and an impressive captain's chair at the head. There was also space for a playpen in front of the wide window and well out of the way of the work areas of the room.

Daisy put Hazel into this second playpen and by a little tactful persuasion got Giles to join her while she set about finding refreshments for them and the other members of the household. She gave the children biscuits to be going along with and moved the big kettle over on to the hot spot on the Aga. As she did this, her sister-in-law pushed open the door.

'Ah, here you are. I thought we could all do with a cup of tea.'

'The kettle is boiling.' Daisy didn't mean to sound so brusque; it was just that Edith always managed to wrong-foot her somehow. She had a knack of telling her to do something when she had already started to do it and it grated on Daisy. She felt it made her look as if she could not think of something off her own bat but needed instructions. She told herself a thousand times that she probably didn't mean it; it was just that she was fifteen years older, headmistress of the local primary school and used to telling people, including Richard, what to do.

As Edith put the teapot on the hob to warm and began to spoon tea into it, she said over her shoulder, 'I expect you want to get the children to bed. I'll do this.'

Daisy hadn't actually got as far as thinking about bed for the children though a glance at the clock told her that Edith, as usual, was right—it was actually well past their normal bedtime. 'Yes,' she agreed, 'but I have to give them something to eat first.'

Edith looked across at the children. Daisy could see her taking in the partially eaten chocolate wheaten biscuit in each small hand and the liberal smear of chocolate across Hazel's face. She found herself explaining, or excusing—she wasn't entirely sure which. 'They were hungry. I just gave them a biscuit each to keep them going while I got them something else.' She ran her mental eye quickly over the possible menu for the children and decided on baked beans on toast, the good old standby that always seemed acceptable.

'Shall I pour you a cup?' Edith asked as she prepared to pick up the tray of tea things.

'Thanks!' Daisy did her best to sound gracious as she fumbled with a tin-opener that had seen better days. Inwardly she grappled

113

with the realization that Edith was taking the tea tray out rather than simply calling Richard and the rest of the family to come to the kitchen. It made her feel both excluded and in some way less than family. She plonked the saucepan of beans down on the hotplate rather more noisily than necessary and rammed down the lever of the pop-up toaster.

'We'll have this in the drawing-room while we wait for George,' Edith told her as she picked up the tea tray. Her words reminded Daisy that Edith—in fact, all the family—were on Christian name terms with Dr Wilson. It was only she, who had incurred his displeasure by going to his partner rather than him when she was first pregnant, who was not.

Daisy was still spooning beans into Hazel and cleaning Giles as he fed himself when she heard Edith let George Wilson in and the muted murmur of their voices as she led him up the stairs. She rubbed Giles's face and hands so vigorously with the damp flannel that he protested and tried to push her away. She felt at times that the child carried independence to extremes when he refused any assistance, but consoled herself with the reflection that at least this trait in his character should stand him in good stead in the years to come. Hazel, on the other hand, opened her mouth at regular intervals, rather like a fledgling bird. Daisy wondered sometimes if she would remain so amenable, or whether in another year's time she would be as independent as her brother.

George Wilson didn't stay any longer than was absolutely necessary to make out the death certificate. She heard the front door open and close—so he hadn't accepted Edith's offer of tea. Daisy felt another prick of irritation that her sister-in-law had taken the tray, with the large teapot, out of the kitchen. She hoped that now the doctor had left, she would be back with it soon; she needed another cup to soothe nerves which seemed to be rapidly becoming jangled.

When Edith did bring it, the tea was cold.

'I shan't stay tonight; I'd better get back to Frank.'

Daisy was relieved when she heard this. She found the presence of her husband's older sister in the house unnerving. She was five years older than Richard—that made her seventeen years her senior. Old enough—just—to be her mother. She was in fact more like a mother-in-law than a sister-in-law. This rambling old house had been her childhood home and even after she left it to marry Frank, she had returned constantly, most days in fact, to do things for Richard. Daisy often felt that it was Edith, not herself who was the mistress here. She managed, however, to say with some degree of warmth.

'You are always welcome to stay if you wish. You know that, Edith.'

The older woman inclined her head, the nearest she could bring herself to thank her young sister-in-law. 'No, I must get back.'

Daisy moved the kettle back on to the Aga hot spot and made herself more tea in the small, brown teapot she had discovered in the Oxfam shop on one of her forays for bargain clothes for the children. She poured in too much milk in order to drink it quickly as the children ate. It was what her mother had always called 'nursery tea'; not particularly palatable, but better than nothing, and she finished it at the same time that the children finished their meal.

Wearily she reclimbed the formidable staircase and, collecting their nightclothes, took them into the bathroom. After she tucked Hazel into her cot and told Giles that he must remain in his bed, she reflected that children were never so lovable as when they were pink and scrubbed and in their nightwear, *except when they are asleep*, her weary brain reminded her.

Downstairs she set about the task of getting a meal for Richard and herself, and she knew it would need to be something a little more ambitious than baked beans on toast.

Richard was morose and taciturn as they ate. Daisy thought this only natural as his father had just died and forbore to chatter.

'Death duties?' she repeated blankly. Richard had broken the silence with the

116

comment that he wondered how things would stand for them as his father had persistently resisted the idea of doing anything about the inevitability of the heavy death duties that would accrue for his heir.

'Let's wait and see,' Daisy murmured soothingly. 'Giles is upset. He keeps talking about his grandpa and wanting to see him. It's difficult explaining to a two-year-old.'

'He'll soon forget,' Daisy thought he said as he pushed back his chair.

'I shall have an early night . . .' she told his retreating back. 'It's been an exhausting day.'

As she passed the little sitting-room where they often sat when there was just the two of them, she heard Big Ben and knew he had turned on the radio. Come hell or high water, Richard must listen to the news, or at least appear to listen to it; more often than not, he went to sleep. She called through the door, 'I'm having a bath!' and didn't wait to hear his, 'Leave the water.' His parsimonious attitude to bathing was something she still had difficulty coming to terms with. She smiled slightly to herself. At least she would be first in this time.

CHAPTER THIRTEEN

'Sell the business?' Daisy gazed in total disbelief at her husband. 'But you can't!'

117

'No one can stop me—if I want to.'

'But your father built it up, made it into what it is today. And—and your grandfather started it.' She stared at him and Richard stared back. 'But, why?' she finally said, so softly it was almost a whisper.

'Death duties,' he answered tersely.

'Oh. But do you have to pay them all? I mean, what about Edith?'

'I, not Edith, inherited,' Richard pointed out.

As if she needed reminding. The scene when the family solicitor read out Thomas Dobbs's will was etched in her memory. She would never forget Edith staring at poor old Mr Parvill in blank disbelief. She had turned first so white that Daisy had thought she was about to faint, then scarlet as she vented her rage on each of them in turn; the lawyer for drawing up the will, Richard for being the chief beneficiary and finally Daisy.

'You are the one to blame. You influenced my father, you schemed and smarmed up to him—you . . .' At this point Edith's husband Frank intervened, taking her by the arm and leading her firmly from the room. As the three people left sat in shocked silence, they could hear her still screaming abuse at her hapless husband.

'I—I didn't . . .' Daisy stammered. She wanted to say that she had never done anything in any way to influence her father-in-law; she had not discussed his will with him in any way. But she had been fond of him, they had got on well and at times she had found a warmth in him lacking in his son. It didn't seem to her that Edith had so much to complain about. She had been left a nice house plus a bequest of several thousand pounds, and with a husband who was well enough off to be described by some as rich, she had no actual need of the business. Surely she hadn't expected to inherit it and have Richard running it for her?

'Your father didn't leave it to you to sell,' she pointed out now as her thoughts came back to the present moment.

'He left it to me under such terms that I do not have much option,' Richard countered. 'Edith wants her cut now, immediately, and there are one or two other small bequests, mostly to people who worked for him, and the money in trust for our children.'

'The money he left Giles and Hazel would be better left in the business anyway, wouldn't it? And surely Edith will be happy to leave hers there for the time being. I would have thought it would be as good an investment as she is likely to find.'

'Edith does not care one jot what happens to the business. In fact, I think she would be quite happy to see it go down the gurgler. What she wants is her money.'

'But your father, he was so proud of the

business, what he had done with it, proud of his father—your grandfather—how he built it up from nothing. He—he used to talk about Giles taking over . . . eventually.'

'Huh!' Richard gave a snort of derision. 'By the time Giles is old enough to take it over, there won't be a business to run.'

'Well, there certainly won't be if you sell it!' Daisy retorted. 'Couldn't you—borrow?'

'And put myself in hock for the rest of my life?'

He sounded so dispirited that Daisy was moved to say, 'This isn't like you at all, Richard. I never thought of you as the sort of person likely to give in.'

'I am being realistic, that's all. I don't want to sell any more than you want me to. It is—as you said—Giles's inheritance too.' He paused and looked at her, almost as if he were seeing her for the first time. Or the first time in many days. 'One of my problems is getting good staff in the office. You have been missed there, Daisy.'

Daisy wasn't sure she was hearing correctly. Richard was, it would seem, praising her in his rather devious manner.

'Are you asking me to come back?' For a brief moment, she forgot that she now had two young children. Working had never been an option since she married Richard.

'Yes,' he told her without hesitation, yet looking faintly surprised as if he hadn't expected to hear himself say this. 'Let young Lizzie look after the children, and come back and help me keep the business going—for our son.'

'Lizzie can't do everything in this house and look after the children properly,' Daisy objected.

'You do.'

'Of course I don't, Richard. I have Lizzie to help me.'

It was then that Richard delivered his bombshell. 'Edith has offered to come in and help.'

'Edith! But I thought you and she . . . I thought she barely spoke to you, or you to her, since—since your father died.'

'I am trying to save the business for Giles,' Richard pointed out patiently. 'Unless we pull together, I can see no alternative other than selling to pay off the death duties. Edith is willing to supervise the house and the children.'

Even when he told her that, it didn't occur to Daisy that Richard had already discussed this with his sister.

'Why doesn't she come into the business?' she asked now.

'Edith has never worked. She knows nothing about the practical side of running the business. She has no secretarial skills—you have. On the other hand, she is used to running a house.'

'She has no experience of children though.'

Richard shrugged as if to say that any woman knew how to look after children; it was something that came naturally. 'She knows Giles and Hazel,' he pointed out.

Later, with twenty-twenty vision bestowed by hindsight, Daisy knew she should have refused to do this even for a few weeks, but Richard had used her two vulnerable points to win her acquiescence: her lack of self-esteem and her love for her children.

'Very well, Richard. I will come into the office to see you through this difficult period.'

What she had envisioned as a purely temporary arrangement soon became the status quo, and there seemed no way to change things back without causing a gigantic upheaval in the household.

Edith and Frank leased their own house and moved into The Grange. Lizzie left, whether of her own choice or not never seemed quite clear, and was replaced by another maid of Edith's choosing. In other, more subtle ways, Edith took over the reins.

Daisy's temporary employment in the business had extended to nearly four years by the time the flu epidemic struck. Giles, now at kindergarten, had brought the virus home and when both Edith and his wife went down with it, Richard sent an SOS for his mother-in-law to come and help them out.

Ella swept into the house like a blast of

122

fresh air and when she left, she had a convalescent Daisy and the two children with her. By the time she arrived, Edith was already on the mend, but Ella was shocked to find her daughter not only very sick but suffering from a lassitude and depression she could relate to all too well. She knew that something more than a virulent influenza virus was affecting her. Ella's previous visits over the years had been restricted to lunch on Sundays. Ella had thought Edith bossy and overbearing, but had not realized just how much of her daughter's position in her own household she had usurped.

'I can't leave Walter much longer. He is not young and—well, not too good on his own,' Ella told Daisy who was slumped in one of the big armchairs in what was known as the morning-room. Ella was in a straight-backed chair sewing something for one of the children. For once they were unlikely to be interrupted by Edith who had taken Hazel with her to fetch Giles back from school.

'It was very good of you to come, Mother. I—we all appreciate it.'

'That's as may be.' Ella's voice was tart. 'But how are you going to manage when I leave?'

'We'll manage . . . Edith . . .'

'That's just it, Daisy. Edith is managing much too much. I thought this was supposed to be a temporary arrangement, helping Richard. Well . . .' she added when there was

123

no response from her daughter, 'I just hope he is paying you well, at least the same salary you got before you were married.'

Daisy's lips tightened and she turned her head away.

'He's not paying you anything, is he? Fair enough for a short time, a very short time, but you have handed over everything to that sister of his—the running of your house and the care of your children. You've become nothing in your own home. You are not even Daisy any more. Well, Richard can call you what he likes, but you will never be Margaret to me. Where is your self-respect, your spirit?'

'Don't, Mother!' Daisy caught her breath on a sob and made no attempt to stop the tears brimming over and rolling down her cheeks. She fumbled about, but did not seem to have a handkerchief. Ella reached into her own pocket and pulled out a large, white one belonging to Walter.

'Just tell me—honestly—that you like this arrangement. That you enjoy seeing another woman take over your children as well as your household, and I won't say another word.'

Daisy responded by sobbing louder than ever and wailing, 'Of course I don't, but what could I do? Richard wanted me to help him and I felt I should. It's a wife's duty to help her husband, isn't it?'

'What about a mother's duty to her children? Where does that come in?'

124

The only answer was an agonized wail and even louder sobbing. Ella could feel her patience ebbing. 'You need to convalesce. I am taking you back with me. If Richard has any sense, he will realize that you are not much good to anyone in this state.'

'What about the children?'

'The children too. A change of scene won't do them any harm.'

But when it was mooted to Richard, he was adamant that Giles must stay at home. 'He cannot miss school,' he said.

Daisy demurred and Ella pointed out that it would not be too serious for a six-year-old to miss a week or so of school. But there was no changing Richard's mind; Daisy and Hazel left to stay with Ella and Walter the following day.

It was on this visit that Hazel became 'Nutmeg'. Walter, who had no grandchildren of his own, was enchanted by the child. She in turn found him a delightful companion. A man who found time to read to her, play with her, most of all talk to her was a novelty, and within a couple of days they were almost inseparable. Hazel, who had no memories of her real grandfather, was following him around like a devoted puppy and happily calling him 'Grandpa'.

Hazel came dancing into the kitchen one day where Ella and Daisy were busy peeling and slicing apples for a pie. 'I've got a new name, I've got a new name. Grandpa says I'm

125

"Nutmeg",' she chanted.

'How did he get to that?' Ella asked, realizing as soon as the words were out that she knew just how he had reached this new name.

'He says Hazel is a nut and Meg is short for Margaret and I'm called Hazel Margaret so that makes me Nutmeg. He said I'm full of spice too, just like nutmeg.' Her excited treble stopped its singsong chanting and she turned to her mother. 'Why does Grandma call you Daisy and Daddy call you Margaret?'

'Because,' Ella began to explain, 'her name is really Marguerite. That is the name of a flower, a pretty daisy, so when she was a little girl, we all called her Daisy.'

Hazel, now Nutmeg, squealed in delight and clapped her hands. 'That's much nicer than plain old Margaret!'

Ella smiled. 'I think so too.' She turned to her daughter. 'Why did you choose to become Margaret?' she asked. 'I always thought you were quite happy being Daisy.'

'I didn't,' Daisy shrugged. 'Richard said Marguerite was too much of a mouthful and Daisy was common, so he started to call me Margaret.'

'I see.' Ella threw a thoughtful look at her daughter before asking, 'What about you? What would you prefer to be called, or don't you have a say in it?'

'Me? Oh, I haven't really given it much

thought, but if you ask me, I suppose Daisy is what I have been called for most of my life. That is who I think I am, somehow.'

'Then be Daisy,' Ella said firmly. 'As far as I am concerned, anyway. I just couldn't remember to call you Margaret; you had always been Daisy to me, ever since . . .' She stopped abruptly and busied herself with the pies she was making. She was not into dwelling on memories, whether bitter or sweet.

'Why are you making such a big pie, Grandma?' Hazel asked as she reached across the table and grabbed an apple slice that had missed the dish.

'Because someone is coming to lunch.'

'Who? Are they nice? Will I like them?'

'Yes, he is very nice, so I hope you will like him,' Ella told her. 'He is Grandpa's son.'

'Ooh, a little boy coming to play.'

Daisy laughed. 'Not a little boy. He is quite grown up. In fact, I suppose he is a sort of uncle to you.' She turned to her mother. 'How old is James, Mother?'

'Oh, about a couple of years older than you, I think. Actually, I don't know him either. He's been overseas, in New Zealand, for several years.' She looked across at her daughter and added, apparently apropos of nothing, 'He isn't married.'

Daisy felt herself flush. She wished, not for the first time, that her mother did not have such an uncanny knack of tuning into other

127

people's thoughts. Anyway, what was it to her? She *was* married—very much so.

Daisy tried to efface herself over lunch, leaping up to change plates and bring in the next course until Ella, irritated by her behaviour, commanded:

'Do sit down, for goodness' sake, Daisy. Let Sarah do all that.' She almost added that Daisy was indeed behaving like the servant that Richard equated with the name Daisy. She found it irritating when her daughter was in this self-effacing mood. It was something that her young granddaughter was never likely to suffer from.

'I'm not Hazel any more,' the child had announced precociously when she met James. 'I have a new name. Nutmeg. Grandpa Walter gave it to me.'

'He did? Can you explain why?' James responded seriously, and she launched into an explanation of her new name.

'I see . . .' James smiled over her head at Daisy, 'And what does Mummy think about that?'

'Oh, she thinks it's a lovely name,' Nutmeg said airily.

'Mummy thinks it's fine, but I don't think Daddy will,' Daisy told her, feeling a sudden need to let this attractive young man know that there was a daddy in the equation.

He smiled again, once more catching Daisy's eye, and she had the feeling that what he was conveying to her was that the information had been received and noted but he still found her attractive. She found herself blushing and turned away quickly to help her mother with the meal.

James Crutchley was a doctor. He had spent the last five years in New Zealand and when he talked of his time there, it reminded Daisy of her own childhood in Australia.

'Have you come back here for good?' she asked him over dessert.

'I haven't decided. It all depends.'

Looking up and meeting his gaze across the table, Daisy felt that telltale flush warming her cheeks again. Somehow he had made it sound that it depended on her. But this of course was ridiculous; she had met him less than two hours ago. She asked, so casually that she was afraid she sounded uninterested.

'Depends on what?'

'Whether I decide to stay or not.' His smile took the rebuff out of his words.

I deserved that, Daisy acknowledged to herself.

'You sound as if you have the same dilemma as myself, James.' Ella took up the conversation. 'I have never been able to decide whether I am Australian or English. When I am there, I long to be back here, and when I am here, I often yearn to be there.'

'Exactly!' James agreed. 'I suspect the true answer lies in the heart, not the mind.

Wherever you have the most and deepest attachments is where you are truly at home.'

Daisy was to remember this conversation many times in the years ahead as she struggled with her own loyalties and identity.

CHAPTER FOURTEEN

Daisy's convalescence moved forward in leaps and bounds with the arrival of James. Ella, noting this, was worried for her daughter. She could see that there was a strong attraction between the two but could see no possibility of a happy outcome. She wanted to warn them both, but did not know how to do it tactfully. All she could do was limit the opportunities they had to be in each other's company.

Ella was standing at the window looking out on the garden. Nutmeg was in bed; Walter was dozing in his chair, sleeping off a good dinner. She wondered where Daisy and James were. Surely it was too cold to be outside, but when she moved over to the French window to draw the curtains, she saw two figures walking together in the twilight. She could just make out a circle of silver-white light framing them. It could, she knew, be a trick of the light except that she had seen this before and associated it with two people who were meant to be together. This sort of thing had happened to her before. It went with what she called an 'inner knowing', and everything told her that the feeling between these two was more than liking. With the knowledge came anxiety: whatever they did about it, someone was going to be hurt, and if they did nothing, either one or both of them would suffer.

With a quick look at Walter to check he was still sleeping, she crossed the hall to his study where the only telephone in the house stood on his desk. While she waited for her son-in-law to answer, she tried to assemble her thoughts and decide what to say. He was there all too soon.

'Hello, Richard.' Oh, God, she sounded over bright, even to herself.

'Ella . . .?' He sounded surprised to hear her voice. 'Nothing wrong, is there? Margaret and Hazel both well?'

'Oh, yes—fine . . .' It took Ella a moment or two to realize that Margaret and Hazel were Daisy and Nutmeg. 'I just wondered how you and Giles are getting along without them.'

'We are also fine,' Richard assured her. He wondered why his wife had not telephoned herself. 'We both miss them, of course, especially Margaret,' he added, giving Ella the perfect prompt.

'Yes, I am sure you do. Dai—Margaret is really quite fit again now, ready I think to come home. Perhaps you would care to come to lunch on Sunday and collect them both?'

'Thank you, yes, I would. If you are sure she is ready to come back.'

'Quite sure. Only . . . well . . . maybe it would be a good idea if you didn't mention I had called you, give her the impression that you couldn't bear being without her . . .' Ella's voice faded as she imagined Richard scowling into the silence. Oh well, she was just giving him more proof that she was a scatty, emotional person. She had no illusion about his opinion of her. He had firm views about what he referred to as the 'sanctity of marriage', and a woman's place both in the home and in the general scheme of things. Ella wondered how he squared that with getting Daisy to work in his office. But it was amazing, she thought, how people could adjust their views to their own wishes.

She put the receiver back slowly into its rest, suddenly doubtful about the wisdom of her actions. After all, she had bucked the system herself and left an unsatisfactory marriage, but then that was precisely why she knew how tough life could be for women who did not conform. She did not think Daisy had the same hard core that she herself possessed. That probably made her a nicer person, but also much more vulnerable.

When James and Daisy returned to the house from their twilight stroll, Ella anxiously scanned their faces. She thought her daughter had the unmistakable look of a woman in love.

132

My God, she thought, how far have things gone? When she told Daisy her husband had telephoned—a slight rearrangement of the truth—and that he was coming at the weekend to take her and Nutmeg home, she saw her cast an anguished glance at James. He appeared not to notice. At any rate, he made no effort to return it. Ella wished with all her heart that her daughter could learn not to show her inner feelings so clearly on her face.

Nutmeg pouted. 'I would rather stay here,' she said. 'I like staying with you, Grandma.'

'Oh, you will be glad to be home again and see Giles.'

'No, I won't. Giles teases me, but he doesn't get into trouble all the time like I do.'

'Oh, come now, Nutmeg, I am sure you don't,' Ella protested.

'I am afraid she often does, Mother. Giles always seems to do the right thing and say the right thing. Richard doesn't like her being such a tomboy.'

'And sour old Aunt Edith is always telling me off,' the child cut in.

Ella, looking at her high-spirited and frequently untidy granddaughter, could well believe that. She was afraid she had inherited some of her own wilfulness and could only hope it didn't land her in trouble. Alas, Hazel was slapped down by Richard within minutes of his arrival.

'I am not Hazel any more, I'm Nutmeg,' she

told her father.

'Nutmeg! Whatever sort of a name is that?' Giles asked scornfully.

'No name at all,' Richard replied coldly at which the child promptly launched into an account of how she had come by it.

'As far as I am concerned, and everyone else from now on, you are Hazel,' Richard told her.

'I am so sorry. It was all my fault,' Walter explained apologetically.

Richard listened with a slight tightening of his lips. 'I do not care for nicknames,' he began, but was interrupted by Giles.

'I think it is clever, I like it. Nutmeg . . . Nutmeg . . .' he experimented with the sound.

'Well, you will not use it. It sounds quite absurd!' Richard snapped, thinking it was high time everybody was back home; Ella and Walter were both far too soft with the children.

Hazel's lips wobbled, but he turned away from the threat of tears on his small daughter's pouting face. They disappeared when Giles, behind his father's back, mouthed the word 'Nutmeg' to her with a grin.

Ella bustled in from the kitchen to tell them in an overly bright voice that lunch was ready. This diffused the tension and they all trouped into the dining room for what turned out to be a somewhat strained meal. Daisy retreated inside herself, even the children were subdued, and the conversation was kept going only by Walter's valiant efforts to discuss business with

Richard.

Almost immediately the meal was finished, James made some excuse about meeting a friend and said a formal goodbye to Daisy. He would have done the same with Nutmeg, but she hurled herself on to him and he had little choice but to sweep her up in a bear hug. 'Goodbye, Nutmeg,' he said softly. 'I have enjoyed meeting you—and your mother.' He looked over the child's head and smiled at Daisy. She did not return the smile or the sentiment.

Ella was glad that Richard had carried the cases out to the car and was busy stacking them in the boot with his usual care. When Daisy kissed her goodbye a few minutes later, she felt her cling to her as she pleaded, 'Come and stay with me—soon, Mother. It's ages since you've been.'

Watching the car turn out of the driveway gate, Ella wondered if it would have been better to let things take their own course.

Daisy retreated into her thoughts on the way home. Richard seldom talked when driving. Light conversation was not his forte; he gave his full attention to whatever he was doing and only spoke when he had something to say.

Hazel and Giles were chattering together in the back seat, for once amicably, catching up on what had been happening in each of their lives while they were apart. Daisy hoped this would last till they reached home. Richard had a very short fuse when it came to putting up with bad behaviour in the back seat. Daisy was with him on this; driving with squabbling kids in the back could be hazardous, though there were worse things. She remembered bringing the children home from a party when Giles threw up down the back of her neck, causing her to drive off the road into a ditch. A kindly farmer had hauled her out with his tractor.

Daisy let her thoughts drift to her mother. She had really enjoyed her time there; the years had dropped away as she let her mother fuss over her. She smiled as she heard Hazel rattling on about Grandma and Grandpa and relaying again to Giles how she had got a new name. Turning sideways to glance at Richard, Daisy saw him frown and his lips tighten. 'Your name is Hazel,' he reminded her tersely.

Daisy repressed a sigh; she could see trouble ahead over this. Why on earth couldn't Richard lighten up, be a bit more like Walter—or James. Briefly Daisy wondered if Ella could have had anything to do with Richard collecting her but dismissed the thought. There was no reason whatsoever why her mother would want to get rid of either her or Hazel. On the contrary, she loved having them there. Her thoughts then strayed to James. She was painfully aware that she could very easily fall in love with him, so perhaps it was as well she was returning home.

On that thought, Daisy sat up a little straighter in her seat. Ella had told her in no uncertain terms that it was more than time she took over the charge of her own home and children. Daisy knew she was right; she just had to convince Richard.

The opportunity to broach the subject came sooner than she expected. The children were in bed, the last meal of the day finished and she was in the kitchen helping Edith clear up.

'Richard will be glad to have you back at the office,' Edith told Daisy in the slightly superior tone she sometimes felt was kept especially for her.

'I am not going back to the office,' Daisy told her, picking up the tray of coffee and carrying it into the lounge where she began to pour it. She passed a cup to Richard, in itself a minor act of defiance; it was one of the many chatelaine tasks Edith had usurped.

Daisy had to repress a wild desire to giggle when Edith, astonished by this act of defiance, followed her into the lounge with the tea towel she had been hanging on the Aga rail still in her hand. Noticing it, she ticked to herself.

'Did you hear that?' she demanded of Richard. 'Daisy says she is not going back to the office.'

Richard sipped his coffee and looked over the rim of his cup with raised eyebrows, his glance going from one to the other of the two women. He answered with his usual economy of words.

'I have had to manage while she has been away. No doubt the present arrangement can continue. It was, after all, intended in the first place as a purely temporary arrangement. I am very grateful to you, Edith, for stepping in here and making it possible.'

Both women stared at him in surprise. 'But . . . but . . .' Edith stammered. She looked almost forlorn. Daisy, steeling herself for a battle with Richard, felt let down to find that he was actually supporting her.

Edith was the first to find her voice.

'I am quite willing to stay on and help. Daisy may find the house—and the children—too much for her. After all, she is still convalescent.'

Daisy smiled. 'That is kind of you, Edith, but it will not be necessary. I can assure you I am quite fit again. My mother looked after me very well indeed, and I am looking forward to taking over the reins and running the house again.' She glanced at Richard and was surprised to receive a small nod of approval. 'I am sure you will be glad to return home yourself, Edith. As Richard said, we are very grateful to you, but I realize that coping with young children is not easy at your time of life.' Seeing Edith bridle visibly at this reference to her age, Daisy hastily added, 'There is no need for you to rush away, of course,' and could have bitten her tongue.

Edith ignored this and spoke directly to Richard. 'I will probably go tomorrow. You are right, of course, I should be back home. If Daisy finds she is unable to manage, you can always call on me to come back and help.'

Daisy forced herself to smile. She would manage, she told herself, and if ever she needed help again, it would be her mother she would turn to.

CHAPTER FIFTEEN

Ella turned away from the window with a sigh. She was going to miss both her daughter and granddaughter very much. Had she done the right thing, she wondered, in interfering? Instinctively she knew that if it had been Nutmeg, grown up and in her mother's place, she would not have done anything. She recognized in the child a kindred spirit to herself, one who would take risks, fly close to the flame and inevitably get burned from time to time. Daisy was different. The heat would shrivel her up, she needed some sort of shield and Richard, humourless and pedantic, gave her protection from herself. Daisy would not be able to exist if she lost her children, and if she walked out of her marriage, that is precisely what would happen, for Richard would never let them go. Oh no, he would simply call in that insufferable elder sister of his to look after them. Yes, Daisy—who she supposed she must remember to call Margaret, at least in Richard's presence—was safer and better off with Richard.

Her own situation had been very different. William had turned out to be a drunken fool. Worse, a lecher (she rather liked that old-fashioned word; it was so descriptive) and violent. Edwin had truly loved her and offered her a genuine sanctuary in her time of desperate need.

Ella was unaware that she had sighed out loud until she heard Walter get up from his chair and walk across to her.

'Sad they have gone?' Although posed as a question, it was more like a statement. 'So am I. I shall miss them both, especially that imp of a granddaughter of yours who reminds me so much of you.'

'I was thinking much the same thing,' Ella admitted, and hoped she wouldn't make as many disastrous mistakes in life as she herself did. 'I should have married you in the first place, Walter. My parents, it seemed, really did know best.'

Walter did not answer immediately and Ella turned away, but he put his hand on her arm and surprised her by asking, 'Were you thinking the same thing? That you knew best when you packed Daisy off home?'

Partly because she could not move without

pulling her arm free and partly because she was so surprised that Walter should know what she had done, she answered truthfully. 'Yes, I was. I couldn't stand by and watch her destroy her life.'

'You think that falling in love with James would do that?'

'I think falling love with anyone would.'

Walter relaxed his grip on her arm. 'You make falling in love sound like a very dangerous pastime.' His voice was dry.

'In my experience, it is.'

Walter sighed as she turned to leave him. 'Don't rush off to the kitchen or whatever,' he pleaded. 'Come and sit down with me, relax, drink a glass of sherry with me. Let's be Derby and Joan for once.'

'Most things work out for the best in the end, you know,' Walter remarked as he passed her a glass of the dry sherry she liked.

'Meaning?' Ella asked, nodding her thanks.

'Well, if you hadn't taken off to the Antipodes with young William Weston, there would have been no Daisy, or Violet, and certainly no Nutmeg. I wouldn't have married Marion and would have missed having James.' He raised his glass to her. 'To our descendants!'

Ella felt her throat constrict. He was such a kind man and she had treated him so badly. 'Were you happy with Marion?' she asked.

Walter nodded. 'Yes, I was. I had known her

141

all my life. She was my age, we were comfortable together.'

'I don't suppose you would have been able to say that of me.' Ella's lips twisted into a rueful half smile.

'Probably not,' Walter agreed. He leaned back in his chair, looking into his glass. 'I am sorry our marriage did not last long enough for me to be able to convince her that I did not just marry her as a sop to my wounded pride when you ditched me.'

Ella winced at the expression.

'Though I have to admit in all honesty that it helped.' He paused and Ella could see his thoughts were taking him back in time. 'Poor Marion. Her first husband was killed before James was born and she went back to live with her parents. I don't think she found it very easy; they were not easy people, very set in their ways.'

'It must have been hard, bringing up a child in those circumstances.'

'Very. And particularly hard on the child. James was seven when Marion and I were married. We hoped for more children, but it was not to be. I have always considered James my son, particularly after Marion died. He was only twelve then. So, the time we had together was very short; but yes, to answer your question, I was happy with her.'

They sat in silence for a while. Ella knew she had been extraordinarily lucky to have this

142

second chance with Walter. She placed her hand over his. 'I think you did a wonderful job,' she said gently. 'James has grown into a very fine man.'

'But not good enough for your daughter?'

'Oh no—I mean yes. More than good enough. If only . . . but Daisy could not endure losing her children, and she would, Walter, if ever she attempted anything . . . foolish.'

'I know, my dear, it's just that they struck me as so perfectly suited.' He returned the pressure of her hand and smiled at her, somewhat wistfully.

'What an old romantic you are,' Ella told him, leaning forward and kissing him lightly on the lips.

She got up with a sigh and moved towards the door. 'Daisy's children mean the world to her. If she lost them, it would destroy her. She told me that she is not going to work in Richard's office any more; she intends to stay home. I hope she gets her way and that Richard doesn't insist that battleaxe of a sister of his stays on. I tried to impress on her that if she needs help, I am the one to ask.'

'Just so, dear.' Walter smiled to himself. He would back Ella against Edith any day, and somehow he thought that staying here had toughened Daisy up in more ways than improving her health. He felt for James, but no doubt he would return to New Zealand and hopefully find a new love there. Ella was right;

143

it would have been disastrous for anything serious to develop.

He switched on the radio to catch the six o'clock news.

CHAPTER SIXTEEN

Walter frowned as he listened to the news. That Hitler fellow was being obstreperous again, he thought, and he doubted that they were anywhere near prepared to deal with him. Certainly that fellow Chamberlain was no match for him. Walter was one of those people who failed to feel any jubilation when the prime minister made his famous 'Peace in our time' speech. He was glad James was planning to return to New Zealand. Hopefully they would have the sense to keep out of Europe's squabbles. At the same time, he felt that they were going to need all the help they could get to stand up against the might of Nazi Germany. Overcome by memories of the 1914–1918 war, the one they believed at the time was to be the war to end all wars, he pushed himself up from his chair and snapped the radio off before refilling his glass.

James agreed about the probability of another war. 'I have cancelled my passage to New Zealand,' he told them over dinner. 'I've joined the reservists and taken a post at one of the London hospitals until . . .'

The way he allowed his sentence to peter out was more telling to Ella than if he had spelled out the words 'war breaks out'. She knew that he would be in uniform and gone as soon as that happened.

'There didn't seem much point in going back just to be sent back here in a New Zealand uniform,' he pointed out. 'I am afraid poor old England is going to need all the manpower it can get—and of course, all the doctors.'

Walter thought it malevolent, or perhaps just fate, that wars should break out a generation apart. The last one, 'the war to end all wars', had robbed James of his father, and he could only pray that the next one would not rob him of his life. He stared at him, inarticulate with this appalling thought and could only murmur 'yes' into his soup.

'I suppose if New Zealand comes in, so will Australia,' Ella remarked thoughtfully.

'The whole world will be in it—civilians as well as the fighting forces,' Walter told her, his face sombre, 'but Violet and her children should be safe enough in Australia,' he added hastily. 'Maybe you should go back and see them, before things get worse. Take advantage of this lull before the storm.'

'You really believe war is inevitable?' Ella asked, looking from one man to the other. They both nodded and with a deep sigh, she agreed, 'I am so afraid you will both be proved right—whatever Mr Chamberlain says.'

'You know, that is a good suggestion; go before it all blows up. And you can't?'

Ella turned on James. 'That's rich coming from you! Haven't you just cancelled your travel plans to go to that side of the world?' Her angry glance flicked from one man to the other. 'And no, it is not a good suggestion at all; it is simply terrible. No way could I scarper off to safety and leave you, Walter. Besides, England is my birthplace *and* my home.'

'I am suggesting a visit, that is all,' Walter demurred, 'but maybe it is not such a bad idea—scarpering, as you call it. You could take Daisy and the children with you; you would all be safer there.'

'You would come with us, of course?' Her voice was dry. 'No, of course not,' she added as Walter shook his head. 'And even if I did consider it, you don't imagine Richard would let me cart his children off, just like that, do you? And how could I leave you?' As she delivered this tirade, Ella began to collect plates somewhat noisily. 'You must be mad,' she muttered as she carried them out to the kitchen.

Later that night when they were alone in their room, Walter raised the subject again. 'You would be safer . . .' he began.

Ella cut him short. 'You should know me well enough, Walter, to know that I have never

146

played for safety in my life. Much as I would like to see Violet and her children, I am not going. Whatever is coming, we will face it together. You have given me security and . . . and I love you for it, so please, no more talk of Australia.'

Walter smiled to himself; Ella didn't seem to realize that her talk of security was somewhat at odds with her previous remark about safety. But he did not bring her attention to it. Instead, he cherished her remark about loving him. She had never told him that before so even if it was in a roundabout way, it was important.

'I don't want to be with anyone else—or any*where* else,' Ella assured him, dropping a light kiss on the top of his balding head with its Friar Tuck circle of grey hair. She was surprised to find that she meant it and wondered why it had taken her so long to realize how deep her affection for him had become.

With a wave of guilt, she remembered that her main reason for marrying Walter was because it gave her a legitimate excuse to stay in England, close to Daisy who had always been the one who needed her most, if not her 'favourite' daughter. Ella baulked at using expressions like that, even to herself. Even so, if she were strictly truthful, she would rather live in England than Australia. Ella had done her best to be a good wife in every way to

Walter; she felt she owed it to him as some sort of recompense for the way she had treated him all those years ago. Her feelings for him had deepened over the years; they were, as he had said about his first wife, 'comfortable together'. It was both generous and unselfish of him to suggest this visit to Australia. She felt a fresh wave of guilt. She felt she didn't deserve the kindness and consideration he had shown her over the years, but had accepted his offer of marriage primarily for her own convenience. His suggestion that she should leave him, even temporarily, shocked her into acknowledging that it was not gratitude, guilt or even affection she felt; she loved him.

'Why should I want to go back to Australia and leave you?' she asked rhetorically without waiting for an answer. 'Don't you know I love you?'

Walter simply smiled. 'Think about it.'

'I don't need to think about,' she told him, 'I know I love you.'

'You are evading the issue, my dear. I think you should go back, just for a visit, while you can.'

Ella bent down and kissed the centre of his monk's tonsure. 'I'll think about it,' she promised.

'Thank you, my dear.'

Ella was not sure whether he was thanking her for the kiss, agreeing to think about his suggestion or for finally, after so long, telling him she loved him.

After this more than usually emotional exchange between them, life settled down into the uneasy days between the promise of 'peace in our time' and what most people expected— the outbreak of war. It was about halfway through this year in limbo that Walter raised the question once more of Ella going to Australia.

'I don't particularly want to go,' she protested, 'and how would you manage without me?'

She poured him one of his favourite whiskey and sodas. With drink in hand, she turned away from the drinks cabinet and bit back the words that shot into her mind: *how will I manage without him*? She noticed the slight tremor in his hand as he reached for the glass, and she was filled with a sudden, nameless foreboding. 'I'll think about it,' she promised, just as she had done before. But this time, he was not mollified.

'Do more than think,' he almost snapped, half to himself. 'I want to know you are safe.'

At least, that was what Ella thought he said. Repressing the wave of irritation and foreboding, she turned away and returned to her preparation of the evening meal.

She had barely left the room when she heard the sound of a tumbler falling to the parquet floor. She knew he had dropped his whiskey and, snatching up a cloth, she

149

returned with an irritated 'tcch'. The glass was where she expected: on the floor. The hand that had held it hung limply and Walter's head had dropped forward on his chest. Ella knew he was dead.

CHAPTER SEVENTEEN

'Mother, you can't be serious!' Daisy stared at Ella with a blend of horror and disbelief that was almost humorous, or would have been if the circumstances had been different. 'I know it was a terrible shock to you, Walter dying so suddenly, but you can't hie off to the other side of the world—not now, with war clouds looming.'

'It is precisely because war clouds are looming, as you so dramatically put it, that I am going.' Ella looked tired, drawn and obstinate. 'Walter wanted me to. In fact, we were discussing it, or perhaps I should say arguing about it, just before he died. I was refusing to go . . . then.' She paused and looked at her daughter. 'Why don't you come with me?'

Daisy sighed impatiently. 'Mother, you know I can't—the children—'

'Bring the children with you. That's what Walter wanted.'

'What on earth do you mean?'

150

'He wanted me to go to Australia and take you and the children with me. He said you would be safer there.'

'Oh, Mother, you must know that is out of the question. Do you think for one moment Richard would allow his children to go to the other side of the world, just like that?'

Ella shrugged; truly she did not. Nevertheless, she persisted. 'You could come with me, see Violet, let the children see Australia at least.' She had some half-formed idea that if she could get them there, they might stay.

Daisy shook her head. Like so many gentle and unassertive people, she could be stubborn at times. 'Richard would never let the children go. Please, drop the idea.'

'I have told you, Daisy, it was Walter's dying wish—literally. It was the very last thing he was talking about. I have to go. Besides, I would like to visit Violet; it is a long time, too long, since I saw her. Her children, my Aussie grandchildren, must be growing up.'

Daisy sighed, 'If you must go, you must—I know I can't stop you—but please, go quickly so that you get back while you can.' Struck by the thought that she might not intend to get back, Daisy added: 'You will come back, won't you?'

Ella didn't answer.

'Promise me, Mother, you will come back.'

'I intend to,' was the only answer she

151

received.

'Good,' Daisy murmured, but watching her mother's face, she was convinced that her mother had been aware of something she herself had missed in those few moments when Ella seemed so far away.

Walter had left the house to James and his investments and shares to Ella. Knowing that the house was not hers made it easier to leave emotionally, and the fact that she had an income of her own—not large, but sufficient—made it easier financially.

It was frustrating how long it took to sort things out and arrange her passage. When everything was settled and she was simply waiting to leave, she accepted Daisy's invitation to spend the last couple of weeks with her.

Because both Ella and Daisy were determined that only good memories should remain with them, it was a happy time that passed all too quickly. Daisy was pleased to see that her daughter was as much the mistress in her own home as she was ever likely to be with a husband as dominating as Richard. She spent as much time with her grandchildren as possible, revelling in their company, particularly in that of Nutmeg who she had to remember to call Hazel in front of Richard. In this child she recognized someone like herself, a recognition that appeared to be mutual, for the child was never so happy as when she had her grandmother's undivided attention. When the time for the final parting came, she clung to her tearfully. 'Promise you will come back!' she begged.

'I will do my best,' Ella told her, suddenly chary of making a promise that might be impossible to keep.

Daisy was seeing her off at the station on the first leg of her long journey. Ella had refused to consider tearful dockside embarkation scenes, so at the last minute, just as her train was drawing into the platform, she reached into her bag and drew out an envelope. She thrust it on Daisy. 'Keep that safe, and open it if I don't come back—only then!' she admonished, her voice rising to be heard over the noise of the train.

'Oh, Mother, of course you will come back!' Daisy shouted back, her voice choked with emotion. She thrust the letter into her own bag and when she got home decided to hide it in the secret drawer of a beautiful little escritoire she had. Holding it in her hand, she fought the desire to open it there and then. With an effort she resisted and quickly hid it to save herself from further temptation. Ella, she was sure, would demand it back *when* she returned. She refused to think 'if'. It was to remain in its drawer unopened and unread for more than ten years.

The war years were, in many ways, good to Daisy. Richard was busier than ever at his factory. Providing boots and shoes for the men who fought for England was a vital part of the war effort, and he took on the running of the local home guard in what spare time he had.

Daisy too found she was more than fully occupied. When the large house was filled with evacuees, mostly mothers and young children, she discovered a totally unexpected talent within herself for coping with other people and for emotional situations that were often more than potentially explosive. She also 'dug for victory' as the posters urged and found a primitive satisfaction in this close contact with the earth and nature and a very real pleasure in harvesting her own vegetables. As a member of the local Red Cross, she learned basic first aid and wondered why nursing had not appealed to her as a career. In addition to this, she somehow managed to put in several hours a week in the office at Richard's business and fill her larder shelves with the fruit preserved from the trees in her own garden. The one dark shadow in her life was that her mother was still in Australia. She had, as Daisy had feared, left it too late. As the war escalated and more and more ships were sunk, she had been forced to stay.

In some ways, Daisy was relieved her mother was safe, but she missed her and was sorry she was not around for the growing years of her children. She thanked God for their relatively safe home deep in the Warwickshire countryside. The war for her children merely meant a household of evacuees and parents who were so busy they did not have too much time to oversee what went on, a combination that led to an untrammelled and relatively free childhood. It was, therefore, even more shattering when war hit home one sunny August afternoon.

August 1940 was when the Luftwaffe's assault on Birmingham began. Richard was one of the first of more than five thousand people killed or seriously injured before it was to end in April 1943. He was in Birmingham for business and had decided to go by car, for as the recipient of a petrol allocation for business purposes, it seemed foolish to struggle with a tedious rail journey. Birmingham was the target of a daytime raid and Richard, his business finished, was driving out of the city when his car was blown to oblivion by a direct hit.

Hazel was five years old and Giles seven. Always closer to his father, Giles was more affected than his younger sister whose strange reaction was to insist that from now on, she would be known as Nutmeg, the name her father had banned. Daisy guessed that it was some odd, childish way of ensuring that nothing happened to her grandmother who had always called her that—still did, in fact, in her letters. The time staying with Ella and Walter had been a very happy one for the child

155

and she had been hurt and cross when Richard had insisted that she be called Hazel and not what he referred to as 'that ridiculous nickname, "Nutmeg".'

Giles had nightmares for a long time after Richard's death. Daisy, with even more to worry about, did not fall apart. In fact, she was surprised and rather shocked by her calm acceptance of things. Once the initial shock and horror had passed, she picked up the reins of her busy life and simply carried on. She was beset by sharp twinges of guilt, however, when friends referred to her bravery; she knew deep down that amidst her many jangled emotions, bravery was the least in evidence.

When she did break down, to her shame, was when James turned up looking very handsome in a captain's uniform. He came ostensibly to offer her his sympathy; in reality because he couldn't keep away. His uniform reminded her that they were at war and if Richard, a civilian, could be a casualty, there was a high probability that James could as well. When he put his arms round her and endeavoured to comfort her, Daisy sobbed unashamedly into his smart uniform, finding more than comfort in the feel of his arms but not daring to confess that her tears were as much for him as for Richard.

Before James left, Daisy offered him an open invitation to spend his leaves with them. 'Where else would you go?' she demanded, 'with Walter gone, my mother in Australia and your house rented for the duration. We are the nearest thing to family, so feel free to come here whenever you wish.'

James wanted to point out that the relationship between him and Daisy was very tenuous and in fact not a blood one at all, but he thanked her and promised he would remember.

Giles had no such inhibitions; he scowled at James. 'You aren't actually related at all, are you? You are just my grandmother's husband's son.'

'I am afraid I am not even that; I am your grandmother's husband's *stepson*,' James pointed out, smiling at Daisy over his head. Daisy didn't see the smile; she was too busy chiding Giles for what she considered his rudeness.

'I am sure he had no intention of being rude, did you, Giles?'

Giles grunted, shuffled his feet and looked uncomfortable. He wanted it made clear that James had no right to be there—he didn't want any other man there—taking his father's place in the household, however briefly.

Understanding this, James was particularly careful in the presence of the children. But Hazel had no such reservations as Uncle James was one of her very favourite people. In fact, she wished he *were* her father.

James took Daisy at her word and gratefully

spent most of his leaves with them. The friendship grew and deepened between them, and because he valued having this base, James was careful not to step over the borderline of friendship. He was not sure how Daisy felt about him, or of the depth of her feeling for Richard, and he was aware of the simmering hostility in Giles. Better to have Daisy's friendship than nothing. An added complication was her very full and busy life; when she wasn't fully occupied at home, she was working in the business.

To Edith's horror, Daisy sent the children to the village school along with the evacuee children. Her more egalitarian Australian upbringing saw this as the sensible thing to do, but by the time Giles was ten, she was unable to withstand her sister-in-law's nagging any longer and reluctantly agreed that maybe it was time for him to go to a good prep school in preparation for Shrewsbury. This was Richard's old school where he had been entered for some time. Fortunately, Edith did not consider Hazel's education of prime importance although she frequently referred to her tomboyish ways. Daisy would have liked to tell her that being her husband's older sister did not bestow on her the divine right to interfere, but she knew this would unleash a spate of hurt protestations about doing it in the best interests of Richard's children.

Fortunately for Hazel, Edith seemed to

think there was little chance of turning her into a lady, and when the suggestion that Hazel should be sent to the school she herself had attended as a boarder produced such a storm from Hazel, supported by Daisy, she climbed down and mentioned a small private school at Kenilworth where she could board weekly.

Giles stopped being openly hostile to James and took to being extremely polite, to the extent of calling him 'Sir'. Hazel laughed, 'I'll never be so polite,' she told him. 'Giles is just silly.' She took his hand and added confidingly, 'I like you coming, Uncle James. Mummy always cooks nice food and wears something pretty when you are here.'

'Does she now?' James responded. He looked over the child's head at Daisy who blushed and mumbled, 'Don't be silly, Hazel.' Hazel looked from one adult to the other, wondering why her mother seemed cross and James pleased. She had only told the truth.

Later that evening, James and Daisy sat companionably in the dusk, delaying the moment when the heavy blackout curtains must be pulled and sipping coffee that owed more to dandelions and chicory. James returned to the subject:

'Do you, Daisy?' he asked softly. 'Was it true what little Nutmeg said?'

'About what?' Daisy prevaricated.

'That you wear pretty dresses when I

come?' When he got no answer, he persisted, 'Is it, Daisy?'

'Well, I . . . I just try to be a good hostess,' she mumbled, hoping the flush spreading up her throat and cheeks was not visible in the failing light.

James reached out and took her hand. 'You are the very best,' he told her, 'but I am afraid it's coming to an end.'

'Don't take any notice of Hazel's chatter. Don't let it stop you coming . . .' Daisy was filled with alarm. Surely he didn't think she was—well, trying to trap him, wanting more than he was prepared to give.

Abruptly James jumped to his feet and, still holding her hand, he pulled her to him. 'But I did take notice, and it gave me pleasure—and hope. Something to take away with me. I'm being sent overseas; that's why I shan't be coming for a while. Can I hope that when I come back—'

He never finished the sentence. Daisy wasn't sure who initiated it, but somehow they were kissing each other. One kiss led to another—and another—and later that night, Daisy discovered that being made love to by James was entirely different to anything she had known in her married life.

CHAPTER EIGHTEEN

'If you love someone, be sure to let them know while they are alive,' Ella had said to her when Walter died. 'Thank God I did, but I regret so much that it was the only time in all our years together that I did. I sometimes think the most painful part about losing someone is our inability to put the clock back and fill in the gaps.'

Now James had gone and she no longer had his leaves to look forward to. Pleasant anticipation was replaced by gnawing anxiety about his safety. If he never came back, she would be haunted forever by the things she had left unsaid. She was ashamed when she thought of her silence when she lay in his arms; she should have assured him that she would be there for him when he came back, and told him she loved him. The trouble was she hadn't been sure—until he had gone and it was too late.

When she heard he had been wounded, she was relieved he was now safely out of the war, but when she learned that his injuries had been so severe that he had lost a leg, she felt guilty all over again.

Hazel frowned in bewilderment. 'How can you lose a leg, Mummy?' she asked. She could see how a boot could be mislaid but not a whole leg.

'It was so badly wounded they had to cut it off,' Giles chimed in while Daisy was still working out a suitable answer. 'Don't they teach you anything at that silly school of yours?'

'They don't teach us about cutting legs off,' Hazel retorted, her eyes filling with tears. 'Poor, poor Uncle James. Will he have to have a wooden one?'

Daisy wrote to him regularly, but his letters seemed distant and stilted and the military hospital was a long way off. Then he was moved to a convalescent home in Shropshire and she was able to visit him. They were uncomfortable with each other as he didn't mention his wound and neither did Daisy. She wondered if in time-honoured tradition he had fallen for one of the nurses and found her visit an embarrassment.

'Have you anywhere to go when you leave here?' she asked tentatively. He shook his head. 'Then please come to us. There is plenty of room; the evacuees have gone home and . . .' She was going to add that she could fit him up with a downstairs room but wondered how he would take such a direct reference to his disability; it seemed the one thing he had no wish to discuss.

He surprised her by accepting her offer. 'Thank you, that is kind of you, Daisy. I won't be able to get into my own house for a while as

162

the lease still has some time to run, I believe.'

Daisy was able to fetch him a few days before the war in Europe ended on 9 May 1945. He had one trouser leg pinned up and was walking with crutches.

He stayed until early July. He was not an easy guest, only lightening up to Daisy with the children, particularly Hazel whom he still called Nutmeg. It seemed to her that whenever she tried to be cheerful about the ending of the war, he reminded her that it was only the war in Europe that was over; there was still Japan.

Daisy too had her problems, not the least that she was more or less permanently exhausted. Coping with shortages and lack of help and having to rush back and forth between home and the business left her little time and even less energy to enjoy herself. She sympathized with James but found the way he had turned inward and away from her, or so it seemed, both hurtful and isolating. If he had not taken her completely by surprise and if he had been a little less distant, she might have given a different answer when he had astonished her by asking her to marry him out of the blue.

'Come and sit down with me and have a last drink before I leave tomorrow,' James had pleaded, following Daisy into the kitchen where she had been engaged in her usual struggle of getting an appetizing meal out of very few ingredients. She had turned and smiled at him, wiped her hands on a tea towel and followed him into the study, still in her apron. This room had been sacrosanct to Richard when it had been his chamber. They still called it the study even though it was now used as a family sitting room. It was the easiest room to heat in winter, and pleasant now in July. The bay window had a window seat curving round it, chenille curtains were never drawn back tightly and it was here, hidden by their heavy folds, that Hazel loved to curl up with a book. Hazel had been about to reveal herself when James had begun to speak. Agog, she had curled up tighter and listened. Afterwards she tormented herself by speculating that she could have made her mother answer differently had she revealed herself.

James had poured two drinks, from Richard's carefully hoarded whisky supply, she noted. She had sat down and watched him bring one glass at a time to the small table in front of the sofa. He was getting quite dexterous with his crutch and she knew he would resent offers of help.

They had sipped their drinks in a companionable silence. Daisy had been thinking how she would miss him when he left when he had taken her by surprise by asking without any preamble, 'Will you marry me?'

'Marry you . . .' Daisy knew she sounded as

if it was the very last thing she expected to hear. 'Oh, James, how can I?'

He stared at her. 'Don't sound surprised. You must have known I would ask you.'

Daisy shook her head and took too large a gulp of whisky. 'No—I—I didn't, actually. I—I thought . . .' She shook her head again and murmured, 'I don't see how I can.'

'What on earth do you mean, Daisy? I thought it was understood . . . last time I was here—before . . . I was wounded. You came to see me in hospital. You asked me here to recuperate. What has changed things? Is it this?' He nodded towards the leg that wasn't there.

'Because of your leg? Of course not, James. You don't think I am that shallow, surely?'

'Then give me a legitimate reason. I've loved you since the moment I met you and I thought you had begun to feel the same about me.'

'Oh, James, I do.' There was a pause before she said, 'I don't see how I can. Not if you are going back to New Zealand. Giles—'

'I asked for a legitimate reason, Daisy. Don't put the blame on Giles.'

'You don't understand; you are getting it all wrong. I have to be here for the time being. Giles . . .' Daisy knew she was making a mess of this.

'I don't think I am the one getting it wrong; I have never made any secret of my feelings

165

for you, nor that I intended to return to New Zealand as soon as it was practical. I have been offered a position at Dunedin Hospital. New Zealand is a wonderful country, I want to go back there. And I want to take you and the children. It would be a new life in a new country, one that hasn't been shattered by war.'

'You don't understand, James. I just can't. Richard left Giles the business and this house. I have to see that both are looked after for him until he is old enough to take it on himself.'

'The house can be leased and a manager put in the business.' James's voice was curt. 'It seems to me that you are using this as an excuse to turn me down.'

'That is quite unfair. If you really wanted to marry me, you could stay here and manage the business.' Even as she spoke, Daisy knew this was a forlorn hope.

'Daisy, I am a doctor. I am trained to save lives, not make boots and shoes. And I have had more than enough of England. I enjoyed my time in New Zealand, it's a wonderful country and I want to go back. I intend to go back and this time I shall apply for New Zealand citizenship.' He added this last part defiantly.

'You are saying that what you want to do is all that really matters.'

'Yes, because I know it is in the best interests of all of us. The children—'

166

'How do you know what is in their best interests? They are not your children.' Daisy stopped; she had the feeling that she had gone too far. But words, once said, cannot be pulled back.

'If that is how you feel then it seems there is nothing left to say but goodbye.'

Daisy stared at him; she felt he was being totally unreasonable. What was happening to the love he was supposed to have felt for her all this time? James stared back, and in that moment they were strangers.

He inclined his head in a stiff little bow, turned away, and with as much speed and dignity as he could muster, left the room.

Behind her curtain, Hazel stuffed her fist into her mouth to make sure she did not betray herself by making any noise. To her horror, Daisy burst into tears, convincing her that she must not reveal herself. She did not crawl out until long after her mother had left the room. For years she would feel angry when things were not going according to plan in her life and remind herself that they could all have been enjoying a different life in New Zealand if she had only burst out from her hiding place and begged her mother to accept.

After James left, Daisy did her best to erase him from her thoughts. She worked harder than ever and tried not to grumble about the everlasting shortage of everyday things and the perpetual need to make do and mend. She

167

looked forward to her mother returning at last from Australia, but on 15 August 1945, the very day the war with Japan finally ended, she received the news that Ella was dead. It was a shattering blow coming on top of her break-up with James.

*   *   *

The sound of the telephone bell ringing below in the hall had woken her. Her first thought was that there was an air raid, and then she remembered that the war was over; Japan had conceded defeat only yesterday—the bedside clock said it was five minutes past three in the morning. She tumbled out of bed and without slippers or robe hurried down to answer the summons.

'Hello . . . hello . . .' She could hear a woman's voice overlaid by crackle and static, almost obliterated by the echo that followed each word. 'Daisy—is—that—you?'

Daisy's first reaction was that although the voice sounded like that of her sister Violet, there was no way it could be her, for all international phone calls had been stopped immediately on the outbreak of war. Then she remembered the service had been reinstated on 23 June, barely six weeks before.

'Daisy—are you there—can you hear me?'

'Violet, is it you? What on earth are you doing at this time of night?' Then she

168

remembered that it wouldn't be any time of night in Australia but the middle of the day. An icy fear clenched her heart; there could only be one reason for Violet to telephone.

'I am sorry. I know it must be the middle of the night—you were probably asleep—but—it's—mother.' As she finished speaking, the eerie echo of the word 'mother' reverberated in Daisy's ear.

'What's the matter? Is she . . . is she ill?'

'It's—it's worse than that. She . . . dead.'

Once more the word bounced in Daisy's ear to echo again when she repeated it.

'Dead! She can't be—she's coming home . . .' Even as she spoke, her brain told her it had to be true; otherwise Violet would not be calling her at this time of night. 'What happened?' she managed to croak after a long pause.

'A massive heart attack—a few hours ago—nothing anyone could do.' The line was fading out. 'I'll write.'

The line went dead. Daisy looked at the phone in her hand. *She never said goodbye.* Even as she thought this, she wondered who to: Violet or her mother?

She shivered. Even though it was August, the night had a chill to it and she was wearing only a flimsy nightdress and nothing on her feet. As if in a trance, she moved to the hall closet and pulled out an old coat which she draped round her shoulders, then, still

169

barefoot, she padded to the kitchen where she switched on the electric kettle to make herself tea, the tried and true remedy for trouble of any sort. She was still sitting at the kitchen table, the cup clasped between her fingers, long since empty save for leaves and dregs, when the old grandfather clock in the hall struck six-thirty. She knew she must move; Hazel would be down soon and she needed to pull herself together before she told her.

Half an hour later, she stood at the window of her daughter's bedroom, staring out at the sunlit garden. Hazel was still asleep. It seemed heartless to wake her, but when she turned around, she saw that the sound of the curtains being drawn back had roused her. Hazel's eyes flew open and her face broke into a smile when she saw her mother.

'Hello, Mummy, is it time to get up already?' She stretched then pulled herself up to a sitting position. 'I had such a wonderful dream—you'll never guess. Grandma was back here and she was sitting on my bed, talking to me. It was so real. She didn't get back in the night without me knowing, did she?'

Daisy stared at her daughter, unable to speak for a moment. She swallowed, endeavouring to get a grip on herself. This was not the first time Hazel had known something she couldn't know or dreamed something before it happened. She took a deep breath, swallowed again and sat down on the child's

170

bed. Painfully aware of Hazel's intense scrutiny, she sought for words to break the news gently, but they just weren't there. She could only croak, 'Grandma died last night.'

Hazel stared at Daisy, her lips trembling and tears spilling down her cheeks. 'She must have come to tell me,' she finally whispered.

CHAPTER NINETEEN

Daisy reached out and clasped both her daughter's hands in her own. 'Darling, did you hear me? Did you understand what I said? Aunt Violet telephoned me in the middle of the night to say that Grandma had died. It was very sudden. She had a heart attack and was gone—just like that.'

'Yes, Mummy, of course I understand.' She brushed at her tears with the back of her hand and, making a valiant attempt to smile, whispered, 'I think she came to tell me. She looked lovely, really happy.'

Daisy smiled and hugged her daughter. It was a strange coincidence that Hazel should dream of her grandmother the very night she died; she didn't want to think it was anything more.

It was a few weeks later when Hazel looked up from her homework and sniffed loudly. Daisy was about to ask if she had a handkerchief when she forestalled her by asking, 'Can you smell that lovely scent, Mummy?'

Daisy shook her head. 'No, I can't smell anything. What sort of a lovely smell?'

'Oh, flowers, perfume—lily of the valley, I think. Remember how Grandma loved them, said she couldn't grow them in Australia—too hot and dry—so she had a big bed of them at her house to make up for it. I think it was her favourite scent. Mine too.' She looked round the room with a rather vague expression, sniffed again then sighed contentedly. 'I expect she was letting us know she was still around. What do you think?'

Daisy didn't know what to think. She had smelt nothing out of the ordinary, but if it consoled her daughter to believe her grandmother was still around, she saw no reason to disillusion her. How like Ella she was becoming, in both looks and character. Her mother used to call her strange flashes 'in-knowing' and appeared to enjoy her gift although she never took it too seriously, or if she did, she didn't flaunt it. Daisy, on the other hand, had hated it when her mother had made one of her pronouncements; it had scared her when she was young, mainly because they came true. On very rare occasions, Daisy had a dream that seemed to foretell forthcoming events and she had even had the odd intuitive flash which she could only explain as 'just

172

knowing'. She had kept these to herself, preferring to deny any so-called psychic sense she might possess; to acknowledge it was too scary. This no doubt explained why it was Hazel, not herself, whom her mother chose to approach.

As that thought slid into her mind, she hastily obliterated it. To accept the thought that her mother's spirit was still around might have been comforting, but not the thought that Hazel had inherited her grandmother's gift.

*　　*　　*

Looking up at her son—at seventeen, he was considerably taller than she was—the absurd thought crossed Daisy's mind that he was so unlike herself that had she not been present at his birth, she would not have known he was her son. Now, as a young adult, he was more like his father than ever, 'a real Dobbs', people were apt to say. This went for his character too; he already seemed middle-aged and, Daisy thought, took life far too seriously.

He was talking to her now—lecturing, rather—as if he was her elder. She didn't mind this so much as she was used to it. After all, both her children tended to look on her as the juvenile in the family, but today she thought that what he was saying was really none of his business.

'Please give me that letter.' She was pleased

to hear the firm note in her voice. 'Where did you get it from, anyway?'

'It was on your desk.'

'Didn't it occur to you that a letter on my desk was my business and not actually anything to do with you?' She extended her hand for the envelope he was holding. He had removed it from its envelope to read so could not use the excuse that it was lying open and he 'could not help but read it'.

'It is about Hazel.' Grudgingly, he extended his hand so that she could take the letter.

'Ye-e-s?' Daisy failed to see the reasoning behind his belief that because the letter was about his younger sister, it gave him the right to read it.

'I wondered what you were going to do about it.'

'I haven't decided yet. I will talk to Nutmeg when she comes home this weekend.'

'And that's another thing, Mother. Isn't it about time you dropped that ridiculous name and referred to her as Hazel?'

'I shall do that when Nutmeg asks me to,' Daisy retorted, stung by his stress on the words 'ridiculous name'.

Giles's response was a sigh. 'Mother, you don't seem to realize that Hazel is only fifteen, a child still, and you are her mother. It is up to you to deal with this properly.'

Giles's patient voice sounded pompous to Daisy; it was also familiar. Richard had spoken to her in just such a voice, each time managing to sap a little bit more of her self-esteem during the years she was married to him. She surprised herself as well as Giles when she rapped back, 'Please remember I am your mother too, and if you consider yourself an adult then Nutmeg certainly is too at fifteen, allowing for the fact that girls mature so much earlier than boys.' Defiantly she used the nickname again.

Giles flushed, but the angry retort Daisy expected did not come. Minus the pompous bluster, he sounded tolerably pleasant and much more like a young man of seventeen. 'Well, what *are* you going to do?'

'I have told you, Giles. I shall show Nutmeg the letter and see what she has to say. It is Thursday today, so she will be home tomorrow for the weekend.' She pushed the letter into her pocket and turned to leave the room, throwing back over her shoulder as she reached the door, 'I will keep you informed.'

She retreated to her own private sanctuary, the little room where she wrote her letters, sorted out accounts and paid bills, did her sewing and, as now, escaped to when things tended to overwhelm her. Mothering teenagers, she was discovering, was a very different ball game from coping with young children. One minute that was exactly what they were—children—the next they were disconcertingly adult. With a sigh, she pulled

175

the letter out of her pocket and reread it. Her daughter, the headmistress wrote, had been 'apprehended playing with an unsavoury pack of cards and it appeared money was involved'.

Daisy could not imagine what an 'unsavoury' pack of cards could be. Surely cards were cards, but as Nutmeg had always had a healthy financial sense, one of the few attributes inherited from her father, she was quite prepared to believe that money had been involved and no doubt to Nutmeg's advantage. She pushed the letter back into its envelope and shoved it firmly into one of the pigeonholes on her desk. Tomorrow would be soon enough to seek answers. Whatever Giles said, she did not intend to do anything until she knew both sides of the story.

At 4 p.m. the following afternoon, Daisy was outside the school gates to collect Nutmeg for the weekend. Anxious to get things sorted out before Giles confronted her once more, she broached the subject as soon as the car drew away from the school.

'I have had a letter from Miss Andersen,' she began.

'Oh, about the tarot cards.' Nutmeg laughed. 'She had no idea what they were. I think that was the crux of the problem.'

'No doubt. She referred to them as "unsavoury" and suggested you were using them for financial gain.'

'Wrong on both counts, Mother dear! There

is nothing intrinsically bad about tarot cards. They are just a tool for tapping into the subconscious.'

'Really?' Daisy was afraid she was getting out of her depth.

'I suppose you would call them a fortune-telling device.'

'I suppose I would. And have your friends paid you to tell their fortunes?'

'Well, yes and no. I have been doing readings for them, but no one has paid me—well, not in money anyway. They . . . er . . . well, they do me favours.'

'Such as?'

'Maths homework—you know how I hate that. Occasionally, just occasionally if there is nothing I really want doing, they pay me in kind—sweets, chocolate, that sort of thing.'

'I see,' Daisy repeated, not sure what else to say. She rather felt the headmistress had overreacted to a relatively innocent pastime. On the other hand, tarot cards . . .

'How did you get . . . caught?' she asked, adding as an afterthought, 'and where did you get the cards from?'

'Matron walked into the dormitory after lights out. We were doing it by torchlight and she must have seen the beam. She read the riot act and confiscated my cards. She must have gone straight to Miss Andersen because I was summoned to her office first thing the next morning and there they were, lying on her desk. I asked for them back, but she refused. Even when I told her my grandmother gave them to me.'

'Your grandmother gave them to you? But Hazel, how could she? You haven't seen her for years and . . . she is dead now.'

'But she did—well, sort of.'

'Sort of? Either she did or she didn't.'

'Well, to be absolutely truthful, I found them when I was with her in her room one day. They were a miniature deck, wrapped in a silk handkerchief and in a little wooden box. She said I could have them and told me to put them away and that when she came back home, she would teach me how to use them. I hid them in my drawer and forgot all about them till just recently when you made me tidy my room and I came across them.' She paused thoughtfully. 'I remember smelling Grandma's lovely lily of the valley scent when I found them, so I thought I must be meant to do something with them. I took them out, looked at them and somehow I knew what they meant and how to use them. So, I took them back to school and, well, you know the rest.' She paused and then added, 'Thing is, Mum, I want them back. They were a present from Grandma. That woman has no right to keep them.'

'No, she hasn't,' Daisy murmured without much conviction, anticipating what her daughter was about to say.

'She wouldn't give them to me, so you will have to ask her for them.'

Daisy glanced sideways at her daughter who was staring straight ahead through the windscreen. Even so, she recognized the stubborn set of her jaw and knew she would have no alternative but to do as she asked. She had an uncomfortable feeling, but she refused to acknowledge it as premonition, feeling that somehow or other, this whole business would prove to be more than just a letter from a headmistress.

Daisy sighed. 'I'll telephone Miss Andersen and make an appointment to see her.' She had no great desire to confront the formidable Miss Andersen and wondered if she would have the nerve to actually demand the return of the cards.

It was a wet weekend, and more to stop her daughter mooning about the house bemoaning the fact that it was too wet to do anything, Daisy asked if she would help her in some clearing out.

'Gee, Mum, is that really the most exciting thing you can think of?'

'To tell you the truth, it is, just at the moment,' Daisy admitted.

Hazel slid off the wide seat in the bay window. The rain was coming down in relentless sheets from a leaden sky. Giles was swatting in his room—at least, that was what he said he was doing. She was bored with her book, and her newly discovered tarot cards were in the headmistress's study. Sighing dramat-ically, she agreed with obvious reluctance. 'OK, then. What have you in mind?'

'Your clothes and my desk.' Daisy had already decided what the biggest priorities were.

'One condition then,' Hazel bargained. 'You don't throw away any of my clothes unless I say so.'

'Done!' Daisy agreed. 'But you mustn't throw away anything out of my desk without letting me see it.'

They worked through the clothes first and when they had finished, Daisy was astonished to find that the reject pile was actually larger than the 'to keep' pile. A moment's thought, however, told her that this was not really so surprising; the more clothes Hazel declared unwearable, for whatever reason, the more new ones Daisy would have to buy.

'OK, Mum, now for your desk.' Hazel grinned and rubbed her hands together in anticipation.

The wastepaper basket was overflowing with old and worthless scraps of paper, things long since dealt with, when Hazel pressed idly on a small panel below the numerous pigeonholes. To her surprise, it sprang forward, revealing a hidden drawer.

'Hey, look at this, Mum. Did you know

180

there was a secret drawer here?'

'Yes, but I had forgotten all about it.' Daisy's admission was cut short by Hazel's exclamation as she pulled out an envelope.

'A letter! Addressed to you, Mum.' She waved the envelope tantalizingly in front of Daisy. 'A letter from a secret admirer, hidden away. How romantic!' Her teasing note changed to puzzlement as she added, 'It looks like Grandma's handwriting.' Turning it over in her hand, she looked to see who it was addressed to. 'Marguerite Dobbs—Daisy,' she read. 'Only to be opened after my death.' She stared at it for a moment before reluctantly placing it in her mother's outstretched palm. 'Go on, open it,' she urged, but Daisy tucked it into her pocket.

This was the letter her mother had handed to her all those years ago. She had forgotten its existence till now, and if she had remembered, would not have known where it was. Her fingers closed protectively over the envelope and she shook her head. 'I'll open it later,' she said and pushed it firmly down into the pocket of her skirt. Her gut feeling told her that whatever she had to say, it was for her eyes alone.

CHAPTER TWENTY

Alone in her bedroom, Daisy sat down heavily on the bed and drew the letter out of her pocket. Her fingers trembled slightly as she tore the envelope open. She was not sure it was because receiving a message from the dead was slightly unnerving, or because she was afraid of what the letter might contain. She was totally unprepared for the contents:

My dearest daughter,
I have always tried so hard not to make it obvious that you always held a special place in my heart. I have wanted so many times to enlighten you about your parentage, but the time never seemed right. I have concluded that the only right time is now—when I am gone. What you do, or do not do with this information is your affair; I know I can rely on you not to cause pain to anyone else. I am not telling you because I expect you to DO anything, but because I feel you have a right to know. Your sister Violet is in reality your half-sister. Your father was my very dear friend Edwin Sanders who you knew as a child as 'Uncle Edwin'.

I made a terrible mistake when I married William Weston. It took me a long time to accept the fact that his charm was skin deep and that his main interest in me was to persuade my father to settle an income on him that would make him comfortable for the rest of his life. He underestimated my father's astuteness, so we ended up in Australia, far from rich. I was a foolish and ignorant girl blinded by romantic notions and the prospect of adventure. It was totally self-centered of me to break my engagement to Walter who was, then and always, a good man. Fate, God, what you will, was extraordinarily kind to me in giving me a second chance with him.

You are bound to ask why Edwin and I did not marry. Quite simply because he already had a wife. I did not know this when I fell in love with him, but I did when I conceived you. He was a good man; kind, gentle and clever, so please do not judge him harshly. He had 'problems' in his marriage, as his wife was a semi-invalid. I had problems in mine. When circumstances threw us together, the outcome was predictable, if not inevitable.

Forgive me. I should probably have told you long ago. The truth is, I did not want you to think badly of me.

Wherever I am, I shall always love you.

Daisy's first reaction was anger, then disbelief. How could her mother, always so upright, so straight, so insistent on honesty, have lived a lie of this magnitude all these years? Maybe it wasn't true and she had been deranged when she wrote this. But no, her mother had kept her wits very much about her until the day she died; Violet had told her that. Then surprisingly, a flicker of pleasure touched her. She remembered Edwin Sanders as everything her mother had said he was. Physically, her biological parents were similar; tall, slim and fair, just as both she and Hazel were. Maybe this explained her mother's particular attachment to Hazel. She wondered if she should show this letter to her. After all, Edwin was her grandfather. It did not occur to her to share the information with Giles; he was so very much a Dobbs in looks and personality. He would either be furious or dismiss the information out of hand—or both.

After a great deal of thought, Daisy decided that it would serve no helpful purpose to tell anyone. When Hazel asked about the letter, as of course she would, she would tell a white lie and say that her mother was saying goodbye in the event of being unable to say it face-to-face. Unable to throw away this last communication from her mother, Daisy returned it to the secret drawer, confident that no one would look there again.

Over the next few days, Daisy found herself

looking at her daughter, searching for resemblances to Edwin. Later in her bedroom, she peered in the mirror, looking for the same thing in herself. Maybe her memory of him was growing dim, but all she could see was a woman who reminded herself of her own mother.

She did not sleep well that first night and in the early hours of the morning got up to read her mother's letter once more. Eventually, on the thought 'least said, soonest mended', she returned the letter to its hiding place once more and decided to ignore it. She could see no pressing need to reveal its contents to anyone, or to dwell on it herself.

*   *   *

Daisy's interview with the forbidding Miss Andersen did not go well. The first thing she noticed when she answered the brisk, 'Enter!' and stepped into the principal's office were the offending cards on the desk. As she sat down, Miss Andersen tapped them with a forefinger and, curling her lip slightly as if there were a very bad smell under her nose, asked, 'Were you aware, Mrs Dobbs, that your daughter had these in her possession?' Daisy shook her head. 'Now you are aware, do you know where she obtained them?'

'I think my mother gave them to her,' Daisy stammered, twisting her hands in her lap.

Immediately, she wished the words unsaid when she saw the look of horror on the other woman's face. 'I—I don't really know . . .' she stammered, 'but that is what Hazel told me when I asked her.'

'Your mother!' The principal could not have sounded more scandalized if Daisy had said her daughter had stolen them. 'I can hardly believe that, Mrs Dobbs. You are aware, I suppose, what these are?'

'Yes, they are tarot cards.'

'Tarot cards!' Miss Andersen spat the words out. 'Once known as "the Devil's picture book". They are used for fortune-telling, a thoroughly evil pastime, and *that*, Mrs Dobbs, is what your daughter was doing with them.'

Daisy mumbled a barely audible assent; truly she did not know what to say. But feeling that both her daughter and her mother needed defending, she took a deep breath, locked her fingers together and tried to ignore her thumping heart as she answered as calmly as she could. 'I do not think Hazel meant any harm. It was just a little fun with her friends. If you will give me the cards, I will see that she does not bring them to school again.'

'Indeed she will not, Mrs Dobbs. Quite frankly, I am appalled by your laissez-faire attitude to this, but no doubt if the cards originally belonged to the child's grandmother—your mother, I presume—it is a degenerate pastime embedded in the family. I understand this "sort of thing" tends to be handed down from mother to daughter.'

Daisy's tolerance was wearing thin. She rose abruptly to her feet and held out a somewhat shaky hand. 'The cards, please, Miss Andersen. I have given you my word that my daughter will not bring them to school again.'

'Indeed she will not, Mrs Dobbs.' The principal repeated, tight-lipped. She rose to her feet, pointed to the deck of cards and said in an icy voice, 'Take them by all means, and take your daughter home as well.'

Daisy stared blankly for a minute. 'Do you mean . . . are you telling me that you are *expelling* my daughter?' she gasped in disbelief, 'for playing cards?'

'Not ordinary cards, Mrs Dobbs, tarot cards, and telling fortunes for material gain is hardly playing.' She pressed a buzzer on her desk and a communicating door to the next room opened so swiftly that Daisy felt sure the mousy little woman who almost fell into the room must have had her ear to it. Daisy knew her as the principal's secretary and general dogsbody.

'Kindly fetch Hazel Dobbs from form five and tell her to pack her belongings as quickly as possible then go down to the front hall where her mother will be waiting for her.'

Miss Smith threw an anguished glance at Daisy and fled.

'I will say good day to you, Mrs Dobbs.

187

Please wait for your daughter in the front lobby. In the circumstances, I will excuse a term's notice, but the fees paid for this term will not be refunded. Take these with you, please.'

Daisy had forgotten the prime cause of this interview, but now she reached out and picked up the deck of cards to which Miss Andersen was pointing; apparently she was incapable of contaminating herself by touching them. Without another word, she turned and left the room.

'Well, Mum,' Daisy murmured under her breath as she sat on a hard, uncomfortable chair in the cheerless lobby, 'you amaze me. I have learned more about you in the last couple of days than in my whole lifetime. It seems I never really knew you.'

Daisy got up without speaking when Hazel appeared, humping a couple of bulging bags. Outside, when they had stowed them in the back of the car, she said in a tight voice. 'You have everything, I hope, because we are certainly not coming back here.'

'I hope so. Have you got my cards, Mum?'

'I have,' Daisy assured her as they settled into their seats. 'I am not sure which Miss Andersen was most anxious to be rid of—you or the cards.'

Hazel shot her a sidelong glance but did not say anything. Daisy appeared preoccupied with the road ahead and they rode in silence for a while.

'The problem now, Hazel, is what do we do with you?'

Hazel bridled at the implication that she was a problem to be dealt with. She bit back the inflammatory retorts that buzzed in her brain and remained silent. Given time, she was sure her mother would redirect her fury to the real villain in this scenario—Miss Andersen.

They travelled in silence and her mother was turning the car in at the drive gate when she asked, 'What do *you* think we should do?'

'We-e-ll . . . I don't want to go back to school. Oh, I know I can't go back to that school, but I don't want to go to *any* school.'

'But you are not quite sixteen,' Daisy pointed out as she drew the car to a halt. 'Come on, let's discuss it over some lunch. I feel the need of sustenance after confronting that . . . *woman.*'

Hazel smiled inwardly, sure that her mother had been about to refer to the headmistress in much stronger terms. She felt her normal optimism bubbling up. Mum was OK, really. The grin spread to her lips as she hauled her bags out of the car.

'Now, suppose you tell me what you think you should do next?' Daisy asked later over cheese and tomato sandwiches and coffee.

Hazel chewed thoughtfully. 'Do you want to know what I think I *should* do, or what I really *want* to do?'

'Is there a difference?'

'Of course there is, Mum. If I tell you what I think I should do then I will just be saying what you want me to say, but if I tell you what I really want to do then you will probably blow your top.'

'I will?' Daisy had never seen herself as the sort of person who ever 'blew her top'. On the contrary, she was a very restrained person, or so she thought, who hardly ever got carried away in any direction. For the briefest of moments, the memory of James asking her to go to New Zealand with him surfaced from wherever it was she thought she had buried it. Perhaps always being so careful to do the right thing was not the virtue she believed. She sighed. 'Tell me what you want to do with your life and I will do my very best to listen carefully and evaluate what you say.'

Hazel chewed her lip, frowned and seemed to be wrestling with her thoughts. 'If you really want to know, I just want to write books,' she finally blurted out.

'Write books!' Daisy exclaimed. 'But, shouldn't you stay at school for that?'

'You promised to listen,' her daughter reproached.

'I am sorry. It's just that . . . well . . .' Daisy shrugged, realizing that she was about to repeat herself. She had a feeling that someone with aspirations to be an author should stay at school and work for university entrance, a

190

college degree. She bit her tongue to keep these thoughts to herself.

'Mum, I have been writing since I could wield a pencil,' Hazel pointed out. 'Remember all those stories and poems and things I wrote for you when I was little?' Daisy nodded. 'Well, I never stopped writing, I just stopped showing you most of the stuff.'

'Why? Why did you do that?'

'Oh, I guess I got critical of myself. Didn't want to bore you. But I never stopped writing. I have always kept a diary, and until she died, I wrote to grandma regularly. My diary wasn't just the "went to the dentist today" sort either; it was a journal. I wrote about my thoughts and feelings as well as the things that happened. I hate school, always have, and I don't think I would like college much better—just more of the same, I suspect. The only university I want to go to is the university of life.' She had heard that phrase somewhere and stored it away to use when applicable. It resonated with her inner feelings.

Daisy sighed. 'Yes, but . . . you could go to the technical college,' she suggested hopefully. 'No . . . ?' she added when Hazel merely shook her head at the suggestion.

'Mum, have you heard what I am trying to say? I don't want anything to do with any sort of school system anymore. I just want to learn about life, and then I will have something to write about.'

'And have you any suggestions for the course you will take in "the university of life"?'

'Well, I did have an idea, but I don't know whether you will agree to it. In fact, you probably won't, even if Auntie Violet—'

'What on earth has Violet got to do with this?'

'I want . . . well, I thought it would be interesting—educational . . . a really great experience if I could go out to Australia and stay with her.'

'I agree, it would. But I think you are too young to go so far at the moment.'

Daisy wondered how long Hazel had been incubating this idea. They stared at one another, neither one willing to back down. Finally, Daisy got up and began clearing the table. 'I'll give it some thought,' she said aloud, wondering what acceptable diversion she could drag up. Wishing with all her heart she had her mother, or even Richard, still around to discuss it with.

At that moment, Giles erupted into the room. He stopped in his tracks when he saw Hazel.

'What are you doing here?' he wanted to know. 'You both look very solemn. Have you finished lunch?' he interjected as he looked at the table. 'Not been expelled, have you?' he threw over his shoulder as he collected food for himself.

'Sorry about lunch,' Daisy murmured

192

guiltily. 'I thought you were out for the day.'

Her apologetic mutterings were almost drowned by Hazel's defiant reply.

'Yes, I have been expelled. Are you satisfied, Mister Perfect?'

Giles gaped at her. Even though he knew her to be much more of a rebel than he was himself, he had not really expected this. 'Gee, what did you do?'

'Nothing. I didn't really do anything. I just got caught with grandma's tarot cards.'

'I suppose you were trying to tell fortunes, or something daft like that.'

'Yes, that is exactly what happened.' Daisy shrugged to express her disbelief and helplessness. 'I don't know what to do with her.'

'Send her to another school, of course.' He reached out for the cheese. 'I can't believe that stupid Andersen woman could really take them seriously,' he chortled. 'Maybe someone once predicted a handsome husband for her and he never turned up.'

Daisy smiled, thinking this might well be true, but Hazel scowled ferociously. 'I am not, *not* going to another school,' she stamped her foot petulantly and glared at her brother, 'so don't suggest it.'

'OK, OK, don't. Stay home and learn to be a good wife to some unlucky man.'

Daisy could see a sibling clash looming darkly on the horizon. 'She wants to go and

193

stay with Aunt Violet in Australia.'

Giles rubbed his hands together and beamed facetiously. 'Great, then we will have some peace.'

Hazel leapt at him in fury, threatening to pull his hair out.

Daisy's patience was wearing very thin; it had been an extremely trying morning. 'Just shut up, Giles, if you can't say something pleasant and constructive. I think she is too young to go to the other side of the world on her own.'

'Go with her, then.'

'And leave you?'

Giles pondered this. While in some ways it might be fine if they both went, he knew that it would be pretty difficult for him to manage without his mother for the next year or so.

'Why don't you enrol on a secretarial course and do that for a year? It would be a great help to you later on if you really want to write books, and if you did that, you would probably be able to get a job in Australia if . . .' he held up his hands, 'OK, OK, *when* you go.'

Daisy was surprised, and a little hurt, that Hazel had apparently confided her literary aspirations to Giles and not to her, but what he suggested made good sense and a glance at Hazel told her that she was prepared to consider this.

CHAPTER TWENTY-ONE

Hazel spent two years at the local technical college, honing her skills. She passed all her tests with flying colours proving, as she pointed out to Daisy, how much better you could master anything if you were interested and had a goal. Although she sometimes threw 'when I go to Australia' or similar phrases into the conversation and had initiated a correspondence with her cousin Maureen who was fairly close to her in age, that was as far as her Australian aspirations went. She got a job in the offices of the local paper and though it was not on the journalistic side, she was thrilled to be even so vaguely connected with the world of writers.

Daisy was delighted that Hazel had found work locally and she allowed herself to believe that she had forgotten her earlier ambition to go to Australia. She had taken a pile of clean washing into her daughter's room and was placing it on the bed when she saw the open book. She knew it was the one that bore the heading on the front in bold letters: *Nutmeg's Journal.*

Even as she did it, Daisy felt thoroughly ashamed of herself, but she read quickly through the open page before replacing it.

I have been working in 'The Advertiser' offices now for well over a year. It is high time I got on with my life. If I stay much longer, I shall be in such a rut I won't be able to move. Worse—I could do something utterly stupid and fall in love, end up a dull little housewife and never realize any of my dreams. I haven't told Mum as she seems to get so uptight when I mention Australia, but I have written to Auntie Violet as well as Maureen and I can go there when I arrive—no problems. I have also applied for an assisted passage. No problems again as I am young and healthy and Mum was actually born there. I shall be sorry to miss Giles's twenty-first birthday bash, but I am certainly not giving up my £10 passage for that! I guess the time has come to break the news to Mum.

This should have prepared Daisy when Hazel broke the news to her, but she dropped into one of the hard chairs at the kitchen table with a thump and stared at her daughter.

'Just say that again, Hazel, I don't think I quite understood. Giles's birthday is only a few weeks away. Of course you will be here.' She pushed away the cup of tea Hazel had thoughtfully put in front of her in the hope that it would cushion the shock of her announcement that she would not be here for her brother's twenty-first birthday party.

Determined that one of them at least, and preferably her, would remain calm and in control of the situation, Hazel sat down on her side of the table, picked up her own cup and sipped slowly before explaining.

'No, I shan't be here, I'm afraid. I have been notified that I have a passage on a ship sailing for Australia just a week before his birthday.'

'Well, you will have to change it.'

Hazel shook her head. 'I can't do that. I've waited ages for this. It would be another age before I got another chance—if I did.' She reached out and helped herself to a cookie. 'Mmm, these are nice, Mum. Did you make them this morning?'

'What do you mean, you have a passage to Australia?' Daisy resisted a sudden desire to throw her cup of tea across the table at her maddening daughter. 'How could you afford it?'

'Assisted passage. It is only going to cost me ten pounds. I'm not quite sure whether Australia wants me, or if the British government is pleased to get rid of me, but what I do know is that I only have to cough up ten pounds. Think of it, Mum. Ten pounds to take me to the other side of the world. A month long cruise for the price of a train ticket to—oh, I don't know—somewhere in the British Isles, anyway.'

'It sounds good, almost too good to be true.

I am sure there must be a catch in it somewhere.'

'Mum, you really are the wettest wet blanket in the world. Couldn't you just say, "How absolutely marvellous and how sensible of you to take advantage of such an offer"? Well, of course there is a downside; there is to everything, as you always point out. Recipients of this assisted passage scheme are expected to stay two years at least. What they really want is people like me—young, healthy, qualified—to settle there and boost the population.'

'Two years. You mean you won't be home for at least two years. We shan't see you for all that time. Oh, Hazel, I shall miss you.' Daisy's voice broke as she realized just how much she would miss her daughter.

'You could always come out to see me, Mum.' Hazel sounded wistful. She too knew she would miss her mother. 'Aunt Violet would love to have you. You know she would.'

Privately, Daisy wasn't entirely sure of that, but she knew Hazel was right; she could go out to Australia, if she really wanted to. Technically, she was still an Australian citizen.

'Why on earth didn't you tell me sooner?' she demanded. Daisy was shocked, hurt and not a little angry when she realized how little time there was left before Hazel sailed.

'Because you would have done everything you could to talk me out of it.'

Daisy, admitting that she probably would

198

have done, guessed Hazel might have been more than a little afraid she might succeed.

The next three weeks rushed by in a frenzy of shopping, packing and emotional farewells. By the time she and Giles drove Hazel to Southampton, Daisy felt wrung out. As she waved frantically to the speck on deck that she presumed was her daughter before the great liner finally moved out of her berth, she felt the tears she had managed to keep out of sight welling in her eyes so that all she could see was a mist.

'Oh, I do hope she will be all right.' Her voice was choked and Giles caught her arm as she stumbled against him when they turned to go home.

'Course she will, Mum, Hazel is tough. She will be absolutely fine.'

'But that cabin, so many of them having to share. I hope they are—well, nice girls.'

Giles kept the thought to himself that they probably were not, at least not by his mother's standards.

'She is a grown woman now, you know.'

'I suppose so.' Daisy sounded doubtful, wondering just how old was 'grown' in a mother's eyes. She doubted if she had ever achieved that status in her own mother's mind.

'We must think about your twenty-first party,' she told Giles as they drove home. She was making a supreme effort to think of something positive, but she found herself adding wistfully, 'Such a pity Hazel won't be here for it.'

'Yes, I am sorry too that she won't be here.' He wondered if this was the right time to tell her. A sideways glance at her preoccupied expression suggested it was not. Perhaps at dinner. They had barely arrived home when there was a phone call for Giles, inviting him to join a group of friends for a pub meal. He was on the point of refusing, but Daisy, guessing from the half of the conversation she could hear that it was an invitation, mouthed to him that he should accept.

'You go, dear. I am very tired. I shall have a snack and an early night. Plenty of time to discuss your party.'

Giles smiled at her and forbore to tell her that it wasn't exactly the party he wanted to talk to her about.

CHAPTER TWENTY-TWO

Daisy felt her world was shrinking around her. Certainly, her family was. The large house seemed empty without Hazel who was, Daisy reflected, one of those people who seemed more than she was. Full of vitality and fun, she filled a room. True, Giles was living at home now, taking his place in the business, but the two of them seemed to live almost separate

200

lives, meeting only occasionally at meals.

Daisy had been looking forward to Giles's twenty-first birthday party and visualized herself organizing a sort of super version of the children's parties of the past. She was stunned when he told her that he didn't want her to do any organizing, didn't even want it at home.

'But Giles,' she protested, 'where else would you have it?'

'At the country club, Mother, a dinner dance. Don't worry, you don't have to do a thing, not a thing. The people there told me they will even arrange for a cake.'

'Oh, I see.' Daisy sounded bleak. 'But . . .' She had been going to say she loved organizing parties and had been looking forward to his twenty-first for a long time. Until that moment, her only disappointment had been in Hazel missing the celebrations.

'You can concentrate on shopping for a new dress and getting your hair done.'

Daisy glared at him, wondering if he was being deliberately patronizing. She gave him the benefit of the doubt and decided he was merely trying to be kind. But even shopping for a special gown did not have the same savour without her daughter's company.

Sitting with her head under the dryer, trying to concentrate on the magazine in front of her, Daisy wondered how she had managed to end up so bereft of female company. The answer, she supposed, was that she had relied too much on Hazel. She hadn't felt lonely in the war years; she had been so busy and had felt needed. Now, only Giles needed her at all, and that merely as an efficient housekeeper. She had actually offered to go back and help in the office, but he had laughed indulgently.

'Mother, dear, the business is not that desperate. Things have moved on since you went in to help Dad out.'

Daisy bit her lip and thought that at least he could have been a trifle more tactful. She mentally toyed with the idea of joining the Women's Institute or one of the church groups but jettisoned the idea when Giles said, 'If you want something to do, why don't you join the WI?'

'Because I am not that desperate,' she snapped back and went to her room to read a book.

Next day, an airmail letter arrived from Hazel. Daisy's spirits lifted as she picked up the flimsy, pale blue missive from the doormat below the letter flap. It caught her eye immediately among the white and buff envelopes; most of the white ones were acceptances for Giles's party and she put them to one side for him to open himself. It was only a fortnight away now and Daisy, having nothing else to do, was ready as she would ever be with her dress hanging in the wardrobe and her hair appointment booked for the morning

202

of the party.

She deliberately resisted her first impulse to tear open the aerogram and devour its contents. Instead, she made herself a cup of coffee, carefully slit the folds with a knife and took both with her into the lounge.

She sipped her coffee and opened up the single, thin sheet. Hazel's bold and generous writing filled the page, shrinking as it got near the bottom, and she realized she was running out of room but not things to say. Daisy smiled. Even this was so like her daughter.

Well, Mum, as you can see, I am here at long last. I had begun to think that the voyage was a life sentence. I wanted to get here, even though I was enjoying the trip and didn't really want it to end. Sounds crazy, but I am sure you know what I mean. (*Daisy did.*)

Aunt Violet and Maureen and Simon met me off the ship. We all recognized one another at once. Not surprising, I suppose, as we had sent photos over the years. Maureen is only a year older than me and she is the only one still at home, Simon is up at Queensland and Lydia in Western Australia, so there is plenty of room for me here.

Aunt Violet is not a bit like you, not in looks or ways. She seems tanned and tough. (Oh, dear. That does not sound very nice!) What I mean is that she is very Australian whereas no one would ever guess that you only came to England in your late teens. I thought one was only supposed to feel dislocated after travelling by air, but I found it harder to find my land legs than my sea legs at the beginning of the voyage!

I won't describe the house because Aunt Violet says you know it since it is where you both lived as children. Apparently, Mrs Sanders, who owned it, was so grateful to Violet (she told me to drop the 'Auntie') for staying with her there until she died that she left it to her in her will. Violet said as far as she was concerned, the boot was on the other foot as she was grateful to the old lady for giving them all a home when she found herself a deserted wife. Oh, dear, I am rambling on and running out of space. Next time I write, it will be a proper letter, not one of these scrappy things, but I just wanted you to know I am here and enjoying life. Give my love to Giles. What do you think of Susan? Violet sends her love.

Lots of love, Hazel.

Daisy sighed and read through the letter again and yet again, and only on the third reading did the mention of 'Susan' register. On the fourth reading, she took in that it was someone here that she was supposed to know—nothing to do with Hazel. Yet another reading told her that it appeared to be something to do with Giles. His girlfriend? She guessed he had one, but he had never confided in her. She sighed. She supposed it would become apparent in time.

It was. She was thinking about the unknown 'Susan' as she spread marmalade on her toast the following morning. Giles seems even more preoccupied than usual, she thought, as she watched him pour milk on his cornflakes. Breakfast was often a silent meal; Daisy was never at her best first thing in the morning and Giles usually had his head in the newspaper or his mind on the office and the day ahead. It was surprising, therefore, when he cleared his throat and said in a brusque voice, 'I—I want you to meet someone.'

'Susan?' Daisy asked absently, speaking directly from her thoughts.

'Well . . . yes, it is actually, but how did you know anything about her?'

Daisy thought he sounded put out. It gave her a secret kick.

'I just . . . knew,' she told him airily with a slight shrug.

Giles looked at her suspiciously. Had it been his grandmother or sister, he would have thought they were using their so-called second sight. His mother made no such claims.

'I wondered when you were going to tell me about her.' She managed to sound aggrieved.

'I'm telling you now,' he snapped. Hearing how bad-tempered he sounded, he managed a smile. 'I would like you to meet her. I—we . . . well—'

'You mean it is serious?'

Giles nodded. 'Yes, very. In fact, we . . . well, we intend to announce our engagement at my twenty-first party.'

Daisy bit back the sharp rejoinder she felt like making and contented herself with raising her eyebrows. 'That is serious. I hope you are quite sure about this, Giles?' She would liked to have met the girl before things were a fait accompli.

'Of course I am sure. I inherit the business and this house when I am twenty-one, as you know, Mother. If I am old enough to do that, I am also capable of selecting a wife.'

Daisy thought the idea of 'selecting' a wife sounded sensible but calculating. She would rather have heard he was madly in love with this 'Susan'. His reminder that he would inherit the house in a few weeks' time sounded a warning bell somewhere in her subconscious, but she smiled brightly. 'I hope I shall meet her, Giles, before your party. Perhaps you could bring her to dinner one evening?'

'That is exactly what I was about to suggest. Would next weekend be convenient?'

Daisy nodded, reflecting wistfully how very

like his father Giles was becoming. She would have liked to put her arms round him, hug him and wish him joy in the future, but instead they were discussing a suitable evening for dinner. 'Fine, just fine. Saturday or Sunday?'

'Saturday, I think.'

This surprised Daisy. She somehow imagined that all young things liked to play on Saturday evenings, but beyond a barely perceptible lift of her eyebrows, once more that she was not aware of doing, she merely nodded.

'I shall look forward to meeting her on Saturday, Giles.' So she was, but with mixed feelings.

They were still mixed by the end of the evening they met. She didn't dislike Susan at all—there was nothing about her to dislike—but neither did she feel a rush of affection for her; there was nothing about her to inspire it. She was a thoroughly nice, middle-class girl, dressed well, but not in any eye-catching way. She was obviously intelligent and well educated, the product of one of the better boarding schools for young ladies, she learned over dinner. She knew how to use the correct cutlery and make pleasant conversation. Her father was a local businessman, owning a large flour mill. Daisy could see that she was a very suitable wife for Giles.

'Goodnight, Mrs Dobbs, and thank you for asking me. It has been a lovely evening.' She held out her hand to Daisy before shrugging into the coat being held out, rather impatiently, by Giles.

'Goodnight—and thank you for coming.' Daisy wondered why she had said something so stupid, yet somehow it seemed to be required of her. She sighed as the heavy front door closed behind them and when she heard Giles's car start up began collecting coffee cups. She sighed again, feeling far too tired to do any more clearing up until the morning. She did not feel the pleasure she felt she should about her son's engagement. This was a beginning; it should be joyous. If it was not, then it was probably her fault, or so she told herself as she made her way to bed.

Daisy wrote to Hazel the following day and told her she had met Susan and thought she and Giles were very well suited. When Hazel's reply came, it was typical, Daisy thought: *You say you think Susan and Giles are very well suited* . . . her daughter wrote. *I suppose that is your nice way of saying you think she is dull.* Daisy smiled to herself as she read the letter but had to admit the truth of that. Giles was her son and of course she loved him, but all the same, she did think at times that he was a good deal too serious for his age, a seriousness verging on the pompous. She learned that Susan was six months older than Giles. Like him, she seemed sensible and mature to the point of being, as Hazel had suggested, dull.

208

Or was that too harsh? Considering them both, Daisy decided that they were middle-aged when they should be young—probably the very quality that had drawn them together and made them eminently suited.

The twenty-first party was, Daisy supposed, a success. The venue, the local country club, was sumptuous and dignified, if a trifle staid. Daisy, who had seldom been there, had not even known that it had this large room which was used for such functions. Giles looked prosperous and handsome, as did his fiancée, the champagne flowed without anyone getting unduly affected by it and the general opinion seemed to coincide with her own that it was a very suitable match. Daisy wished Hazel was there to share the occasion. Her absence highlighted the fact that Daisy was very much on her own with her mother and stepfather both dead and her daughter on the other side of the world. But she didn't actually admit this to herself until Edith pointed out that Daisy had always tolerated her sister-in-law chiefly for Richard's sake. Considerably older than herself, Daisy had always found her humourless and domineering and she realized now that she had resented the part this woman had played in her family life when the children were young. She had no illusions that Edith liked her either, seeing her as a poor manager and a feckless wife and mother.

When she loomed over her now, she was an

extremely tall woman and said in an unctuous tone, 'Such a pity Hazel isn't here. I should have thought she could have postponed her trip until after her brother's twenty-first celebrations. It would have been nice for you too to have her here.'

Daisy thought she appeared thinner, more desiccated than ever. She had not worn well, she decided, rejoicing in the liberation of these thoughts without any accompanying guilt. She was still being talked at, she realized.

'But then she always was a headstrong sort of child, so different from Giles,' she continued.

Daisy merely smiled rather vaguely. There was little point in springing to Hazel's defence, for Giles had always been his aunt's favourite and nothing she said would change things.

'What do you plan to do now, Margaret?' It was so long since she had answered on a regular basis to that name that Daisy half turned to see who Edith was addressing.

'I am sorry, Edith. I am not quite sure what you mean.' She was confused by the question as well as the name.

'Well, I understand the wedding is to be fairly soon. No point in them waiting, since Giles inherits the house now he is twenty-one. Surely you don't plan to live with them?'

'No, no, of course not. I . . . well, I haven't decided yet.' Daisy gripped her champagne glass in sheer panic. She had not decided because she hadn't given it a thought, assuming that it would be a year or so at least before Giles and Susan were married. But Edith droning on in her irritatingly superior voice sparked an idea.

'You could of course go and visit your sister in Australia (she pronounced it 'Orstralia' and somehow made it sound like the sort of place no one in their senses would dream of visiting) and see what Hazel is getting up to at the same time.'

Daisy bit off the retort that she didn't expect her daughter to be 'getting up to' anything, certainly not in the way Edith inferred.

'Yes,' she agreed, 'that actually is what I intend to do. My sister has been asking me to visit her for some time.'

CHAPTER TWENTY-THREE

When Giles told her that he and Susan had fixed their wedding day for a mere five months ahead, Daisy knew this was indeed the right time to visit Violet in Australia and, of course, to catch up with Hazel—she was missing her daughter more than she would have believed possible. Any doubts she may have entertained were dismissed when she saw the look of relief that swept across Giles's face when she announced her intention.

211

Daisy toyed with the idea of going by air but decided against it. The main object of the trip, after all, was not to be where she was; getting to her destination was secondary. She booked her passage on a ship leaving ten days after the wedding, judging this would give her ample time to clear out her belongings while Giles and Susan were on their honeymoon in, predictably, Venice. They planned to be away for two weeks, so she would be on the high seas by the time they returned.

As Susan's parents, together with their daughter, were organizing the wedding in every detail, there was little more for Daisy to do than get herself an outfit. She felt the twenty-first party had been a sort of dress rehearsal for the wedding as she searched the better shops and boutiques for something that Giles would approve of and she might actually like herself. She wished Hazel were here to help her. While she was about it, she indulged in new clothes for the voyage and her visit to Australia. With only herself to please, this was enjoyable.

It was after one of these shopping sprees that she returned home to find a blue aerogram with an Australian postmark waiting for her. Knowing it was from Hazel, she tore it open eagerly and skim read it while the kettle boiled for a reviving cup of tea.

Hope the wedding goes off well and wish

I was going to be with you. It was nice of you to suggest I come home for it and then we travel out here together, but not really practical, Mum. For one thing, I have a job, and don't forget I agreed to stay here for at least 2 years when I scored a £10 passage (I bet yours will cost a lot more) and I wouldn't really want to be away so long. I have friends here and I feel I belong. Aunt Violet has been very good and says that I can stay here as long as I like. That's great because I get on really well with Maureen. Did you know Edwin Sanders had a son? He is actually quite young and very nice indeed; we get on really well.

Just what did that mean? Daisy asked herself as the flimsy sheet of paper blurred in front of her. Edwin Sanders, the man her mother had told her about in that last letter, was her father. Then this son of his that Hazel got on 'really well' with must be her own half-brother—Hazel's uncle. If that was so, he must be old. Well, a lot older than Hazel; he was probably *her* age.

She forced herself to read on through the remainder of the letter which was mostly inconsequential chitchat except for the 'PS' squashed in at the very bottom after her daughter's signature: 'By the way, his name is Tim—Timothy Sanders—and I really do like him very much'.

In a desperate but futile hope that she was not remembering her mother's confession correctly, Daisy retrieved her letter from the secret drawer where she had kept it all these years. Her fingers shook as she unfolded it. No, there was no denying her mother's words. Edwin Sanders was her father, Hazel's grandfather and also, it would appear, father to this middle-aged man, Timothy Sanders who her daughter was so fulsome in her praise for. By this time, Daisy's imagination had Hazel madly in love with him and facing a broken heart when the truth of their relationship was revealed. Why, oh why had she not shown Hazel the letter when she first read it? But of course, she had not guessed then that it would be of any importance to anyone but herself.

After an almost sleepless night in which she tried to remember what degree of relationship barred two people from marrying and whether the same rules applied in Australia, she also fought the voice in her head reminding her that no one but she knew about the relationship anyway, so ... if she kept quiet ...

A strong cup of tea and a couple of aspirins gave Daisy the strength to sit down and write to Hazel, simply begging her not to do anything drastic before she got there, but she didn't add that that included marrying her uncle. When Daisy wrote how much she was looking forward to seeing her again, she wondered just how true that was, given her knowledge.

*   *   *

At Giles's wedding, Daisy felt as if she was taking part in some great drama. She floated through the day in a dreamlike state, playing her role of mother of the groom. The champagne, like everything else, was excellent. Afraid she may already have imbibed too freely to help her through the task of listening to what seemed far too many and too ponderous speeches, Daisy thought she had better switch to orange juice. She didn't want her tongue to slip and make some foolish remark, letting Giles down, or worse, be indiscreet about Hazel when she was repeatedly asked by well-meaning friends if she would soon be the mother of the bride. She heaved a sigh of relief when at last it was time to wave the happy couple off on their honeymoon.

Daisy was surprised to see that their car appeared pristine clean. No confetti sticking to treacle smears, no old boots dragging behind. Giles must have not only hidden it well but had a trusted accomplice. Not quite trusted enough though, for they drove away to a splendid cacophony. The hub caps had been filled with pebbles or coins. She smiled and

215

wondered how far they would get before Giles dealt with them—if it was coins, salvaging them would assuage his annoyance.

As the noisy car disappeared and they were all left behind feeling flat, the saying: 'Your son is your son until he gets him a wife, but your daughter is your daughter all her life' floated through her mind. Giles's marriage was, she knew, as much a defining moment in her own life as it was in his.

With this thought and the realization of all there was for her to do in the next ten days, all speculation about Timothy Sanders and his relationship with Hazel was relegated to the backburner of her mind.

Daisy arranged for her larger personal possessions to go into storage, including the bureau with the secret drawer, but without its letter. This she secreted at the bottom of her jewel case. She decided to sell her car and repurchase when she returned to England; at this point, she had no idea how long she would be away.

She said farewell to her friends and arranged for Mrs Johnson, who came in three mornings a week to help with the housework, to open up the house for the newlyweds. Finally, she was on the train to London where she would catch the boat train for Southampton, glad, as she settled in a corner seat, to have nothing to do and no one to do it with.

'Are you coming or going?'

Daisy, leaning on the deck rail watching the last minute preparation for departure and hoping her luggage was safely on board, did not turn her head at the voice somewhere near her right shoulder. She didn't want any interference as she savoured her aloneness in this moment which, to her surprise, she was finding emotionally charged.

'I'm not sure,' she mumbled, hoping her lack of friendliness would encourage him to move away. But when she stole a glance around, she realized that was a forlorn hope; there were too many people packed too close up here on the deck for anyone to move far.

'What I meant was, are you going back home, or is England your home and you are leaving it?'

In this longer sentence, Daisy thought she detected something familiar in the timbre of his voice, but this was absurd. However, she turned her head to answer him this time.

'England has been my home for slightly more than half my life. Before that—'

Her voice died away and she stared at the man at her side, seeing his face in profile, for his attention was now below on the dockside. He waved rather vaguely as if he couldn't actually see the person he was waving to then turned back towards her. For a moment, they stared at one another then, overcome by a swirling sensation, Daisy gripped the rail so hard that her knuckles went white. For a dreadful moment, she thought she was going to faint, or worse, fall overboard. 'James!' she croaked.

'Daisy! Is it really you?!'

She nodded, 'I—I think so.' She shook her head as if to clear it, 'but I feel I must be dreaming or something.'

He smiled. 'Well, at least you didn't say, "this is a nightmare!".' He stared at her as if he too was not sure whether this was real. 'You haven't answered my original question. Are you taking a trip, or maybe emigrating?'

'I am going to stay with my sister,' she explained, 'and visiting Hazel. She is in Australia at the moment.'

'Hazel—ah. Yes, little Nutmeg.'

'Not so little, and no longer Nutmeg. She calls herself Hazel these days.'

'And—what was his name—your son?'

'Giles. He is married. That is one of the reasons I am coming out to Australia. At twenty-one, he inherited the business and the house. It seemed a good point in all our lives for me to . . .' She had been about to say 'come back home' but wasn't sure if that was what she really meant. She turned back to him. 'And you—what are you doing? If I remember, neither of us quite knew whether we belonged

218

in England or the Antipodes.'

'I definitely belong in New Zealand now. I took out citizenship years ago. My wife—'

'You are married, then?' Daisy cut in. Turning back to the scene below so that she missed the tightening of his lips and the slight shake of his head, she only heard:

'Not now,' in the sort of voice that did not encourage questions.

She wanted to ask about his wife, what exactly he meant by that terse remark, but embarrassment kept her silent.

Remembering he had lost a leg in the war, she found herself glancing down involuntarily. He must have a good prosthesis, she thought; he looked perfectly normal as he stood by her. She did not even remember which leg it was, let alone notice anything wrong.

'It was the right leg, and it hasn't grown back. I just have a very good artificial one.' His tone was dry as he interpreted her glance.

Daisy felt her cheeks glowing. 'I—I . . .' she stammered, and quickly asked about his career. 'You are still doctoring, I suppose?'

'Yes, I am still doctoring, as you put it. I specialized in amputees. Fellow feeling, I suppose you could call it. I do a lot of work with the victims of road accidents, particularly children.'

'I see,' Daisy murmured. She would have liked to say something more congratulatory, but everything that sprang to mind seemed too trite. She tried to change the subject. 'Whereabouts do you live?' she asked.

'Christchurch. I am a consultant at the main hospital there.' Abruptly, he turned from the rail. 'Well, Daisy, it is a real surprise to meet you again. No doubt we shall bump into one another as we are confined to this ship for the next few weeks.' With a brief nod, he moved away.

Daisy, watching, thought that apart from a slightly stiff gait, you would never imagine that he was so handicapped. He left her feeling that in some way, she had done or said the wrong thing. She felt both guilty and snubbed and told herself that she really hoped their paths did not cross too often on the long journey to the other side of the world. She wondered if he was travelling alone—and what exactly he had meant when he said he was not married now.

CHAPTER TWENTY-FOUR

Feeling tired and very flat, Daisy turned away from the railing. It was obvious the ship was about to leave; the tugs were in position to escort her out to sea and passengers were hurling coloured streamers over the side, the last symbolic tie with England.

Making her way through the crowds, she went down to her cabin to find, with relief, that her cases were there. She unpacked the few things she would need immediately and lay down on her bunk. Listening to the sounds of the ship, she remembered the last time she travelled on an ocean liner. She had still been in her teens then, full of anticipation as she set out on this exciting adventure. She had only planned a couple of years in England, but it had turned out to be the start of an entirely new phase of her life. Now here she was, nearly twenty-five years later, returning for what was supposed to be a visit. She felt her life was changing drastically yet again, and she wasn't sure she was prepared for it.

When she had travelled the opposite way all those years ago, she had shared a cabin with her mother and had made shipboard friendships with three other girls round about her own age. They kept up with one another for a while after they arrived in England, but over the years, the friendships had dropped away as each of them became involved in other things. She wondered if anyone else had stayed there as she had, or if they had returned home after a couple of years. She had paid for privacy on this trip, so the tiny cabin was her space and hers alone. Remembering James's abrupt departure, however, she thought she might have preferred company.

She was a good sailor, or had been on that earlier voyage, so she had no qualms now and actually found the movement of the ship and the subdued throb of the engines as it made its way slowly towards the open sea relaxing. She closed her eyes; it had been a frenetic rush getting organized to leave so soon after the wedding. She dropped off to sleep, wondering if James really was travelling on the same ship, or if it had been a hallucination.

An insistent tapping roused her. Rolling off the bed, she opened the cabin door to come face to face with him. For a moment, she thought she must still be asleep and it was all a dream. She stared at him, absently running her fingers through her hair in a futile attempt to improve her dishevelled appearance. The action restored her to wakefulness and reality and seemed to cause him amusement.

'I'm sorry if I disturbed you,' his lips twitched in a manner that suggested he was not in the least sorry, 'but as you are travelling alone, I wondered if maybe you would permit me to escort you to dinner?'

'Thank you, that's very kind of you, but I'm not dressed for dinner.'

'Neither am I, as you can see. There is an hour to go before it is served, anyway. I suppose you could say I came to make an appointment.'

Daisy stared at him in confusion, wondering if she was properly awake. The last time she had seen him he had not sounded as if he expected or wanted to see her again until they docked at Melbourne, yet now he was offering to escort her to dinner. 'Well, yes, all right. That would be—nice,' she said at last, groaning to herself at the churlishness of her response.

To make up for it, she took pains over her appearance, changing her clothes more than once to create the right impression. She wanted to look attractive and well dressed but also to achieve a casual chic and not in any way appear to have gone to a great deal of trouble—a tall order as that was precisely what she was doing. She was looking at herself critically in the mirror when he knocked again.

The voyage seemed to Daisy to be time set completely apart from the rest of her life. They were isolated in the capsule world of the liner; the days bore no relation to her past and certainly no connection to the future, living each one as it came, giving herself up to the pleasure of having no pressing duties, no meals to prepare, no more urgent social obligations other than the captain's cocktail party and the ever present enjoyment of James's company.

Much of their conversation consisted of bringing each other up to date with the events in their separate lives since they parted. He laughed uproariously at Daisy's account of Hazel's expulsion from school. 'Good old Nutmeg, I always knew that kid was a character,' he applauded.

Their renewed friendship remained just that. Beyond a light 'goodnight' peck, James never tried to kiss her or suggest in any way that they might reignite their earlier relationship. Sensing a reserve in him about his own life, other than the surface details of his work, the hospital and Christchurch as a place to live, Daisy did not ask direct questions and it was only on their final evening aboard ship that he told her about his marriage after Daisy complained: 'You know everything about me, James, but you haven't really told me what happened to you when you went back to New Zealand.'

'Well . . .' he said after a pause, as if he was considering how much to reveal, 'I took up the appointment I had been offered at Dunedin Hospital. Janet was a sister there, a war widow with a ten-year-old son, Christopher. She lived with her parents so that her mother could look after Chris while she was at work.' He gave a small shrug. 'I guess it was a case of propinquity.' He paused, remembering. 'No, that is not entirely true.'

Daisy, surprised and a little ashamed by wishing there was no more to it than that, wanted to make some sour remark about doctors marrying nurses, but before she said anything, he picked up his train of thought and continued.

'No, it was not that we were thrown together in our work—it was rather more like a popular romance, best women's magazine stuff. I was taken ill with a serious infection in . . . in my . .

224

. stump. She nursed me. It was only later on when I was fully recovered that we worked together. Overall, it was four years before we got married. Or to be more accurate, that I could persuade her that I might make a passable stepfather for young Christopher. By the time we were married, he was going on for fifteen and she was finding it hard coping on her own with a teenage son. Her parents, I think, were finding it even harder. I have to admit, being turned down in an earlier application to be a stepfather had sapped my confidence, or I might have persuaded her earlier.'

Realizing that beneath his dry tone, he was teasing, Daisy began to protest, but he cut her short with a smile.

'Don't take that remark to heart. You were probably quite right at the time. I was not in a fit state to take on a ready-made family then and later, with the wisdom of hindsight, I could acknowledge that you did have a certain obligation to Giles and his inheritance until he was of age to take it on himself. Had I not been so steeped in self-pity, I might have seen that and we could have worked something out. Instead I stormed off back to New Zealand and, ironically enough, found myself in the step-father role anyway.

'What neither Janet nor I realized at the time of our marriage was that it was more than life with a teenager that was wearing her down;

she was in the early stages of the leukaemia that killed her.'

Daisy laid a hand on his arm. 'Oh, James, I am so sorry.' Her sympathy was genuine, yet underneath it, she was shamefully aware of a stirring of pleasure that he was, after all, free. She stifled it and asked, 'Christopher, is he . . .?' her words petered out as she realized she was not quite sure what it was she was asking.

'He is a doctor now, doing a couple of years as an intern in Auckland. I am leaving the ship there and visiting him before I go back to Christchurch. I can't have shaped up too badly as a stepfather after all because we are now excellent friends.'

When he mentioned leaving the ship, it was on the tip of Daisy's tongue to propose that he leave the ship at Melbourne, but it was not in her to put herself and her wishes forward in that way. If that was what James wanted to do then he would do it without prompting. Her mother had once pointed out to her that what people called 'good luck' was merely the courage to seize the moment and snatch at opportunities that were offered. It was something she found very hard to do. 'Look before you leap' was much more her philosophy in life. She knew that this was just one of the many ways in which she differed from both her mother and her daughter. She kept silent now and could not know that James had toyed with the idea of suggesting it himself, but, fearing a rebuff, remained silent.

They did, however, exchange addresses and promised each other to remain in touch. 'Try and get over to New Zealand while you are in this part of the world,' James urged.

'I will,' Daisy promised, thinking it unlikely that she would make the trip out here again once she was back in England.

'Have you thought of staying in Australia?' James asked, almost as if he had tuned into Daisy's train of thought. 'After all, you were born and brought up here, so it should be just as much your home as England, and what about Nutmeg? She might decide to stay here.'

'I'll cross that bridge when I come to it,' Daisy told him and changed the subject. It was in fact a bridge she had gone at least halfway across many times in her thoughts. She had a feeling that Hazel might want to stay here. As always when her thoughts jumped ahead to the future, she was apt to rein them in. She had no wish whatsoever to have any part of her mother's gift of precognition which to her had always seemed to predict something unpleasant so that as a child, she had half believed that Ella actually made things happen.

CHAPTER TWENTY-FIVE

'Mother was so obstinate.' Violet's voice drifted across the shade-drenched veranda.

'She called herself "strong-minded",' Daisy murmured drowsily from the old cane lounge. She was finding it hard to make the right responses to her sister's conversation. The thirty plus temperature contributed to her feeling of lassitude as did the feeling of actually relaxing in a deckchair without the movement of a ship at sea. She hadn't expected to be in this dreamlike state when she was finally on dry land after the weeks at sea. It was hard to keep her eyes open and stay with it.

In spite of her fuzzy state of mind, she was acutely aware of her surroundings. She knew that if she opened her eyes fully, she would see the lemon tree with its yellow fruit hanging among glossy leaves. The scent of the blossom, promising yet more fruit, hung tantalizingly on the air, blending with the grass and eucalyptus smells that were so uniquely Australian. The tree was an old friend and unlike most things, which seemed to have shrunk in her long absence, it was bigger and better than she remembered.

A little further away, the sprinkler flicked its life-giving jets across the parched lawn with hypnotic regularity.

The undisciplined grapevine climbing the veranda posts and wandering across the trellis toward the roof was just as she remembered— thick and cool, giving shade at this time of the year, but in winter its leaves fell, letting in the sunlight so that the veranda was still a favourite place to sit. The lavish bunches of sweet sultana grapes were small and green now, but soon they would be ripe and honey sweet and it would be possible to sit here and reach out for a bunch.

A willy wagtail hopped about the lawn and Vi's geriatric and rather staid tabby, stretched out on the top step of the veranda, watching it through thin slits, only the slight twitching of its tail betraying awareness.

Daisy did her best to stay focused on her sister's voice, but the summer sounds were insidious—and hypnotic. The buzz of insects, the rhythm of the sprinkler, the distant hum of traffic, then as if it were welcoming her home, a kookaburra laughed. The sound brought her wandering attention back to the veranda and her sister's voice.

'If she hadn't been so pig-headed, she wouldn't have ended up here in Australia like she did.'

'Mother?' Daisy reeled in her thoughts with an effort.

'Of course! Haven't you heard anything I've been saying? You haven't changed a bit, Daisy.

You're still a dreamer fifty years on!'

'Well, you haven't changed either. When you latched on to a subject, you always chewed at it like a dog with a bone!'

'Yes, well . . .'

That, Daisy knew, was about the nearest her sister would get to capitulation.

'People don't change, not really. Here we are, two middle-aged women arguing just like we did as kids. No, people don't change; they just get more so as they grow older. Grandma Ella may have called herself "strong-minded", but I can tell you, when she got old, she was a stubborn, pig-headed old bat!'

'Just like I said, once you get hold of a subject, you hang on. Why do you call her "Grandma Ella"? She was our mother, for heaven's sake.'

'I suppose I got into the habit of calling her that when the kids were little. That's what they called her to distinguish her from their other grandmother, the Australian "Nanna". Not that it was necessary; no way would she be called that.'

Daisy smiled. Impossible to imagine her patrician mother being called Nanna. 'Did they tag her name on when they talked to her?' she asked.

'Heavens, no! Nothing more or less than a formal "Grandma" would do.'

When her sister frowned, pursed her lips and pushed her hair back with an abrupt gesture clearly remembered from their shared childhood, Daisy realized that she was genuinely upset. She wondered why, but the warm sun was making her too indolent to bother finding out. Closing her eyes, she let her thoughts slide back to her childhood in this house. She remembered it as a golden time of perpetual summer, and her lips curved in a soft smile.

'You wouldn't smile if she had lived with you until she died! You shipped her over here, got rid of her, yet with all your money, advantages and conveniences, you had the means to cope with her much better that I could!'

'Just a minute!' Daisy cut in. 'First, I didn't "ship her over" to you. She came because Walter wanted her to and when he died suddenly, she had the money to do it. She wanted to see you, but it was Walter begging her to come just before he died. He more or less died saying it. I think she felt it was his dying wish and she must honour it, plus of course she really wanted to see you and your family,' Daisy added quickly, feeling maybe she was being less than tactful. 'He thought she should come and stay for the duration. He actually wanted her to bring my children with her. He was very worried about the war and what it would do to "ordinary" people. I remember Mother saying that the prospect of war had literally worried him to death.'

'Mother didn't usually do things to please other people, but why didn't she bring your children?'

'You are very hard on her, Violet. I can remember her doing a great deal for others; Walter thought the world of her. So did my children, particularly Hazel. She was terribly upset when she died. The reason they didn't come out here was that Richard would not consider it. We were looking forward to her coming back, but she was trapped here by the war, so please, no more about me shipping her off to you.'

'I always thought you had paid her fare, just as we thought it was only for a visit.' Violet looked surprised by her sister's vehemence, as was Daisy herself.

'Didn't she tell you it was her inheritance from Walter that paid?'

'Well, no. She never said anything much about money.'

'So you formed your own conclusion.'

'Well—yes. Then when war broke out, she stayed, whingeing every now and then about being stuck here, and telling us how much better everything was in England.'

Daisy snorted. 'Not in wartime; she was much better off here. There were lots of things she loved about Australia—both of us did. It was meeting up with Walter again that made her stay, just as I stayed because I married Richard. She talked about coming back to see you and your kids every time Australia was mentioned. When Walter died, she had the money to do it and no pressing reason to stay in England.'

'She might have gone back, I suppose, if it hadn't been for the war and torpedoes.' Violet sounded doubtful.

'Well, I didn't pay her fare. I've told you, she inherited the money. She knew that was what Walter wanted her to do, so she came. I am sure she would have been back if it hadn't been for the war. You talk as if I wanted to get rid of her. I didn't, I missed her and looked forward to her coming back.' Daisy remembered getting the news that her mother had died out here in Australia. It had been just one more blow in the dark days of the war and its aftermath.

'Easy to say that when she stayed here, in this house, until the day she died. Pretty difficult she made life too at times.'

Daisy could believe that. Her mother and Violet had always managed to clash. She wanted to say that she herself had never found their mother *that* difficult, but as she had no wish to quarrel with her sister, she closed her eyes and feigned drowsiness. 'The trouble was,' she murmured with a flash of insight, 'it was so hard for her having half her family in England and the other half here.'

Violet gave another unconvincing and inelegant 'hrrrmph'.

233

Daisy's thoughts drifted to her mother. Back here in Australia herself, she realized for the first time how difficult it must have been for her mother to have her loyalties so divided. She opened her eyes a slit and looked across at her sister, so unlike herself, and wondered how much she knew or guessed about their family history.

The soothing background sounds and the warm sun were combining to waft Daisy into that vague and pleasant spot between waking and dreaming. She imagined she could hear the sounds of their childish voices arguing and laughing—plenty of both in those days. The younger by four years, she had always been aware somewhere deep down that she held a special place in her mother's heart. She was also the one who most resembled her physically. Knowing this, she had never understood as a child why Ella also seemed harder on her than on Violet.

It was when she finally read the letter her mother left with her when she sailed on what she had originally intended as a brief visit to Australia, that Daisy had begun to understand.

She had never forgotten the look in her mother's eyes in the moment that they said their last goodbyes. Had she known she would not return? No, that was fanciful; she was imagining this was her mother's far-seeing at work again. She had always quashed any idea that this faculty had been passed on to her, for

234

she could see no benefit in advance knowledge of events that usually turned out badly.

Although she could empathize to a certain extent with her sister's simmering resentment, Daisy hoped it would not last. She closed her eyes and feigned sleep, but the effect of jet lag and the warm peace of her surroundings overcame her, and on the fanciful thought that returning to this garden was like re-entering the security of the womb, she slipped into complete oblivion.

* * *

'Hi, Ma!' Daisy woke with a start at Hazel's voice. Hazel was standing in front of her chair, looking down on her. 'You always seem to be asleep. It must be a reaction from all the work of getting Giles safely married.'

Daisy opened her eyes and smiled at her daughter who, after taking a day off to meet her when she arrived, was now back at work. 'I am certainly not always asleep,' she began indignantly, 'and anyway, as far as hard work getting Giles married, I didn't have to do a thing. Susan and her family did all that.'

Hazel grinned. 'Yes, Susan is a good organizer. Poor old Giles will be managed to death.' The prospect seemed to please her. 'He was always such a bossy sod, and priggish with it. It will be a just comeuppance.'

Daisy felt she should remonstrate with her

daughter, but thinking of her son—so very like his father—she found she was smiling.

'Come on now, Mum. You can't laze here forever. Time to get dressed in your best bib and tucker. Tim is coming over tonight especially to meet you.'

CHAPTER TWENTY-SIX

Daisy took the hand held out to her and looked up into the face of the young man standing in front of her. She stared blankly. *This could not be Edwin's son. It was surely Edwin himself as she remembered him all those years ago when she was a small child. Besides*, she thought illogically, *he was too young. Edwin's son was supposed to be at least her age, if not older, but this young man was only in his twenties*. Realizing she was still clinging on to his hand as if it were a lifeline he had held out to her, she relinquished her grip and tried to pay attention to what he was saying.

'I believe you knew my father, years ago.'

'Yes, yes, I did.' Daisy repressed a crazy desire to add, 'He was my father, actually, so that makes you my brother'. Aware of Hazel standing by, watching her closely with a slightly puzzled expression, she went on, 'How is your father?'

'My father is dead, Mrs Dobbs. He died in

1937.'

'Oh, oh, I am so sorry to hear that,' Daisy stammered, wondering why no one had told her, or perhaps they had and she hadn't taken it in. 'Then my mother didn't meet him again when she came out here?' She was overcome by the poignancy of it, and the realization that it was her father they were talking about, her father who was dead. She shook her head slightly as if to clear it of confusing thoughts and memories.

'He was an enormous help to my mother— well, to all of us, at the time of my father's sudden death.' Daisy felt a need to establish what everybody believed to be her parentage. At the same time, she wanted to quiz Timothy about his family.

'I am afraid I never really knew him. I was only eighteen months old when he died.' He smiled at Daisy who hoped she didn't look as bemused as she felt. 'You probably have more memories of him than I do?'

'Yes, yes, I do. And I can tell you this, you are extraordinarily like him to look at. For a moment, I felt I had slipped back in time.'

'Yes, people who knew him always tell me how like him I am. I can remember as a small boy, I used to get the family photograph album and pore over it, looking for photos of him taken at whatever age I happened to be at the time.'

There were so many questions she wanted

to ask this delightful young man; how he came to be the same age as her daughter when he was actually her own brother. She contented herself with asking, 'Are you a lawyer too, Tim?'

'Yes, though I can hardly say I followed in my father's footsteps as there was such a long gap between his death and me growing up. But—yes—I am in the firm that my father and his friend George Atwell formed as young men. It was Sanders & Atwell with no Sanders in it from my father's death until I qualified and took his place.'

Daisy smiled, thinking privately that it must have been rather hard on Tim to be steered from birth onwards into replacing his father. 'I don't think I ever met your mother,' she murmured, knowing perfectly well that she had not.

'You would not have done; she was Dad's second wife. His first wife was an invalid for many years, so you probably didn't meet her either.' His smile was wistful. 'I always felt it was sad that he died before he really knew me. Sad for him as well as me, I mean.'

Daisy murmured agreement and wanted to say that at least he had known her.

'Mum married again a couple of years ago. She was a New Zealander; she went back there for a holiday and met up with her childhood sweetheart who had been recently widowed and they sort of took up where they left off.

They live in New Zealand, so I don't see much of them.'

'So, you are on your own?'

'I prefer to think of it as independent,' Tim told her, his smile cheerful now.

Daisy turned to her daughter. 'Mention of New Zealand reminds me, I met James on the ship coming over.'

'You mean Uncle James, who lost his leg?'

Hazel looked sharply at her mother, wondering if her casual mention of the man she had nearly married was genuine or assumed. 'Why didn't you bring him here? I'd just love to see him again.' She turned to Tim. 'He called me Nutmeg because I am Hazel Margaret,' she told him. 'I only reverted to Hazel when I grew up.'

'He still asked after Little Nutmeg,' Daisy said in a dry voice, 'and the reason I didn't invite him here to catch up with you is because he was sailing on to New Zealand. He was meeting his son in Auckland.' She stressed these last words, wishing she had not mentioned James. She was grateful to Violet interrupting them to say the meal was ready.

Daisy could see that Hazel was quite at home here with her Australian relatives and was ashamed of the twinge of jealousy that caught her unawares. Hazel appeared to be part of this household as much or more than in her home in England. Tim too was obviously part of the family and though she was watching

239

anxiously for some special closeness between him and Hazel, she failed to detect any.

Almost as if she had spoken her thoughts aloud, Tim looked across the table at her and said with a smile, 'This house has always been a second home to me and Violet like a second mother.'

'Well,' Maureen chipped in, 'that's only fair as your grandmother was just like an extra grandmother to us. More of a grandmother, really, than Nanna Biggs, and we didn't know Grandma Ella at all until she came to visit before the war.'

'Your gain was my loss,' Hazel told them. 'I really missed Grandma and was looking forward to her getting back when the war was over, but of course, she never made it. There were no other grandmothers around for us; Dad's mother had died before we were born and there was only his starchy old sister who was heavily into "children should be seen and not heard" and was no fun at all.'

'You are probably seeing your grandmother through the rose-tinted spectacles of time and distance. You might not have found her so easy if she had always lived with you.'

Violet's voice was dry, reminding Daisy how she had complained about their mother earlier. Daisy was pleased when Hazel answered, 'I don't think it would have made much difference. I did stay with her for quite a while when I was small, before Grandpa

240

Walter died. We wrote to each other when she came out here. I always loved her,' she repeated. 'I think we were made in the same mould.'

'Perhaps you were,' Violet agreed after a short silence. It did not, Daisy thought, sound like a compliment.

'I think grandmothers are important,' Tim said quickly. 'I spent most of my holidays with my grandmother Sanders because Mum was working and her mother, my other grandmother, was in New Zealand. Bendigo became my home town and Melbourne where I went to school, so I jumped at the chance to practise law here after I qualified.'

Daisy wondered why she hadn't heard about him from Violet if, as Tim had said, he had always been a part of this family. But then, her sister was a notoriously bad correspondent, confining her letters to Christmas and birthdays and not saying much even then.

'Yes,' Daisy murmured. She remembered that when old Mrs Sanders died, she had left this house to Violet who had lived in it since she was a small child and looked after the old lady till her death. She too had spent her childhood here, so returning to it really was like coming home. She wondered why it had never occurred to her before that Edwin Sanders bringing her mother Violet and herself here was more than a quixotic action.

Tim smiled across the table. 'You seem so

241

familiar, I feel I know you, yet I had never met you until today . . .'

'So you couldn't have, could you?' Daisy interrupted.

'No, I couldn't. All the same . . .' Her brusqueness surprised him, but his voice was gentle and when he smiled and added, 'I expect it is because I know Hazel and there is a strong family resemblance,' Daisy felt reassured.

'Yes, that's probably it,' she agreed, searching in vain for some other subject to talk about; family resemblances were not a comfortable topic.

Daisy covertly watched Tim and Hazel, searching for any sign of romantic attachment between them, but she could not find any. It seemed to her that they were excellent friends, but that was all. Violet also seemed to have an interest in them; she caught her watching them several times, and when she was not observing the young people, it seemed to Daisy that she was watching her. When she smiled tentatively back at her sister, Violet looked quickly away.

By the time the meal was over, Daisy was beginning to wonder if she was really seeing these nuances in the behaviour of other people, or if she herself was getting quite paranoid.

Daisy was shocked to learn that Edwin Sanders, the man she now thought of as her father, had died so long ago and wondered

242

why on earth Violet had not told her. She was finding quite a lot to wonder about in her sister's behaviour. Surely she did not really harbour a grudge because their mother had lived with her over the war years. It had not been deliberate, after all, and she had genuinely expected and wanted her to come back home. Yes, she could be difficult, but not, as Daisy remembered, *that* difficult, and Hazel harboured only good memories of her grandmother. She had come here nurturing rosy thoughts of coming back home, but now it seemed as if this was not her home at all, whatever memories she had. She had to admit that she and Violet had never been what might be called 'close' as sisters, even as young children. They had always been so different and sibling rivalry had never been far below the surface. Violet had also been very aware of her few years of seniority.

Thinking back to their childhood, Daisy asked, 'What happened to Rosie, Violet? I remember her looking after us as small children.'

'I doubt if you do,' Violet all but snapped. 'You were only a baby.'

'I'm sure I do,' Daisy insisted, wondering in the face of such certainty from her sister if she really did, or if she perhaps just remembered hearing her talked about. 'Well, what did become of her?'

Violet glared at her. 'Does it really matter,

Daisy?'

'I shouldn't have asked if I hadn't wanted to know.'

Violet sighed and when she answered, she leaned forward slightly towards her sister and answered in a sibilant hiss, 'If you must know, she married our father.'

'Married our father?' Daisy sounded what she was—stupefied. 'Don't be ridiculous, Violet, our father died. Besides, he was married to our mother.'

Violet pushed herself up from the table with a look at Daisy that should have caused her to turn into a pillar of salt at the very least. 'I am afraid you are the ridiculous one, Daisy. He left our mother and Rosie eventually joined him. As far as I know, they lived happily ever after.'

'Why was I always led to believe he died?' Daisy wanted to know as she followed her sister towards the kitchen where she was making a great fuss of making coffee.

'Because you were too young, and too much of a gabble-mouth, to be told anything different.'

'I was so young I couldn't gabble!' Daisy pointed out angrily. 'But you were just the age to let cats out of bags, so why were *you* told?'

Violet had the grace to look sheepish. 'I wasn't. Not then, anyway. I found out for myself when I was older.'

'I see . . .' Daisy was somewhat mollified by

244

this explanation but couldn't help but wonder how much more Violet had found out—or could find out, if she put her mind to the task. She was silent for a moment, absently piling dirty dishes on to the draining board before asking, 'Are they . . . well, are they still around?'

'They moved up to New South Wales some years ago. Dad might be dead, for all I know, but Rosie is probably still alive.'

'I thought I liked Rosie . . .' Daisy murmured, but was cut short by Violet pointing out that she was too young to like anyone.

'You were just a baby. You can't remember her at all.'

'Then I must remember you talking about her and saying you liked her.'

'Yes, I did, and Mother did too. She told me she couldn't have managed without her when she and Dad first came out here. She was on the same ship, coming out to her father, but he didn't turn up to meet her. Never did turn up, in fact. That's why she and Mother joined forces.'

'I always thought I remember her looking after us after Dad . . .' Daisy stopped herself saying 'died' and replaced the word with 'went away'. 'But I expect you are right that I just remember hearing about her.'

'Well, she did stay with us for a while. I don't know exactly what happened, but I think

245

he came here to collect us all—there was an almighty bust-up and he left without us but with Rosie instead. Don't ask me any more questions. I only know that much because I was awake and heard the row.'

Daisy looked at her sister, wondering what else she heard in the course of this row. 'If all that is true, Violet, why hasn't anyone put me straight before?'

'What was the point?' Violet shrugged. 'It was better for you to think our father was dead. He is now, anyway. Divorce was frowned on in those days. Even the innocent party, as I suppose our mother was, could be the butt of gossip and censure.'

Daisy noted that Violet now said her father was dead. She let it pass; there was something else her sister had said that she had to query.

'What do you mean, *"you suppose she was innocent"*—of course she was. He went off and left her, alone with two young children.' Daisy's voice rose indignantly.

Violet didn't answer and she repeated, 'Well, he did, didn't he?'

'Ye-es . . .' Violet finally conceded in a grudging voice that grated on Daisy. Her sister really did seem to bear a grudge against their mother. Was there something else she was privy to and keeping to herself? 'Yes, that is true, but he may have had a good reason.'

'How could any man have a good reason to abandon a wife and two small children in a strange country?'

'If she was . . . "interested" in another man, wouldn't that be a good reason?' Violet dried her hands on a tea towel, keeping her back to Daisy. Her voice came out as a somewhat surly mumble.

Daisy opened her mouth to retaliate then shut it again, not at all sure that she really wanted to pursue this conversation.

'Look, Daisy,' Violet turned and faced her sister, 'I was fond of Dad and I don't think that trying to apportion blame is a good idea after all these years. Let's drop the subject, shall we?'

Daisy was about to protest that she was not trying to blame anyone in particular, merely understand what had happened all those years ago, but a glance at her sister's closed expression made her keep silent. The last thing she wanted to do was quarrel with her so soon after her arrival and she was forced to admit they had already come perilously close.

CHAPTER TWENTY-SEVEN

By tacit agreement, the subject of their parents was carefully avoided by both Violet and Daisy over the next few days. They were having a restorative coffee in Myers Department Store after a shopping spree when Violet suggested they take an early morning train to Melbourne and 'do' the shops in the state capital. Daisy readily agreed; it was easier to keep off controversial subjects with her sister when they were out and about than sitting around the house.

'You mean we could visit the Melbourne Myers? Is it bigger and better?' she asked with mild irony.

'Bigger. Not necessarily better,' Violet bridled. 'Don't forget the very first Myers store was opened here in Bendigo by Sidney Myers in 1911 and now they are Australia wide.'

Daisy had forgotten, but noting that her flippant comment had annoyed her sister, she said soothingly, 'Quite an achievement, wasn't it?'

She had come to Australia with some vague, half-formed idea of returning to her birthplace and settling down, but Violet seemed determined to treat her as a visitor from overseas and a temporary one at that. Hoping to keep things on a pleasant footing, Daisy smiled brightly at her sister. 'That would be fun, Vi—a day in Melbourne, I mean. I always enjoy shopping, don't you?'

'When I have plenty of money in my pocket.'

Daisy sighed. She knew her sister thought that she had married a rich man and therefore had money to burn. Truth to tell, she only had a reasonable, but not large fixed income left her by Richard as Giles had inherited the bulk of his father's estate. She had tried explaining this without success.

As they rode down on the train to Melbourne early the next morning, Daisy was surprised when Violet returned to the subject of their father; in spite of what she had learned Daisy still thought of Bill Weston as her father.

'I didn't quite tell you the truth yesterday,' she began.

'Oh?' Daisy queried, wondering what Violet was referring to.

'About Dad. I said he *might* be dead, for all I knew. That's not strictly true. He is dead— now. But he only died quite recently and I knew quite well he was dead. In fact, I went to his funeral.'

'Oh,' Daisy repeated the monosyllable, but in a different tone this time. There didn't seem much else to say at this point, so she waited in silence for her sister to enlarge on this rather surprising piece of information.

'Yes, I have kept in touch with him over the years, with them both—Dad and Rosie. I loved her, perhaps more than I did Mother. She certainly did more for me when I was little.'

Daisy gasped, a small intake of breath that did not escape Violet who retorted in what Daisy was beginning to think of as her usual prickly manner.

'There is no need to look shocked; it's the truth. Anyway, you were always the favourite.'

Daisy opened her mouth to hotly deny this, but her protestations were cut short.

'Of course you were—and you know it. Anyway, to get to the point, Rosie never forgot my birthday, just a card, but it always came. When I was in my teens—oh, about fifteen, I suppose—I decided to reply.'

'Did she put an address in then?'

'No, of course not, but the envelope was postmarked, so I looked it up on the map and discovered it was a little town in New South Wales. I went to the post office and got the telephone directory for that area and looked up W. Weston. There were a couple, but on a hunch, I tried the number that was under W. and R. Weston. I was lucky first time and that's how I started a regular correspondence with them.'

'You mean they really were married?'

'Of course they were.'

'But, but that means there must have been a divorce and—' Daisy bit off the words. *Mum was free. Why couldn't she and my father have married*?

'Of course there was. Dad may not have been a saint, but he wasn't a bigamist,' Violet snapped, her tone implying her sister was either hypercritical or just plain stupid.

'I suppose I don't really remember Rosie,' Daisy admitted, 'but I certainly remember the Sanderses and a happy childhood.' Why, she wondered, had she never questioned the

250

reason for their kindness.

'Yes,' for once, they were in agreement, 'which is why I stayed on and looked after the old lady.'

'It was very good of you,' Daisy murmured, crushing the unworthy thought that her virtue had paid off as she had inherited the house.

'And it was not for any material reward I might get; I really loved her,' Violet protested, making Daisy wonder if she had expressed her thoughts aloud.

'We both did.'

Daisy thought this was the end of the conversation till Violet broke the silence between them. 'They had children, you know.'

For a moment, lost in her own thoughts, Daisy failed to realize who she was talking about. 'Who did?' she asked.

Violet made an exasperated sound halfway between a sigh and a click of the tongue. 'Dad and Rosie, of course.' There was a tone of exaggerated patience in her voice. 'We have two brothers and a sister. Well, half-brothers and half-sister.'

'You—we have?' For a moment, Daisy had almost said: *you have, but not me*.

'Rosie lives in Melbourne now. She would love to see you again, Daisy.'

'In Melbourne,' Daisy repeated rather stupidly. After all, she had a perfect right to live where she liked and Melbourne was home to many thousands as the capital of the state of

251

Victoria. But she wasn't sure she wanted to see Rosie. As Violet had been at pains to point out, she couldn't really remember her, but she did know she had deserted her mother. She didn't intend to voice these thoughts and exacerbate the tension between Violet and herself as it was obvious her sister wanted her to meet Rosie, in fact had probably already promised to organize a meeting. 'Yes, I would like to see her again.' Daisy tried to inject some enthusiasm into her voice and hoped Violet would not detect any insincerity.

'She has invited us for afternoon tea.'

'We're going to her house?' Daisy felt she had been manipulated and sizzled with repressed anger. It appeared this day in the city was not a casual shopping trip at all but had been carefully orchestrated by Violet and Rosie between them. Through tight lips, she gritted, 'How nice.'

'We can spend the morning shopping,' Violet decreed cheerfully, taking her sister's enthusiasm for granted, 'have lunch then go to see Rosie. She doesn't expect us until after two o'clock, so that gives us a nice long morning and we can spend plenty of time with her before catching the late afternoon train back to Bendigo.'

'Yes,' Daisy agreed weakly, feeling, not for the first time in her life, that she had been steamrollered into a course of action of someone else's choosing.

The morning passed pleasantly enough, browsing through the large department stores with a break midmorning for coffee. Now her programme had been accepted and was underway, Violet was a pleasant companion and Daisy gave herself up to enjoying herself. By the time they needed to think about finding their way out to Rosie's place at Richmond, they were both well loaded with parcels. Violet wanted to get a tram, but Daisy insisted on a taxi. 'I'll pay,' she promised. Violet grunted rather ungraciously but accepted this evidence of who was the well-to-do sister. They rode there in silence, both preoccupied with their own thoughts.

Daisy looked forward to this meeting with very mixed feelings. Truthfully, she could not remember anything much about Rosie, and the knowledge that she had left her mother and subsequently married the man she had believed was her father put her on the other side of some imaginary line in Daisy's mind, into a place where she was not prepared to like her. She paid off the taxi and followed Violet to the door of the neat, terraced house, wishing herself anywhere but where she was.

CHAPTER TWENTY-EIGHT

The door opened as they reached it and a cottage loaf of a woman with whiter than white hair, a face criss-crossed with the pattern of a life lived to the full and beaming a welcome greeted them. Daisy's churlish thoughts melted as she submitted to a warm hug. She even smiled at Rosie's emotional: 'Daisy, my little baby!'

'Not so little and no longer a baby, but yes— still Daisy.' To her own surprise, she returned the hug.

Inside the house, Rosie stood back and studied Daisy. 'Oh, but you are so like your mother!' she exclaimed. Daisy had been told this before but couldn't see it herself. To her mind, the one like Ella was Hazel.

'You should see my daughter. Now she really is like her and I suppose would be round about the age Mother was when she came out to Australia and first met up with you,' said Daisy.

'And a lucky day that was for me. Fifteen, I was, a scrawny thing. Though you wouldn't believe that now, sent out to a father who never turned up to meet me, never did turn up, in fact, alive *or* dead. I would have been in real strife if your mother hadn't taken me under her wing. I owe a lot to her.'

'She owed a lot to you too, Rosie,' Violet cut in. 'You more than repaid anything Mother ever did for you.'

'Yes, well . . .' Rosie looked flustered recalling how her relationship with their mother had ended. It would be less than tactful to bring that into the conversation.

Daisy was surprised to hear herself say, 'Violet tells me you and Dad were married,' and wondered what demon prompted them. She watched a deep flush creep up Rosie's neck and suffuse her cheeks and felt ashamed of herself. She usually took on the role of peacemaker, smoothing over the gaffes of others whether malicious or accidental.

Rosie squared her shoulders and looked Daisy in the eye. For a moment, they stared at one another like two roosters staring down prior to a scrap, Violet told her afterwards. 'More like a couple of old hens,' Daisy had corrected her, a wry smile lifting the corners of her mouth.

'Yes, Daisy, we were married,' Rosie was the first to break the silence, 'and quite happy we were too, most of the time. Neither of us had any great expectations, you see. Bill always said your mother expected too much of him. She was full of romantic notions he couldn't live up to.'

'Did you know Mother eventually married the man she jilted to marry my father and come to Australia?' Violet's voice rasped as if she were holding back angry thoughts. 'She only came back here to see me after he died.'

Daisy looked at her sister with a new glimmer of understanding. Was this why she was so angry with their mother? Not because she had landed herself on her for the duration of the war, but for her perceived rejection of her when she married Walter and stayed in England.

'Oh dear, the lengths the Good Lord had to go to in order to get you two into the world,' Rosie murmured on a theatrical sigh.

Daisy chuckled at this mental picture of the Heavenly Puppeteer moving her mother across the world like a chess piece just to bring her and her sister into being. She met the twinkle in Rosie's eye and her preconceived idea that she wasn't going to like her did a quick somersault; she liked her very much. No wonder her mother had thought so much of her in those first difficult days in Australia.

'I'm really glad, Rosie, that everything turned out all right for you and that you and . . . that you were happy.' With the knowledge of her own parentage in her mind, she couldn't quite bring herself to say *you and my father*.

During this brief exchange, the kettle had come to the boil and broke into the brief silence with a piercing whistle. 'There's the kettle,' Rosie announced unnecessarily. 'I think a nice cup of tea would go down very well,' she smiled encouragingly at Daisy, 'and you can tell me how life has dealt with you since I last saw you.'

Daisy thought that was a bit of a tall order as her entire life had been lived since she and Rosie were last together. 'How do you do it?' she asked as she bit into a feather light scone.

'Do what?' Rosie was baffled.

'Make such superb scones. Mine are like golf balls compared with these. I've never tasted such good ones.'

'I don't suppose you have; your mother had a very heavy hand with scones and pastry. But then she hadn't been brought up to cook, or do anything that you could say was useful which was why she was so glad to have me along with her when we went up to that farm beyond Bendigo. Now, fill me in with what's happened in your life, young Daisy.'

Thus challenged, Daisy felt strangely tongue-tied. 'Well . . . we all lived with old Mrs Sanders after—well, when Mum was on her own. I had always had a yen to go to England; it was where my parents came from, so I always thought of it as home.'

'I don't see why,' Violet interrupted. 'I never did. Australia has always been home to me.'

'Well, Australia was home to me too, but that didn't stop me wanting to see where I had originated.' Daisy tried to explain how she had felt.

'You do talk some tosh, Daisy.' Violet grimaced with impatience. 'You were born here the same as me, you were raised here, you went to school here, but all you ever thought about was going to England, "back to England", you used to say. So silly. You had never been there, so how could you go back?'

'I probably was silly, full of romantic ideas about "the old country", but that is how I was and I can't change what I was then, can I?' Daisy did her best to suppress her irritation with her sister and turned deliberately towards Rosie. 'I suppose I was lucky in a way. Not everyone has their dream come true.'

'Not everyone has such daft dreams,' Violet muttered half under her breath.

Studiously, Daisy ignored her and Rosie cast her a quelling look.

'Anyway, I ended up marrying my boss and having two children.' Daisy decided brevity was the best defence against Violet's constant interruptions.

Rosie sighed. 'Sounds just like a Mills and Boon romance, but I suppose there was really much more to it than that.'

'Well, yes . . .' Daisy admitted, 'that's just the gist of it.' She felt like saying that her life with Richard had not been in the least like a romantic novel but chose to talk about her children instead. 'Giles is married now. That's why I came back to Australia—for a visit.' She paused, realizing that that hardly sounded like a legitimate reason and tried to explain. 'He inherited the house and the business, you see.

When he became of age and got married, I felt it was time for me to leave him to it.'

'You mean your husband left everything to your son, and not you?' Rosie was shocked.

'Don't worry, he was a very rich man, so I am sure he left Daisy well provided for.' Violet's voice was tart.

Daisy glared at her, wondering how Violet had come to assume with such certainty that she, Daisy, was rich. She didn't know how to refute it without sounding pettish, or worse—a total humbug.

Rosie came to her rescue, rolling back the years to talk to Violet as if she were still barely five years old. 'What her husband left Daisy is none of your business, or mine,' she snapped. 'Now, tell me about your mother, what happened to her, and about that daughter of yours. I understand she is a dead ringer of her grandma.'

'Yes, she is very like her, in every way— looks and character. Hazel loved my mother and got on very well with her as a small child. She wrote to her throughout the war and was looking forward to her coming back.'

Violet gave what sounded like a derisive snort. 'Did you know,' she turned accusingly to Daisy, 'that Hazel dabbles with the tarot cards. She says her grandma Ella gave them to her. I find that hard to believe—Mother messing about with something like that.'

'Oh, but she did,' Rosie chortled. 'I

introduced her to them and taught her how to use them. I had an old deck that had belonged to my mother and we whiled away a few hours with them on board that ship. I never let on to your mother, but I made a few bob on the side reading other passengers' cards for them. Most people on board were pretty uncertain about what was in store for them in the future and I had plenty of takers.'

Daisy laughed cheerfully, to the surprise of Violet who had thought to shock what she thought of as her sister's prim English soul. 'So you, Rosie, are the mastermind behind all this. Hazel was turned out of her boarding school for possessing and using a deck of tarot cards, given her, she said, by her grandmother. I found that a bit surprising at the time, but now you have explained it, all is clear, as they say.'

'You had better teach her how to use them properly.' Violet meant to sound withering, but both Daisy and Rosie took it seriously.

'Indeed I must,' Rosie said and Daisy murmured something in agreement. Violet sniffed. She personally had no use whatsoever for such arrant nonsense.

'You told me your mother married the man she jilted to come out here with your father,' Rosie adroitly changed the subject. 'Now *there* is a real romantic story for you. Had he waited for her all those years?'

'Well, not really,' Daisy admitted. 'He had married someone else, a widow with a son . . .'

A shadow crossed her face as she thought of James. Nothing at all romantic there. Twice she had let him go out of her life. 'But she seemed very happy with him.'

Rosie nodded with satisfaction.

Their reminiscing was brought to an abrupt halt by Violet looking up at the clock on the mantle and announcing that they had better move if they were to catch their train.

Daisy hugged Rosie as they left, surprised to find that she was really sorry to be leaving. She promised to come again and bring Hazel with her. What an odd thing family relationships were, she thought as she settled into a corner seat opposite Violet on the homeward train.

CHAPTER TWENTY-NINE

'Mmm—sorry.' Daisy's lids had drooped and she had fallen asleep. It had been a big day in every way, physically and emotionally. She opened them now and looked across the railway carriage towards her sister who looked very much awake and was obviously waiting for an answer to some question Daisy had missed.

'Well, what did you think of Rosie? Do you remember her at all?' Violet sounded as truculent as Daisy had come to expect.

'I liked her. I can't say I remember her, but

even if I did, it would be a different Rosie. She would have been so young when I last saw her.'

'About twenty, I suppose,' Violet told her after a moment's thought. 'I remember her very well. She looked after me most of the time, not only up at the farm but later on when Mother brought us to the Sanders's place. In fact, she is about the only person I can remember looking after me when I was small.'

Daisy thought this was a bit unfair on their mother but didn't argue the point. It seemed all too easy to get at odds with her sister.

'I guess Mother was lucky meeting up with her.' She wasn't really one hundred per cent sure about this in view of subsequent events. She frowned slightly as she took her mind back down the years. 'I don't really remember anything about . . . Dad, either,' she admitted, hesitating slightly. 'My early childhood memories really begin when Mother brought us to Bendigo. I remember the growing up years as pretty happy.'

'Oh, they were,' Violet agreed, 'thanks to the Sanderses.'

'You don't give our mother credit for much, do you?' Daisy was stung into retorting, wondering why her sister carried such a whopping great chip on her shoulder about Ella.

Violet shrugged. 'I give credit where credit is due,' she retorted cryptically.

Daisy sighed and closed her eyes, feigning

weariness. When she opened them a short time later, it was to see that Violet really was dozing. With relief, she gave herself up to watching the scenery changing from suburbia to country as they drew away from Melbourne.

Daisy surprised herself by how much she liked Rosie, but it was the instant regard for a new acquaintance, not the renewed liking for an old friend. She smiled inwardly at the thought of the young Rosie and Ella whiling away the long hours on board ship with Rosie's deck of tarot cards. She had not entirely believed Hazel when she had said that her cards had come from her grandmother, but now it seemed her daughter had spoken the truth. She could understand why her mother had kept quiet about them when she thought how they would have been received in middle-class English society; her own husband, Richard, would have reacted in exactly the same way as Hazel's headmistress. In fact, he might well have been even more scandalized to discover what his daughter was dabbling in and she indubitably would have been blamed. It was a good thing he was not around to see Hazel expelled from school, she reflected, and the thought was immediately followed by guilt; one should never feel glad because a person was dead, whatever the circumstances and however long after they died.

By the time they arrived back at the house, Daisy was limp with exhaustion and her head was aching with a rhythmic thud. Pleading weariness, she excused herself and closed the door of her bedroom with a sigh of relief.

'Have a cup of tea and a couple of aspirins,' Violet suggested, not unkindly.

Gratefully, Daisy took her advice and smiled her thanks when her sister added several biscuits and a banana to the tray of tea. She was, she thought, well meaning; it was just that she seemed to have such a thing about their mother.

With her bare feet stretched out on the bed and her back propped up by a bank of pillows, Daisy reviewed the day. She had been annoyed with Violet for setting up the meeting with Rosie, yet in the end, she had enjoyed it. In all fairness, she was probably far more suited to Bill than her mother had been; she had schooled herself out of thinking of him as her father since she had learned the truth of her parentage.

Because the tea seemed to have done the trick and she hated taking any form of medication, she left the aspirins untouched but ate the biscuits and the banana and drained the small teapot. Stretching thoroughly then consciously relaxing, she closed her eyes and felt a pleasant lethargy overtaking her and her mind slipping into the dreamlike state that often precedes sleep. As she drifted off, she had the oddest feeling that James was in the room with her.

She woke a few hours later, surprised to find that she was fully clothed except for her feet, that it was dark and she was decidedly hungry. All trace of her headache had gone. Swinging herself off the bed, she pushed her feet into her slippers and opened her bedroom door. As she did so, the phone began to ring. Violet had gone to bed, so she hurried to answer it. 'Hello, James.'

'Daisy? How did you know it was me?'

'I—I didn't,' Daisy lied, falling into a lifelong habit of denying any trace of the gift her mother had shown. 'I was asleep when the phone rang,' she added as if that explained everything. She was glad when James did not call her on it.

'Sorry to be ringing you so late,' was all he said, apologetically.

'It's not that late, only . . .' Daisy glanced quickly at her watch, 'just after ten.'

'It's late here—just after midnight.'

'Ah, yes, I had forgotten you are a couple of hours ahead of us.' She wondered what had prompted him to call at all. 'Vi and I have been in Melbourne all day. I was whacked when we got back and went to bed almost straight away. I had just woken up, as a matter of fact, when the phone rang. There is no one about, so I guess Violet made an early night of it too and the young ones are probably out.' She stopped abruptly, feeling she was gabbling and not giving James a space to speak, let

265

alone explain his late night call. When he did not say anything, she spoke again, somewhat tentatively. 'It's good to hear your voice, James. What . . .' her voice faded out uncertainly.

'Nothing in particular.' He answered her unspoken question as if she had voiced it. 'I just felt a need to hear your voice, find out how you are, that sort of thing. I didn't realize how late it was until I had got your number.' The explanation sounded weak, even to him, but it was true for all that. He had just had this sudden urge to speak to Daisy. He had been annoyed with himself ever since the ship left Melbourne that he had let Daisy disembark with nothing settled between them. The excuse he gave himself was that it would be difficult to change his plans to meet his stepson in Auckland—James intended to spend the last week of his holiday with Christopher before heading off on the last leg of his journey back to Christchurch.

He tried to explain all this to Daisy, but it sounded more like a garbled excuse—for quite what, he wasn't sure; not leaving the ship with her in Melbourne, perhaps. He wanted to tell her how much he wished she were with him but ended up by merely asking how she was. It was wishing they were together that had given rise to an irresistible urge to hear her voice.

'I'm fine, thanks, James.' Daisy tried to inject some warmth into her voice. She was afraid she sounded cool, even prim, in her desire not to gush and betray how very pleased she really was to hear his voice. 'I've been meeting up with relatives and—things.' Rosie, she thought, would not appreciate being called a thing.

'How about adding a trip to New Zealand to your itinerary?' James suggested. 'While you are in this hemisphere.'

'Yes, I'll think about it,' Daisy answered with a caution that irritated even herself, so she was not unduly surprised when James sounded impatient when he reminded her: 'That's what you said when I mentioned it on the ship'.

'Yes, James.' Daisy was appalled to hear herself murmuring this. Had nothing except the name changed from the years of saying, 'Yes, Richard'?

'Come on, Daisy. Thinking time is over. If you plan to come, you must do something about it.'

'Yes, I suppose you are right. It is silly to go back without seeing New Zealand. I'll make inquiries.' God, she thought, I might be talking to a travel agent. *Why couldn't I tell him how much I want to see him again*?

'If time is important to you, fly over,' James advised, unwittingly falling into the role she had assigned to him, but in reality anxious to get her committed while she sounded positive. He nearly added: 'he who hesitates is lost'.

'I'll look into it,' Daisy promised. 'Perhaps Hazel would come with me. It would be fun to have her along.'

'Yes, I would love to see little Nutmeg again.' James thought that the unlikelihood of her allowing Daisy to change her mind would outweigh having a third person along and he would genuinely like to see the grown-up Hazel. By the time they wound up their conversation he was already planning to see if Christopher might have some holiday owing and could join up with them.

As Daisy replaced the receiver, Violet appeared in the doorway of her bedroom, hair tousled, looking somewhat bemused as she pulled the tie of her robe. 'I thought I heard the phone ring. Who was it?'

'It was for me, actually,' Daisy hurried to explain. 'A call from New Zealand.'

'New Zealand! Who do you know there?' She couldn't have sounded more amazed if Daisy had said Mars.

'It was James.'

'James? James who?'

'Mother's stepson. Well, not really. I mean, he was Walter's stepson. It's a bit complicated. After Mother and Walter . . . parted . . . he eventually married someone else, a widow with a son, James. He was very fond of Mother and I saw quite a bit of him in England. He was wounded in the war—lost a leg, actually—and when it ended, he came out to New Zealand.'

Daisy stopped, almost breathless, painfully aware that once more she had been gabbling and probably confused Violet more than enlightened her. She hoped her sister meant it when she said 'I see' but guessed she was putting two and two together and adding them up to five.

'What does he do?' Violet asked.

'He is a doctor—a specialist, actually, I believe.' Daisy tilted her chin in an unconscious attitude that said: *so there*!

Violet merely raised her eyebrows in a gesture of surprise and tacit approval.

Daisy was relieved and at the same time annoyed with herself as she didn't need her sister's approval for anything she did. The childhood days when she had always striven to please Violet, who was not only four years her senior but bossy to whit, were long gone.

Violet dismissed the subject with a shrug and turned towards the kitchen. 'I think the phone woke me, but now I am awake, I am ravenously hungry,' she admitted. 'Like you, I was too tired to bother with much to eat when we got home and I soon followed your example and went to bed. How does a midnight snack appeal?'

Daisy admitted it did and was about to protest that it wasn't anywhere near midnight when she remembered that it was actually past the witching hour in New Zealand. With thoughts full of James, she followed Violet into the kitchen.

CHAPTER THIRTY

'Tea, coffee, hot chocolate?' Violet asked. Receiving no answer, she repeated the question with an impatient 'what do you want?' in front of it this time.

'Oh, sorry . . . er . . . hot chocolate, I think, please,' replied Daisy.

Violet threw her a shrewd glance. 'You seem to be in cloud cuckoo land. It's a wonder you managed to wake up enough to answer the phone when it rang. What would you like to eat? I have a yearning for cheese on toast. What about you?'

'Mmm . . . lovely,' Daisy agreed and, anxious to be helpful, moved over to the stove and lit the grill. In a short time, they were seated each side of the kitchen table, companionably munching hot cheese on toast and sipping scalding chocolate. There was a rare feeling of companionship between them. 'This takes me back. Do you remember, Vi, this was one of Mum's favourite snacks when we were kids?'

Violet smiled. 'She never lost her taste for it, either. If ever she was hungry, had missed a meal or, I suppose, was in need of comfort food, she would come into the kitchen and toast herself some cheese and make a big mug of hot chocolate.' She spoke reminiscently and for once, it seemed, without any of the resentment that usually tinged her voice when she mentioned Ella.

'What do you mean—"comfort food"?' Daisy had not imagined her mother anything but perfectly content out here in Australia, away from the stresses of a war-torn Britain.

'Oh, she had times when she felt—I don't know—guilty, probably, because she was out here safe and secure and you and your children were in England. She read everything in the papers about shortages, bombing, etcetera.' Violet glanced across the table at her sister then quickly down again at the food on her plate. 'I'm sorry. I don't suppose I should have said the things I did when you first arrived. I realize now that you didn't push her off on me; she came of her own volition and truly intended, in fact wanted to go back to England. She was—as you said—trapped here by the war. It was a real shame she died when she did and never got back.'

'Yes, it was,' Daisy agreed, leaning slightly towards her sister. 'I really appreciate what you just said, Vi, but there is just one other thing. I never really knew why she died. I mean, she hadn't been sick or anything, had she? It was such a shock when we learned that she was dead—just like that. After all, she wasn't old. Well, not *really* old, was she?'

'Sixty-seven,' Violet supplied. 'Not old at all.'

She paused for so long that Daisy wondered if she were going to give her any more information willingly.

'She dropped dead, right here in this kitchen.' Violet glanced round as if expecting to see her mother lying on the floor and Daisy found her own eyes involuntarily doing the same. 'It was a massive heart attack. Apparently, she had a heart condition. The doctor knew all about it. She knew that there was a chance it could happen any time, but she never mentioned it and made her doctor swear he wouldn't either. I wish we had known. I would have made her take more care of herself. I felt so guilty afterwards.'

'I can understand that, but if you didn't know, you couldn't blame yourself. I wish I had known too. Forewarned is forearmed and all that.'

'I was angry too,' Violet admitted. 'Angry with her, I mean. I knew I hadn't always been as nice as I should have been, or might have been, if I had known.'

'You mean you were angry with her for not telling you? Well, she didn't tell me either.'

'Well, yes, angry because of that, but more because I had resented her and the reason was really nothing to do with her; it was because of you.'

'Of me!' Daisy was genuinely astonished.

272

'But why?'

'Because I knew you were always her favourite. I had known it, I think, ever since you were born, and I never really understood why. After all, she had me first, and it was you coming along that seemed to be the straw that broke the camel's back, if you know what I mean.'

Daisy shook her head. 'Not really. How could I? I was only a baby.'

'It was you who seemed to be the thing that finally broke up our parents' marriage. I loved Dad as well as Mum and missed him when he . . . went. I wondered what I had done; I was sure it all my fault, but later on when I thought about things, I realized the break-up coincided with your birth.'

'Oh, Vi, I'm so sorry . . .' Daisy's voice broke and she wondered how to tell her sister that the problem was nothing of her making but because she, Daisy, had a different father. The only person to blame, she supposed, was their mother. But while she was turning this over in her mind, the door burst open and the young people erupted into the room. They all looked very happy, were very noisy and not a little flushed.

'Hi!' Maureen exclaimed. 'What's this, then? A midnight feast. Didn't you get anything to eat in Melbourne?'

The moment for heart to heart confidences was gone. Violet pushed herself up from the

273

table, her lips in a tight line.

'If you young people want anything to eat, you had better help yourselves. Daisy and I are off to bed—and yes, we did have plenty to eat in Melbourne, but we were both very tired. It was a big day so we had an early night, then the phone woke us and we decided we hadn't had enough to eat so made ourselves a snack.'

'Who rang up?' Maureen asked idly. She was not really worried; anyone she cared about had been with her all evening. She reached for an apple and without waiting for an answer added, 'No, I don't want anything to eat. Hazel might, though. We have been round at Tim's place, eating and drinking all night. Well, we have, but Hazel has been reading.'

'Reading?' Violet sounded bemused. Daisy looked at her daughter and from the expression on her face knew what was meant and guessed another clanger was about to be dropped.

'Yeah, you know. Reading tarot cards, like Grandma Ella used to do. She said that's where she got her cards. I wish she had given me a deck, but I suppose you were always so hung up on them, she didn't dare.' Maureen glanced at her mother; the expression on her face warned her not to enlarge on the subject. 'I'm off to bed. Like you said, Mum, it is late.'

Hazel raised her eyes slowly to her aunt's face with a swift sidelong glance at her mother as she did so. 'I'm sorry, Aunt Violet, but it

274

was only light-hearted fun, really.'

This excuse fell to the ground like a lead balloon. Violet gave a most inelegant snort, threw Daisy a scorching look and remarked sourly, 'If your mother doesn't mind, then who am I to care.' In the doorway, she half turned to throw a grudging, 'Goodnight,' over her shoulder.

Left alone with her daughter, Daisy sighed. 'It would seem your aunt is not kindly disposed to the tarot cards.'

'Maureen knows that and should have kept her mouth shut,' Hazel snapped back. 'She would never have mentioned it if she hadn't been drinking more than her fair share of half a dozen bottles of red wine a grateful client had given Tim. She took his invitation to us to help him drink them very literally.'

'"Us" being?'

'Oh, me and Tim and a friend of his, Derek something or other.' By this time, Hazel too had reached the door and only a little less casually than her aunt, she yawned and said, 'Goodnight, Mum. I'm bushed.'

As Daisy mechanically cleared away the evidence of the midnight feast she and Violet had enjoyed, she reflected on the disturbing fact that Hazel was once more in trouble over those wretched cards her mother had given her. She cursed the interruption for occurring just when she and Vi were reaching some sort of an understanding and finally was cast down by the memory of Hazel's casual 'me and Tim'. She clattered the dishes into the sink and returned to bed with James's phone call relegated to the back of her mind.

Thoughts of him soon made their way to the surface, however, as she lay in bed, sleepless. She blamed the cheese on toast for her wakeful state and tried not to worry about Hazel. From what she could gather, Hazel was getting a deal too friendly with Tim Sanders, but Daisy shirked the idea of explaining why she didn't want her to get too deeply involved with him. He was such a very nice young man that she knew it would be hard to drag up any reason other than the truth to effect a cooling in Hazel's relationship with him.

Daisy was finally dropping off to sleep, in fact, was in that state of relaxation induced on the edge of sleep, almost a meditative mood, when she experienced what psychologists call an 'ah-ha' moment. Of course, she knew the solution. Actually, she had already voiced it when she was talking to James. How, in God's name could she be so stupid as to lie awake worrying over a problem she had already solved? With a sigh, she finally dropped into a deep sleep.

CHAPTER THIRTY-ONE

Daisy overslept. She left her bedroom in her robe and slippers and found Violet in the kitchen moving pieces of crockery from the table to the draining board as if she had a personal grievance against them. Daisy assumed she was still fuming about those damn tarot cards. If there was going to be a showdown, she felt at a disadvantage in her dressing gown, but before she could sneak away to get dressed, Violet turned and faced her.

'If you want a cup of tea, there is one in the pot.' She had the teapot in her hand and gave a slight gesture with it that indicated clearly that unless Daisy did something about it quickly, it would no longer be there.

'Yes, please—I mean, thank you,' Daisy stammered and dropped down in a chair at the table. There was a clean cup and saucer there and she pushed it towards Violet and the hovering pot.

'Is—is Hazel around?' Daisy asked, looking vaguely round the kitchen as if she might see her daughter hiding under one of the chairs.

'She has been up and gone for ages. They both have—she and Maureen.'

'Oh. Why so early? I thought they usually had a lie-in on a Saturday.'

'They do, usually, but they wanted to get the paper early, said they were looking for a flat. Quite who for, I am not sure. Some idea they cooked up between them last night with Tim.'

'What—what sort of idea?'

'They thought up this plan last night to get a flat and all live together. At least, that was the idea as far as I could gather. I might tell you, I don't approve, do you?'

'No, no, I don't.' That was true, anyway, if not quite for the reason Violet supposed.

'Well, it seems to be mostly your Hazel's idea inspired, I gather, by those ridiculous cards of hers.'

'Oh, dear!' Daisy sighed. She wanted to ask what her sister meant by saying that Hazel's tarot cards had inspired the idea. Surely no one would take them seriously enough to make such a major change in their life on their say-so? She drained her cup and pushed herself away from the table. 'I'll get dressed,' she murmured. 'Thanks for the cuppa.' She paused in the doorway as another thought struck her. 'Who exactly is, or are, "all", anyway?'

'Maureen, Derek, Tim and Hazel, of course.'

'Of course,' Daisy murmured and hurried away to get some clothes on. She must find Hazel and put the suggestion to her that they go to New Zealand together. But of course, finding her on a Saturday morning was not that easy.

Daisy made the excuse that she needed to do some shopping but did not run across them in the town. It was late afternoon when the two girls came back. She heard their excited voices as they opened the garden gate and her heart sank.

'Hi. Where's Mum? Any afternoon tea going?' Maureen asked, almost in one breath.

'Your mother is in the garden—*was*, I should say. Here she is now,' Daisy answered, moving across to fill the kettle. She had the feeling that a cup of tea might not be strong enough.

'Oh, Mum, we've found the most super flat!' Maureen did not seem to notice that her news was not greeted with anything like the level of enthusiasm with which it was delivered.

'Yes, two bedrooms, large living room with a kitchen bit at one end and, best of all, our own bathroom,' Hazel enthused.

'Two bedrooms . . .' Daisy, wondering who was going to sleep in them, sounded vague.

'One for the boys and one for us,' Maureen cut in, ignoring, or simply not noticing the tightening of her mother's lips. 'We shall be able to live quite cheaply with four of us sharing the rent.'

Daisy saw one of her lids drop in a wink as she glanced across at Hazel who suppressed a grin. She wondered what they were up to.

'It sounds cheap—in every way. I don't

think I like the idea of you sharing a flat with young men. You should still be living at home, Maureen.' Violet's voice had that 'and I brook no argument' ring to it. She looked across at Daisy for support. 'I can't speak for your mother, Hazel, but I feel sure she will agree with me.'

'Yes. Oh, yes,' Daisy murmured, wishing she didn't sound so feeble.

'But, Mum!' Maureen wailed. Of course she had known that this would be her mother's reaction to such a bid for freedom.

Hazel addressed herself directly to Violet. 'You have been very good to me, very kind and hospitable, Auntie Vi, but I can't lean on you for ever. I never intended that. In fact, I didn't really intend to stay; I just came for a visit, to meet you all. It was wonderful of you to ask me to stay on when Mum said she was coming, but I have to be independent. I am sure you can see that. I quite understand if you don't want Maureen to leave home.' She grinned at her cousin across the room and added mischievously, 'After all, even though she is older, she hasn't had my experience of life.'

Maureen, knowing she was being stirred, bit her tongue, but Violet, who tended to take all remarks on their face value, answered seriously.

'It isn't that I want to keep her at home so much, Hazel, but I don't like the idea of you girls sharing a flat with two young men, and I

280

doubt if your mother does either. Now, if it was just the two of you—'

'You mean you would agree?' Maureen jumped in quickly, suppressing a grin of triumph.

Hazel glanced down at her watch. 'Come and see the flat—both of you,' she urged. 'We promised the agent we would let them know by five o'clock today.'

As the four women hurried out of the house, Violet was grappling with the uncomfortable feeling that somehow she had been manipulated. Daisy, who knew her daughter so much better, was not worried about that; she was merely pleased that it didn't seem that Hazel would be sharing living space with anyone more dangerous than her cousin—for the moment, at any rate.

*   *   *

'It's lovely,' Daisy breathed as she glanced round the small but cosy little apartment. She almost envied her daughter moving in here as Violet was not the easiest to live with. 'But how are you going to manage the rent if there is only the two of you?'

Violet missed this; she was looking critically at the small bedrooms. 'There doesn't appear to be much room for two in these rooms . . .' She stopped and looked from one girl to the other. Both were smiling broadly.

281

'That's what Tim and Derek thought, so they decided to opt out,' Hazel said with a straight face, 'and you did say, Auntie Vi, that you wouldn't mind Maureen sharing a flat if it was just with me.'

When Maureen said airily, 'We both have jobs, so we'll cope,' Violet realized they had never intended to share this place with Tim and Derek, but of course the suggestion that they might had made her agree readily to the lesser evil. This manoeuvre had been Hazel's idea, she was sure. The girl was far too clever for her own good, and Daisy didn't seem to have an inkling.

The flat was vacant and the agent told them they could move in as soon as the bond and a month's advance rent was paid. Violet saw this as a possible means of reneging on the deal, but to her annoyance, Daisy was willing to put the bond money down and the two girls assured them that between them, they could rake up the advance rent.

The next day, Sunday, they moved all their worldly goods and that night, they slept in their new home. Violet, albeit with a grim expression, dished up a large and satisfying evening meal and assured them they could come back any time if they seemed in danger of starving which she was certain would be the case.

Daisy went to bed with a somewhat heavy heart. Not only was she going to miss her daughter's presence in the same house, but she was sure it was going to be a good deal more difficult to persuade her to make the trip to New Zealand with her. In fact, she was not at all sure she was keen on going herself now, unless she summoned the courage to explain to Hazel about her ancestry, and this she was curiously loath to do.

CHAPTER THIRTY-TWO

'It's lucky you and I seem to like each other, isn't it?' Hazel grinned across the untidy little lounge room at her cousin. The small portable radio Maureen had brought from her bedroom at home was churning out what seemed to her a very corny Australian play. 'Do you want this?' She jerked her head in the direction of the set. 'It's pretty feeble, but I suppose if the characters were to behave like reasonable human beings, there would be no story.'

'I thought you were trying to find out how we lived down under.'

Hazel hurled a cushion at her. 'Are you telling me this is true to life? The men are all so full of themselves and the women are total drips,' she complained, 'but if you want it . . .'

Maureen flicked the off switch. 'You were saying how lucky it was we get on so well, before you hurled that cushion at me.'

Hazel grinned. 'What I really meant was that we, who are cousins, seem to get on much better together than our respective mothers who are sisters.'

'Perhaps that is the problem.'

'What is?'

'That they are sisters. Being siblings doesn't necessarily mean you always agree,' Maureen pointed out. 'I'm lucky I really quite like both my brother and sister. We get on fine. Of course, it helps that we don't see an awful lot of one another. What about you? Do you get along with your brother?'

Hazel pulled a face. 'To tell you the truth, I'm not even sure I like him,' she admitted rather shamefacedly.

'There you are then!' Maureen said with the air of one making a point though Hazel wasn't quite sure just what the point was. 'Anyway, that was obvious.'

'What do you mean, obvious?' Hazel demanded. 'I have never said a word against him.'

'No, and you have never said a word for him either, and you quite obviously preferred to stay right here rather than go back home for his wedding.'

'Well, it would have been ridiculous to spend all that money and time and go all that way just to see him tie the knot. I had barely got here, if you remember, and I had agreed to stay two years. That's how I got an assisted passage.'

'You would still have gone if he really meant a lot to you,' Maureen insisted. 'Maybe you have inherited something from your mother— you know, a "let's not get too close" sort of gene.'

'Maybe I have,' Hazel said seriously, not realizing that Maureen was teasing her. 'I suppose I don't really like Giles very much— never have. He is high on bossiness and low on humour which all adds up to a pompousness that doesn't sit well on young shoulders. You should have heard how he carried on when I got expelled from school over those tarot cards. Susan is a bit of a prig too. I suppose that's how she can stand him, how they can stand each other.'

'Then it is a very good thing they have landed up with each other and no one else has to put up with either of them, isn't it?' Maureen said practically. 'How long do you think our mothers will manage without a big row now we aren't there as buffers?'

Hazel stared at her in surprise; such a thought had never occurred to her. 'Oh, they won't do that. Mum never rows; quite the reverse. She is usually the peacemaker.'

'Your mum may be, but mine certainly isn't, and if you ask me, that is part of the trouble: not my mum ready for a scrap but yours always trying to pour oil on troubled waters.'

Hazel sighed. 'She always has done. It

probably has something to do with being married to Dad. He ruled her with the proverbial rod of iron, as I remember. Giles is so like him. She blossomed forth a bit after Dad was killed. Well, in a way she had to; someone had to take charge and we were only kids at the time. To tell you the truth, I was astonished when she said she was coming out here, but I suppose what she was really doing was taking evasive action, as usual.'

'You are a bit hard on her, Hazel. I think your mum is lovely, and what on earth do you mean about taking evasive action? Getting herself out here seems pretty positive to me.'

'Well, she had to get out of the house because it belongs to Giles now and she wouldn't want to be living there under his thumb and seeing Susan take over the reins. Can you imagine? It would be woeful. A pity she is not more like your mother. I can't see anyone bossing her around.'

'They wouldn't boss Grandma Ella either. She and Mum used to have some right old set-tos, I can tell you.'

Hazel looked at her in astonishment. 'I can't really remember Grandma and Mum ever quarrelling.' Her thoughts slid back, a miasma of sadness crossing her face. 'How I wish Grandma had come back. Things might have been different if she had; Mum always listened to her.' She was a little girl again, hiding behind the heavy curtain over the window seat in the sombre study and listening to her mother turning dear Uncle James away. She pulled herself up with a jerk as something Maureen was saying penetrated her wandering thoughts. 'What did you say? What on earth are you saying?' she demanded.

Maureen gaped at her open-mouthed, realizing with a shock that she appeared to have let an outsize cat well and truly out of the bag. 'I—I thought you knew,' she mumbled.

'Knew? Knew what, for goodness' sake?' Hazel was bolt upright now, staring at her cousin. 'Did I hear right? It sounded to me as if you were suggesting—no, saying—that Auntie Vi and my mother . . . had different fathers.'

CHAPTER THIRTY-THREE

'Oh, I don't know what I was saying. I have probably got it all wrong anyway. You know me . . .' Maureen tried desperately to think of something to change the subject when she realized she had put her foot in it in a big way. Because it was something she had known for a long time, she had just assumed that Hazel knew too.

'I do know you, Maureen,' Hazel sat up and glared at her cousin, 'and I know you are not the sort of vague, dreamy person who makes statements they don't really know anything about. Neither do you usually get things wrong, so don't you think it would be a good idea to put me in the picture? After all, if it is about my mother's parentage then it concerns me too.'

'But I don't know if I should tell you. After all, if you don't know, maybe that is because your mother doesn't want you to know . . .' She faltered somewhat at the expression on Hazel's face as she glared at her and was reminded of how Grandma Ella used to look when she was doing battle with her mother.

'I warn you, if you don't tell me whatever it is you know, or think you know, it will be something much harder than a cushion that hits you next time.' Hazel shook the cushion she was holding aloft threateningly.

'All right, just simmer down—and listen,' Maureen gave in, more because of the suggestion that she didn't really know what she was talking about than because of the threat of a hard object winging her way.

'Go on, then, spill the beans,' Hazel snapped irritably as Maureen did her best to gather her thoughts and remember just how she had learned this. It was one of those things that she seemed always to have known. 'Are you going to tell me that Grandma Ella divorced her husband and married again and your mother is the child of her first marriage and my mother of her second?'

Maureen shook her head. 'No, well, sort of.'

'What do you mean? She either did or she didn't, surely?'

'Well, part of that is correct. My mum, as you know, is the eldest. Her father—my grandfather—was Grandma Ella's husband. Mum always said that she was the true love child because she was conceived when her parents were fairly newly married and therefore, presumably, still in love. Calling your mother a "love child" was a sentimental way of suggesting she was a bastard.'

'My mother, a bastard? What on earth do you mean?' Hazel found she was smiling at the sheer absurdity of such a suggestion; her aristocratic, almost regal grandmother would surely never have produced a bastard child. 'Grandma was married when she was born.' Hazel simply could not accept what Maureen was saying. 'Wherever did you get such a ridiculous idea from? You knew Grandma Ella. Does the label "loose woman" fit her?' Hazel's face was pink with righteous indignation.

Maureen wished she had never broached the subject. It was certainly true; the description did not fit Grandma Ella as she remembered her, and to think of Aunt Daisy as a bastard when—as her mother had complained—she had become more English than the English after her life in England as the middle-class wife of a well-to-do businessman was—well, unthinkable. She sighed and vowed to keep a tighter rein on her slipshod tongue in future, but, prompted by an indignant 'Well . . .?' in a no-nonsense voice, she knew that she would have to do her best to smooth things over.

'Haven't you ever wondered why the Sanderses were so good to us all?' she asked.

'Not really, no,' Hazel admitted. 'I gathered Mum was only a baby at the time and I suppose she just grew up accepting the status quo. You don't really think too much about your mother's childhood—well, I didn't, anyway. For years, I just thought Grandma was a widow and that Grandfather had died when she and Auntie Vi were young—Mum just a baby, in fact. I always felt sorry for her— Grandma Ella, that is—but I certainly didn't let it worry me or question the facts, as *I* knew them, in any way.'

She thought for a moment, frowning slightly. 'I'm sorry, Maureen, but I think you are quite wrong. Your theory just doesn't fit. If there had been anything different, it would have come to light when I applied for a passport when I needed my birth certificate. Mum has a special folder where she keeps all such important documents for all of us and when I saw Mum's birth certificate, looked at it actually, there was nothing in the least unorthodox about it. It stated quite clearly that her father was William Weston.'

Maureen sighed. 'Perhaps I made a mistake,' she said in a conciliatory tone. 'Forget I ever said anything.' But she knew she hadn't made a mistake as she remembered quite clearly what Rosie had told her. But Hazel didn't forget. On the contrary, her cousin's extraordinary revelation, for she was sure in her heart that that was what it was, festered in her mind.

*   *   *

'How strange of Hazel to rush off into a flat when you are staying here.' Violet's voice floated back over her shoulder from the kitchen sink where she was washing lettuce.

Daisy, laying the table for their evening meal, repressed the uncharitable thought that her sister meant to rile her; it was the sort of thing she had so often said when they were younger. She bit her tongue and pretended not to hear.

'She has been quite happy living here with us,' Violet went on, the words 'until you arrived' unspoken yet clear enough.

Daisy felt guilty now as well as hurt; somehow Violet had cast herself as the injured party and without saying a word had made it appear to be all Daisy's fault.

'Young people like to be independent these days.' Daisy gave up the pretence of deafness. 'They do get on well together too.' The last bit

291

was tagged on to soothe her sister. It didn't work.

'I don't know about that. It seems to me that Hazel rather dominates Maureen. This flat, for instance. I am sure the whole thing was her idea.'

'Oh, I don't know.' Daisy murmured.

'Of course it was. Maureen would never have thought of anything so ridiculous on her own.'

'Why are you so against it, Violet?'

'For one thing, it is an absurd waste of money, paying rent when she has a perfectly good home to live in, and for another . . . well, to be honest, I would rather know what she is doing, who she is meeting, that sort of thing.'

Daisy sighed and in a rare moment's agreement with her sister, murmured, 'Yes, me too.'

Violet put the bowl of salad down rather too firmly on the table, took her seat opposite Daisy and added, 'I hope there won't be any trouble with those two young men.'

'What sort of trouble?' Daisy wondered as she helped herself to salad. She was even more in accord with her sister now after her last comment.

'What sort do you think? The usual sort, of course.'

Conversation lapsed as both sisters contemplated the trouble their daughters could get into. Daisy's concern for Hazel was centred on her daughter's emotions. She didn't want her to be hurt. But all that was worrying Hazel at that moment was which lipstick to wear.

'Do you think this is the right colour with this dress?' she asked Maureen, looking doubtfully at the open lipstick in her hand then peering anxiously at herself in the mirror.

Maureen studied her critically. 'Absolutely perfect,' she declared, pleased to be asked for advice but a little surprised as it was usually the other way around. Hazel was the confident one and Maureen the one with all the doubts.

'Hmm . . .' Hazel still sounded doubtful but decided to use it anyway.

Tim and Derek were due in a few minutes to collect them for an evening out. She liked them both; they were good company as well as being attractive, but that was the extent of it. She knew that Maureen and Tim really liked each other though Hazel thought they acted more like brother and sister at times. She supposed that came from knowing one another almost their entire lives. They had so many shared memories that she, and even Derek felt a bit on the outer. It might have been easier if they had done the 'right' thing and fallen for each other.

Derek's ambition was to work in England for a couple of years which at least gave them plenty to talk about, comparing similarities and differences between the two countries.

'Do you know anything about New Zealand?' Hazel asked Tim. They were by themselves as Derek was ordering their drinks and Maureen had disappeared to 'powder her nose'.

'Pretty well. My mother lives there.'

Hazel had forgotten he had already told her that.

'It is a different place, you know. English people always talk about "Australia and New Zealand" in one breath as if it is all the same country. Why do you ask?'

Hazel shrugged. 'I know someone who lives there. We knew him in the war and he seemed to think it was next door to heaven. But I suppose it is much the same as here though, isn't it?'

'Some people say it is more like England. As I haven't been to England, I couldn't say.'

Hazel thought her mother would fit in. There were times when her Australian traits had surfaced in England, yet here, back in her home country, Auntie Vi accused her of becoming more of a pom than the poms themselves.

'Mum should go while she is on this side of the world—' she began, but her words were lost when Derek and Maureen came back together with their drinks.

'I thought you had taken root at the bar,' Tim said, making Hazel feel he must have found her poor company.

294

Wondering how she could put the idea into her mother's head, Hazel raised her glass and, dismissing the thought, treated the others to a broad smile. 'To us—and our new home!'

They all drank enthusiastically to this toast; Derek and Tim could see bright possibilities in the lack of restriction the flat offered.

Having decided her mother should visit New Zealand, Hazel's thoughts kept returning to the subject and she turned to Tim in a lull in the conversation and remarked, 'I do know it is divided into two islands and has lots of sheep, judging by the amount of New Zealand lamb consumed in England, probably a few cows too. I seem to remember New Zealand butter also, cheaper than Danish.'

'Your knowledge, as far as it goes, is correct if limited, but why the sudden interest?'

Hazel shrugged. If her mother had reacted differently, they could be living there now, but this wasn't the time to go into all that past history, so she sipped her drink and tried to change the subject.

'I'm due to visit my mother. Why don't you travel with me and take a look at the place?'

Hazel smiled into her drink. 'Actually, I wasn't thinking of going myself. I just thought Mum really ought to go while she is in this hemisphere. Who knows? It may be the only chance she has. The chance of a travelling companion might just push her into it.'

'Yeah, well, yeah, that would be great.'

Escorting her mother wasn't quite what Tim had in mind. He had instead cherished hopes of persuading Maureen to accompany Hazel.

'Whereabouts are you going? Which island?'

'South. Both my grandparents and my stepfather produce some of that butter and lamb you were talking about. My mother and Ralph don't live all that far from Christchurch.'

Hazel almost gave a whoop of triumph. With a bit of luck, she might get her mother delivered into James's hands. 'Perfect,' she told him. 'You can hand her over to James. He is at the hospital in Christchurch.'

Tim was feeling more confused by the moment. 'Who is James, and what is wrong with him?'

'Oh, he wanted Mum to marry him once. There's nothing wrong with him; he works at the hospital. He's a doctor—well, a specialist actually. He's sort of related to us.'

'How can you be "sort of" related?' Tim did not like fuzzy explanations. 'And if your mother turned him down, he may not want to see her again,—or her him.'

'Oh, she will. They met again on the boat coming out here. And he is a sort of relation; he is Grandma Ella's stepson. Well, not even that, really. He was Grandpa Walter's stepson, so there is no blood relationship between us at all.'

296

'I see,' said Tim, not at all sure he did. 'Why didn't she marry him, I mean?'

Hazel shrugged. 'I really don't know. Maybe she didn't love him as much as I thought she did, or perhaps she was scared to throw up her life in England and come out to New Zealand. Maybe she didn't want to uproot Giles and me. It's hard to know why we do what we do ourselves sometimes, let alone why other people do what they do.' She thought for a moment. 'Maybe she feels different now.' She was about to add: 'Now Giles has married and taken over the house' but didn't, feeling that it might make her mother seem grasping. She had probably said more than enough about her mother's personal affairs.

CHAPTER THIRTY-FOUR

Hazel found it a relief to be living in the tiny flat with Maureen. She had been happy living at Aunt Violet's until her mother arrived. She had been looking forward to her visit, astonished and pleased that she had actually made the effort to get out to Australia as she had, under her own steam. But she had felt guilty that instead of enjoying her company, she more often than not sizzled with irritation and found herself being curt with her to the point of snappishness. She had, since a very young age, seen her mother wilt under the onslaught of other people's more commanding personalities. Her father of course was the prime example, her father's sister another, even her own mother.

There had been the years between her father dying and Giles growing up when her mother had to take charge, especially when Grandma had come out here to visit Violet and her family. When Hazel remembered how her mother had blossomed during the war and the years of the early peace, she felt particularly annoyed when she appeared to revert to type as Giles matured. Maybe she hadn't entirely, though, or she would never be out here now. This irritation with what she felt was Daisy's lack of any sense of self-worth flourished when she saw her deferring to others, particularly Violet.

Hazel was still working out in her mind how best to send her mother off to New Zealand when Daisy astounded her by telling her she planned to go and tentatively suggested Hazel join her.

'Gosh—yes, I'd love to,' replied Hazel. Her astonishment that her plans were working out without her interference made her exuberantly enthusiastic. She flung her arms round her mother and hugged her.

Daisy, pleased and surprised, couldn't quite believe it. 'You would? You really would?' Her native caution then made her ask, 'But what about your job, and the flat?'

'I can get another job and the flat won't run away.'

'If you are sure, we had better go and consult a travel agent and work out an itinerary,' Daisy suggested, wondering whether to admit that it was James rather than New Zealand she was going to see.

'Tim told me he is planning a visit to his mother. You know he is a New Zealander. Well, actually, that's not strictly true; his mother is and she went back there to live and remarried. He has grandparents there too. As a matter of fact, he sort of suggested I go over with him when he goes to visit them,' Hazel rattled on.

Daisy was so often silent while she allowed other people to organize her that Hazel didn't notice her anxious expression.

'We could all travel together. That would be great, wouldn't it?' asked Hazel.

'Yes . . . yes, it would,' Daisy murmured weakly. 'When does he plan to go and where does his mother live?' she asked, hoping that he really didn't intend to go for months and that he would be heading somewhere not included in her travel plans, forgetting that she had none as yet.

'I think he said in a couple of weeks, maybe less, and I suppose he would be going to the South Island as his mother and his grandparents both live around Christchurch somewhere.'

'Christchurch. You did say . . . Christchurch?'

'I think we should talk to him before we map out an itinerary.' Hazel, full of excitement and enthusiasm, missed her mother's sudden lack of both. 'He would be able to tell us the interesting places to visit. He might even come with us.'

'Great,' Daisy murmured, totally unable to inject enthusiasm into her voice. Hazel, however, had enough of her own and didn't notice. Daisy's plans to remove her daughter from Tim's orbit were achieving the exact opposite.

'Gee, that's terrific!'

To his own ears, Tim's delight when Hazel told him she too was ready to set off for New Zealand with him sounded overdone and insincere. He could imagine his mother putting two and two together and probably making six when he turned up with Hazel and her mother. He resolved to put more work into persuading Maureen to come too.

'I can't believe Mum decided to go to New Zealand off her own bat. At her age, I don't suppose she is likely to ever go again,' said Hazel.

Tim thought she must be joking; Hazel's mother had not seemed at all old to him, but Hazel looked perfectly serious. 'I don't see why not. Heavens, she isn't that old.'

'Well, I'm sure she wouldn't go again. I'm

300

quite astonished she has gone once. It isn't that she is so old, but her outlook is. She never dares to take the plunge—in anything. She's only here now because my selfish brother and his wife wanted her out of the way. If something happens—Susan falls pregnant or something—and they decide she will be useful to them, they will soon whistle for her. Honestly, Tim, she makes me cross at times. She is so damned unselfish, it's not healthy.'

Tim smiled, but he could see that Hazel really cared about her mother, and he liked her for that. 'Well, if this really is to be a once in a lifetime trip, we must see it is good. I've got a touring map of New Zealand in my car. Let's start making plans.' He looked at his watch. 'It's time Maureen got back from work. I wish I could persuade her to come as well.'

He went out to get the map and when he came back, Maureen was with him. Both were smiling, happy just to be in each other's company. Briefly, Hazel felt like a third leg, then Tim spread the map out on the little table which was so small that the map hung over the edges like a tablecloth. He pointed to a green area about halfway down the South Island on what Hazel called the right side.

'West coast, if you please,' Tim corrected. 'See this large green area?'

Hazel thought it would be hard to miss it with his finger firmly down on the centre. 'Canterbury Plain,' she read aloud from the map.

'That's right. Well, that's where my mother and stepfather and my grandparents live. It's a big farming area.'

'Where Canterbury lamb comes from,' Hazel supplied, playing the smart student in response to his schoolteacher role. 'Those mountains down the centre look exactly like a spine, and what odd placenames. Either the names of English towns or totally unpronounceable.'

'Those are Maori names. I expect the English names were given them by homesick early settlers from those towns.'

'It must have been hard on the women.' Hazel thought of her grandmother coming out to Australia as a young bride, full of romantic dreams. She remembered her saying tartly: 'Well, I soon lost those. There was nothing in the least romantic I discovered about any of it; not the long voyage out, nor the pioneering life when we arrived'.

Tim made her jump by snapping his fingers in front of her. 'Come back,' he told her. 'You are miles away.'

'Only in time,' she told him, suppressing her irritation. 'I was thinking about my grandmother and how it must have been for her when she came out to Australia. You know, I think I might try and write her story.' She had already confided in them her ambition to be a writer. With the same thought

302

running through both their minds, that digging up the past might not be a good idea, Maureen and Tim both tried to bring her back to the present. Hazel, already plotting her first bestseller, felt irritated when Tim pointed out that at that moment, they were planning a trip to New Zealand.

*   *   *

Daisy smiled ruefully to herself at the look of relief that flitted across her sister's features when she said that she was thinking of visiting New Zealand. 'Seems silly not to. After all, I don't suppose I am likely to make this trip again,' she said, unknowingly echoing Hazel's words to Tim. 'I've asked Hazel to come with me and she seems quite keen on the idea.'

'She would be silly not to be, wouldn't she? I suppose you are footing the bill.'

Here it is again, Daisy thought; the suggestion—along with a certain amount of resentment—that I have unlimited resources. 'Well, yes, I suppose so,' she agreed aloud. She hadn't actually considered that aspect. 'I thought it would be nice to have her company. And I have a friend in Christchurch.'

Daisy couldn't remember if she had explained James's existence. She should have done as he was connected to Violet by their mother's marriage as much as he was to her. 'Would you mind very much if I make a phone call? I'll pay for it.'

'Of course,' said Violet.

Daisy wasn't sure whether Violet's 'of course' meant that of course she could make a call or of course she would pay for it. Deciding it probably meant both, she thanked her and went to her room to look for James's number. While she waited for the connection, she mentally rehearsed what she would say and was taken aback when a female voice answered. She left a message for him to call her back and resigned herself to wait.

'Did you get her?' Violet asked when she rejoined her in the lounge room.

Flummoxed by the question, Daisy stammered, 'Yes—I mean no.' Why should Violet automatically assume that her only friends were female? She was still speculating on this when the phone rang. Violet went quickly out to the hall and answered it. Seconds later, she was back.

'Your New Zealand . . . friend. *He* said he had just received your message.'

Daisy hurried to the telephone. She had not imagined Violet's emphasis.

'James, hello.'

'Hello, Daisy. I have just walked in and got your message. You sound breathless.'

She ignored that. 'I was just ringing to say that I'm taking your advice.' It never hurt to let men think you listen to them. 'I decided I should see New Zealand before I leave this

304

part of the world.'

'That's wonderful! You must give me your flight number. I will try and meet you.'

Daisy smiled to herself at his assumption that it would be Christchurch she would fly into. 'Hazel is coming with me,' she added. 'I will give you more details when I have them.'

'That's great! I look forward to seeing you both.'

The slightly too lengthy pause and the slightly too hearty a tone told her he viewed the fact that she would not be alone with mixed feelings. The telephone, she thought, could be very revealing and she wondered how much she had unwittingly given away.

CHAPTER THIRTY-FIVE

'If you ask me, you spoil that girl.'

Daisy was unable to think of a telling reply, so she merely smiled slightly and murmured, 'I don't think so—not really. Isn't one of the pleasures of parenthood spoiling our children, just a little? When we have the chance?'

'That sounds very self-indulgent to me,' said Violet.

Daisy sighed and, remembering Maureen's crestfallen face when she discovered Tim and Hazel were both accompanying her, she responded to her sister with unusual asperity.

'Why don't you try it, Vi? It would be a great experience for Maureen.'

'Because *I* am not a rich woman.'

'Then let me treat her—both of you if you would like to come too.'

'Don't be ridiculous. I couldn't possibly let you—'

'You can say I am being self-indulgent, or you could look at it as a return for your hospitality to Hazel and me,' Daisy persisted.

'But you told me that Tim Sanders is going too.'

'Yes, but he is going to visit his mother and his grandparents; we will only be travelling together.' Daisy secretly doubted if that would be entirely true, but under the circumstances . . . 'Go on, Vi, let her come. You too, of course.'

After a long pause, Violet grunted ungraciously. 'I'll think about it—only Maureen, mind; I have no desire whatsoever to go, certainly not to fly there.'

'Don't think too long, please, Vi. I am going to confirm the bookings and pay tomorrow.'

*   *   *

'Are you quite sure you don't want to come?' Daisy asked Violet again over breakfast.

'Quite sure, but I won't stand in Maureen's way.'

She sounded so disgruntled that it was a few

306

moments before Daisy realized she was actually accepting her offer.

'Considering,' Violet continued, 'that you are in a position to pay for both girls and yourself.'

Daisy put her coffee down in the saucer with exaggerated care. Even she could feel her patience slipping. The cost of the New Zealand holiday was blowing out and secretly alarmed her. Violet's constant, snide remarks about her so-called wealth was getting at her and she was perilously close to losing her temper. She took a deep breath, determined to make yet another effort to make her understand.

'Violet, once and for all, I am NOT a rich woman as you seem to suppose.'

'Not by your standards, maybe, but by mine—'

'Not by anyone's. Richard left me an annuity, everything else went to Giles; the business and the house. Which is why I am here. I didn't relish the idea of being relegated to the servants' wing in the house that had been my home for so long.'

'What do you plan to do when you go back, or are you intending to stay here?'

'Oh, I suppose I will go back,' Daisy sighed. 'There is provision in Richard's will for alternative accommodation to be provided for me and leased to me at a peppercorn rent if I don't wish to live in The Grange.'

'Well,' Violet conceded, 'if you are not rich, you are comfortable, as they say, and secure for the rest of your life.'

'Yes; and so, surely, are you, Violet. You have this house.'

'True.' Violet nodded. 'It was good of Alice Sanders to leave me this house though only what I deserve, really. I was a bit worried for a time after she died that some of her family might contest the will, but Beth lives up in Queensland and her husband is in the money. I don't think she wanted to be bothered with it and besides, she was grateful to me for looking after her mother.

'Then when Edwin married again and started another family, I was worried, but I needn't have been. There again, Tim's mother went back to New Zealand and didn't want to be bothered with it and, like Beth, was grateful that someone other than her was looking after her mother-in-law.' She paused for breath, then, in what seemed like a change of direction in the conversation, rapped, 'Why is Tim really going to New Zealand with you?'

'He is not coming with us. Well, he is, I mean we are travelling together, but as I have already explained to you, he is going to see his mother and grandparents.'

Violet's 'hrrmph' sounded as if she didn't believe that explanation.

They sat in silence for a few moments, each lost in their own thoughts, then both sisters broke the silence between them at the same time.

'Go on,' Violet said, 'you say what you were going to say. I was only going to ask if you were going straight back to England from New Zealand.'

'To tell you the absolute truth, I hadn't thought about it. Well, I suppose I had just assumed I would come back here.' Oh, dear. Now Violet would think she was presuming far too much. Daisy waited for a tart comment that would let her know in no uncertain terms that it was true.

Violet did not answer immediately; she was grappling with the uncomfortable feeling that she had not always been as warm and welcoming as one might expect from a sister. She finally mumbled, somewhat stiffly as if embarrassed by her own feelings.

'Sorry, that didn't sound very nice, almost as if I hoped you would go back to England. I didn't mean it like that. You are more than welcome to come back here; in fact, I—well—I hope you will.'

'Oh, Violet, thank you. I truly don't know what I am going to do. But I think I can say yes, I would like to come back here; that is, if you don't mind.' Impulsively Daisy reached across the table and put her hand on her sister's. 'I have had the impression that you didn't really want me here. You . . . well, you seemed to harbour some sort of resentment towards me. I don't know why. Surely not because our mother came out to visit you and got trapped here by the war?'

Violet stared at her. 'God, no, Daisy. I never really blamed you for that, whatever I said . . .' Her voice trailed away. She glanced at Daisy, then away into the middle distance somewhere, then down at her hands.

'What *do* you blame me for, Violet?' Daisy's voice was so soft, it was barely audible. She could feel sweat breaking out on her palms and was aware of a tight feeling in her chest, but she knew she couldn't stop now; she had to go on and repair her relationship with her sister, if it was at all possible. 'Do you blame me for—for—who I am . . . or who I am not?'

Violet looked up sharply. 'You know,' she said in a flat voice. 'How long have you known? And how did you find out?'

'Mother left an explanatory letter, to be opened only after her death.'

Violet snorted. 'How melodramatic.'

Daisy smiled. 'I suppose it was. But then she was rather given to melodrama, or at least the unconventional which is how she landed out here with . . .' Her voice trailed away; she found she didn't know how to refer to the man who was Violet's father but not her own. 'How did you learn the truth?' she asked instead.

'From Rosie. She told me.'

'Oh, yes, of course. But why? What made you so . . .' Daisy searched for the right word

310

and was surprised when Violet supplied it herself.

'Resentful?'

Daisy nodded.

'I suppose I was jealous. I always knew there was something different about you, something special, and whatever it was, it made Mother prefer you to me, but of course as a child, I had no idea what it could be, other than your innate superiority—or my inferiority. When Rosie told me that Dad was not your father, that you were Edwin Sanders's child, I was so angry. I felt I had been made a fool of all these years; and worse, that I only had what I had, that Alice Sanders left me this house because I was Mother's daughter, not because she had cared for me at all. Stupid, I suppose, but that's how I felt.'

Daisy felt her eyes misting and her throat tightening. 'Oh, Vi, how perfectly dreadful for you, but you are quite wrong, I am sure. Mrs Sanders left you her house because you were the one to look after her when she needed it, just like she looked after us all when we needed it.'

'That's what I tell myself, then I think that if you had still been in Australia, she would probably have left it to you. After all, you were her flesh and blood.'

A thought struck Daisy and she cut in quickly. 'But did she know that, Violet?'

Her sister stared at her. 'I don't know,

311

Daisy. I just assumed she did, but she never gave any indication that she knew. But that doesn't make it any better, does it? It just means that she *should* have left it to you, not me.'

'It doesn't mean anything of the sort.' Irritation flared in Daisy. If her sister was determined to play the martyr, there seemed little she could do. She had tried hard to get on well with her from the moment she arrived in Australia, but it seemed she was never going to be allowed to transcend the circumstances of her birth.

She sighed and stood up from the table. 'Thank you for your invitation, but no, I don't think I will come back here after all. I will arrange to go straight back to England from New Zealand.' She could not stop the sigh that escaped. 'That being so, I had better make sure I pack everything.'

She moved with a heavy step and a heavier heart towards the door, overwhelmed by the sadness and futility of the situation. She had come to Australia with the best of intentions, to renew her sibling relationship with Violet as well as catch up with Hazel. Now it seemed there was little left for her to do but return to England and try and pick up the threads of her life there. Trouble was that now she had come back to this hemisphere, she felt more at home here. She supposed that was normal; after all, Australia was where she had been born, where

312

she had grown up, where her roots were. However, she had a son and a daughter-in-law and it was quite on the cards that she would have grandchildren born and bred in England in the not too distant future. She would look for a nice little cottage not too far away from Giles and Sue, but not too close either, and settle down to being an ageing English gentlewoman.

'Daisy, wait a minute!'

Hope leapt in Daisy; Violet was going to ask her to come back after her New Zealand trip, but it died as quickly when her sister added, 'You had better give me a forwarding address if you are not coming back.'

'Yes—yes, of course. I'll give you the address of my hotel in Christchurch.'

'But you will only be there a short while.'

'Then I'll leave them another address to send mail to if any comes after I've left. I think it highly unlikely there will be any.' She would be with Hazel, and who else was likely to want to contact her anyway?

Daisy was sorting through her clothes when the thought hit her that there was no need to sort through them at all; she simply had to pack everything. With a sigh, she started again, this time laying everything out on the bed.

With cases half packed and the realization that she needed more toothpaste, she decided to go out to the shops and maybe go and see how Hazel was getting on with her packing;

she knew she would not be at work this morning. As she passed through the hall, Violet called her.

'There is a letter just arrived for you, Daisy. It's on that little table near the door.'

'Thanks,' she replied automatically, picking up the letter and turning it over in her hand. It was an air letter from England. The writing was unfamiliar, but when she turned it over to read the address on the back, she saw it was from her daughter-in-law, Susan. How odd, she thought, repressing a sense of unease.

She shoved it into her handbag to read later, aware that she had also felt disappointment as soon as she saw that the letter came from England and not New Zealand. If it had, she thought gloomily, it would probably only have been James reneging on his offer to meet their plane.

She bought her toothpaste and walked round to Hazel's flat. There appeared to be no one at home. She was beginning to feel really sorry for herself and about to leave when she heard the outer door slam and footsteps on the stairs, two sets of footsteps and two excited voices.

'Hello, Mum. What are you doing here?' Hazel asked as she and Maureen rounded the last bend in the stairs.

'I just came round to see if you were here. I—I came out to buy toothpaste.'

'Good idea. They probably don't use it in

314

New Zealand.'

'Don't be silly, Hazel,' Daisy retorted in a testy voice, not in the mood to appreciate teasing.

Maureen looked from one to the other. She could see Daisy looked what her grandmother used to call 'fraught'. She hoped her mother hadn't been difficult—again. She thought it wonderful of Daisy to be so generous and hated it when her mother made some of her comments.

'I'll make us some coffee, or would you rather have tea?' asked Maureen.

'Tea, please, if it's not too much trouble, but perhaps you girls would rather have coffee?'

'Tea suits me,' Hazel said cheerfully, suppressing her irritation. Why on earth did her mother always have to be so self-effacing, and what, for goodness' sake, was the matter with her? Ten to one that Auntie Vi had upset her. Sure, she had an acid tongue at times, but her heart was probably in the right place and her mother was stupid to let her needle her. She was suddenly glad that she was half a world away from her own brother and sister-in-law.

As if on cue Daisy, rummaging in her bag for a hanky, noticed the letter she had stuffed in there.

'Oh, I haven't read my letter yet. It came just as I was leaving.' She held it in her hand, lifting it up to show Hazel. 'It's from Giles and

Susan. Looks like her writing, though. Wonder what she wants.'

'Open it and find out,' Hazel said impatiently. She could see by the way Daisy was staring at the flimsy air letter in her hand that she was afraid. 'Give it to me. I'll open it.'

As Hazel took the letter, she felt some of her mother's reluctance to open it. Susan must want something to have bothered to write. 'Let's just put it in the rubbish, shall we, and pretend it never arrived,' she suggested, only half joking.

Hazel quickly scanned her sister-in-law's neat if rather immature writing and wished that was what she had done. 'It seems you are going to be a grandmother,' she said and pushed the letter away. She passed Daisy her cup of tea with a meaningful look at Maureen who, misinterpreting it, apologized for their lack of biscuits.

But Daisy was not to be fobbed off.

'May I have the letter, please, Hazel,' asked Daisy.

Reluctantly, Hazel handed it over and watched gloomily as her mother read it. Her gloom changed to anger when her mother announced, 'I shall have to go back.'

'Because Susan says she is expecting a baby? I should have thought that was good news,' said Hazel.

'Read the rest of the letter and you will see why I have to go.'

316

Hazel read aloud: 'Susan is pregnant, her parents are away on some luxury holiday and Giles has broken his ankle,' she summarized. 'So . . . why must you go back? By the time you have organized your ticket and spent a month at sea, she will have recovered from the morning sickness that she says is incapacitating her, her parents will be home and Giles's ankle will be mended.'

'I could fly . . .'

'Mum, you *are* flying, with us, to New Zealand, remember?'

'Yes,' Daisy murmured doubtfully. She had almost forgotten. 'I could cancel it, or let Violet have my ticket. I could—'

'Moth-*er*, you could not. You are booked to go to New Zealand.' There was a taut edge to Hazel's voice as she fought to keep her temper. 'They are married. It's up to them to look after each other. If they wanted you there to wet-nurse them, they shouldn't have thrown you out of the house.'

'Oh, Hazel,' Daisy looked aghast, 'that really isn't fair. They didn't—well, not really.'

'They may not have actually shown you the door, but you know as well as I do that as soon as Giles hit twenty-one and inherited, you were only there on sufferance. Marriage to Susan just underlined things. Personally, I think it was unjust, old fashioned and . . . well, unreasonable of Dad to leave things like that in his will.'

317

'Yes, well . . .' Until Hazel put it into words, Daisy had not admitted to herself that that was exactly how she felt herself. Now that her feelings, so long repressed, were bubbling up to the surface, she surprised herself by bursting out: 'Oh, it was totally unreasonable!' She gasped, shocked at her own vehement outcry but was unable to stop. 'But was your father ever reasonable? On anything?'

'Seldom, as far as I recall, but that's past history. You are the one now who is behaving in quite the most stupid, unreasonable and selfish manner.'

'Selfish?' Daisy was stung into retorting. She could accept that she was being stupid, even maybe a little unreasonable, but selfish— never!

'Yes, selfish, Mum. You don't care a damn about spoiling our holiday, treating James like shit—'

'Hazel!' Maureen, who would never dare to talk to her own mother in that way, protested. Embarrassed to be a witness, she turned to leave the room.

'Don't go,' Hazel commanded. 'You are affected by this as well. If Mum backs out—' she gave Daisy a withering look which, added to the mention of James, stung her into protesting.

'I really don't think it's fair to say I am selfish, or to say I am treating James . . . badly.' She couldn't quite bring herself to use the

318

same colourful expression as Hazel.

'But it's true, Mum. You know it is if you are really honest. You see yourself as whiter than white, some sort of noble, self-sacrificing saint. Well, I don't think it is noble, now *or* when you turned James down all those years ago. God knows why he is prepared to even speak to you.' Hazel stopped, appalled. She shouldn't have brought James into this. 'Sorry,' she mumbled. 'I am afraid I sort of lost my temper.'

As Daisy listened to this tirade, one thing slammed her between the eyes: Hazel knew that James had asked her to marry him.

'How do you know?' The question came out as a hoarse croak and fell into the silence. Neither of them noticed that Maureen had left them.

Hazel stared at her mother's white, strained face, ashamed of her outburst. She had never thought she would ever have to confess to that long ago eavesdropping.

'I was in the room, on the window seat, behind the curtain. I wasn't deliberately listening; I just sort of got caught there. I heard James ask you to marry him and go to New Zealand. I was quite excited, then you turned him down with the excuse that you had to stay and look after Giles's inheritance. So bloody noble of you. I could hardly believe it. I always knew that Dad only had time for Giles, but I thought you . . . and now you are about to

319

do the same thing again. You're just a—a professional martyr, Mum. Not . . . noble . . . at all!' The last words came out in short, choking gasps. Before burying her face in her hands, Hazel burst into noisy sobs.

Daisy stared at her without moving, almost without seeing her. She felt perilously close to tears herself, but was honest enough to recognize them as self-pity.

Hazel's tears had subsided to a sniffle when Daisy finally spoke.

'What a pity you didn't come out from behind that curtain, Nutmeg (she did not notice that she had slipped into using the childhood name) and yell some sense into me then.'

'Well, I am doing my best now.' Hazel looked up and managed a wobbly half smile. 'Don't you see? Fate, or whatever, has given you another chance, putting you on the same ship as James.'

'How did you know about that?' Daisy didn't think she had mentioned it.

'I answered the phone to him at Auntie Vi's one day. I was thrilled to hear him—we had quite a chat. Mum, he cares, and if you still care for him, for God's sake don't louse things up again by being noble. You do, don't you? Care for him, I mean.' Hazel's voice dropped to a mumble. 'Sorry, it's none of my business.'

Daisy flushed slightly but did not answer the question. Instead she asked, 'What about

Tim?'

'What do you mean, "what about Tim?" He's a really nice person, I like him a lot. No wonder Grandma fell for his father.' She paused before adding in a low voice, without looking at her mother: 'There's a really strong likeness between you. I noticed it at once, and so did Tim. When I mentioned it to him, he told me the whole story his father told him before he died. Apparently, he and Grandma made a pact not to let the secret die with them.' She looked directly at Daisy now. 'So, if Grandma kept her word too then you must know that you and Tim are half-brother and sister?'

Daisy looked up, swallowed and nodded. 'Yes. It worried me—you and Tim . . .' Her words trailed away and she looked at Hazel in surprise when her daughter gave a great peal of laughter.

'Gosh, Mum, were you worried about consanguinity or whatever it is that stops people marrying their relations?'

'Well, I—'

'Well, you don't have to. I don't think it applies in our case. I mean, we aren't that closely related and in any case, no one would know because your birth certificate has William Weston down as your father.'

'You mean . . .?' Daisy wondered how she felt about this, but Hazel cut in again.

'No I don't, so stop interrupting. Tim is

great; we are terrific friends, but he is more like a brother than anything else. In fact, he is my favourite brother. It's Maureen he is nuts about.' She looked round, noticing for the first time she and her mother were alone. 'I'll dig her out of her room and she can tell you herself.'

'Maureen,' Hazel commanded as she brought her back into the room, 'tell Mum about you and Tim. She's got some weird idea that I—that he and I . . .'

Daisy shook her head. 'I seem to have got it all wrong. I thought it was Maureen and Derek and you and Tim. How does Derek fit in?'

'He doesn't—in the way you mean, Auntie Daisy,' Maureen explained. 'Tim persuaded him to come along to make a foursome.'

'Auntie Vi thinks Maureen is too young to get serious,' Hazel, who could never keep silent for long, took up the story, 'so Tim and Maureen are playing it cool—on the surface, anyway—till Maureen is twenty-one, then they will announce their engagement.'

'I . . . see,' Daisy murmured. 'I gather you and Derek didn't strike sparks off one another?'

'Absolutely not. We really are just friends. I am footloose and fancy free and intend to stay that way for a long time. I have come out here to see the world, not tie myself down.' She wanted to beg her mother to give James a chance but thought that she had said enough, or more than enough, and managed to swallow the words. Instead, she just said quietly, 'Please don't do anything silly, Mum. You're needed on this side of the world at the moment.'

Daisy's only reply was, 'I think I had better go.' As she stood up and moved to the door, Hazel stared at her, afraid she had said far too much, then Daisy added, 'Or I shall never be up to get that plane.'

Hazel stared at her for a moment then flung her arms round her.

'Oh, Mum. Does that mean? Are you coming with us? To New Zealand?'

'Daisy's lips curved in a half smile. 'You've just talked me into it.'

'We shall pick you up at nine-thirty—sharp.' She stepped back and grinned teasingly. 'Auntie Vi is relying on you to be a chaperone.'

CHAPTER THIRTY-SIX

It took Daisy all the way back to come to terms with Hazel's verbal onslaught. It was the charge that she always chose to do what she perceived as the right thing rather than what she really wanted to do that hit home hardest. By the time she reached the house, she had admitted to herself that this was true and made a vow to change. The tremor of anticipatory excitement at the prospect of seeing James again gave her cause to believe she was succeeding.

'I suppose you think I am mean, narrow-minded and domineering.' Violet astonished Daisy by breaking what had been a rather long silence as they sat together over the evening meal.

'No, no, why on earth should I?' Daisy tried to sound convincing. When Violet remained silent, she realized she had to say more. 'I do think that you are sometimes a bit . . . well, repressive, with Maureen.'

'Not wanting her to go on this trip, not wanting her to get a flat. Is that what you mean?'

'Yes, and—' She was about to mention Tim but thought she had already said enough. She changed to: 'No doubt you consider me weak and overindulgent.'

'Well . . .' Violet murmured. 'By the way, what was in your letter? Not bad news, I hope?'

'Not really. Susan is expecting a baby.'

'So, you will be a grandmother. Well, that's good news, isn't it?' She looked at Daisy's face. 'Why don't you look ecstatic? Was there something else?'

'Giles has broken his ankle, Susan has dreadful morning sickness and her parents are off on some luxury holiday somewhere so she can't call on her mother to help.'

324

'So they called on you instead. Knowing you, I suppose that means that you are heading back to England to play the saint instead of to New Zealand where you might just enjoy yourself. Am I right?'

Daisy shook her head. 'Not this time. I have had such a dressing down from Hazel that I have no alternative but to go to New Zealand—as planned.'

Violet stared at her then, surprisingly, laughed. 'Thank goodness for that. I wouldn't like to think of those girls without you to keep an eye on them. That's if you have one to spare—an eye, I mean. From what I gather, you might be the one in need of a chaperone.'

'What on earth are you talking about?'

'I took a phone call while you were out. This "James" person you tried to pass off as some sort of relative; he was checking the flight time and wanted to reassure you that he would be there at the airport to meet you. We had quite a chat. I thought he sounded . . . well, very nice indeed.' Violet's voice took on quite an arch tone and Daisy felt the warm colour rising up her throat and neck. 'Go for it, Daisy—and good luck!'

By the time they boarded the plane, Daisy was asking herself if she had made the right decision. Had she gone home, she knew that Giles and Susan would have been pleased to see her, if only for selfish reasons, but she was not at all sure about James, even less about her own feelings which ricocheted from longing to see him again to a bleak conviction that the whole thing would turn out to be a total disaster. She huddled into her seat and into her thoughts, leaving the young people to their excited chatter. She was very aware that she was of a different generation from them.

If Daisy could have turned back on to the plane when they landed, she would have done so. She moved through the landing formalities like a zombie, then they were through and facing the friends and relatives waiting to meet the passengers. Hazel, of course, was the first to spot him.

'There he is!' Her arm shot up in greeting. 'Uncle James! Here!' she yelled. Slowly her arm came down and she turned to her mother. 'Who is that with him?'

Her voice was low and to Daisy sounded strangely awestruck, but she couldn't think about that now; her heart was thumping, there was a singing in her ears and she knew her lips had stretched into an absurdly wide smile as she and James drew closer through the crowd. It seemed entirely natural to drop her cases and let his arms enfold her.

'Daisy, you've come. Welcome!' His lips moved against her hair and she sighed.

'It was a long journey,' she told him, and both of them knew they weren't talking about the flight she had just taken.

They drew apart reluctantly, aware that

there were introductions to be made.

'This is my niece Maureen and—and this is Tim Sanders.' This was not the moment to go into complicated relationships. 'Dr James Crutchley. And this, of course, James, is little Nutmeg.' She expected a repudiation of the childish nickname from Hazel, but Hazel was gazing at the young man standing by James. To be accurate, they were gazing at each other, both looking quite bemused.

'My stepson, Christopher,' James began, adding, 'This is Daisy's daughter, Hazel.'

'I know,' Christopher said, his eyes still on Hazel. 'She is the little Nutmeg you told me about, but you didn't say she had grown up so beautifully.'

James was about to say he hadn't known that when Tim waved vigorously and shouted to a woman hurrying towards them through the thinning crowd. They fell into each other's arms then Tim disengaged himself and introduced her as his mother. He then took Maureen's hand and pulled her forward. 'This, Mum, is Maureen,' he told her, his face shining with such obvious pride that Daisy wondered how she could ever have imagined there was anything between him and Hazel. It was only when they went off together that Daisy realized Maureen was going to stay with Tim's family. Well, so much for her chaperoning.

James smiled at her. 'Journeys end in lovers'

327

meetings,' he said softly. She nodded in agreement as she and James turned to follow Christopher and Hazel who seemed to know where they were going.

EPILOGUE

Daisy looked up with a smile as Violet crossed the lawn and dropped down in the deckchair at her side.

'What time does James get in tomorrow?' Violet didn't wait for an answer before adding, 'It was nice of you to decide to be married here.'

'It was wonderful of you to suggest it, Vi.'

'Well, tradition has it that the bride marries from her own home and it was a bit of a hike to go back to England. I'm sorry Giles and Susan aren't coming.'

'So am I, but Hazel is here and Tim has agreed to give me away. I bet people will think that strange.' She chuckled to herself. 'You have been wonderful, Violet, making me feel at home here. I'm sorry I was such a poor chaperone to the girls, but . . . well . . .'

'You were otherwise occupied.' Violet's tone was dry, but her smile was warm. 'It all turned out for the best. Maureen met all Tim's relatives in New Zealand and,' she could not resist adding, 'look what happened to Hazel.'

Daisy smiled dreamily. 'It was some holiday.' And that, she thought, was the understatement of the age.

'Why didn't you say anything on the ship?' Daisy had asked when she and James had found themselves alone at last.

James had shrugged slightly. 'I suppose the memory of the last time I had "said something" was too clear. I was afraid that if I did, I might never see you again.'

'Well, you nearly did—never see me again, I mean, by not saying anything. Did you mean what you said? At the airport, about "lovers' meetings"? Or were you just quoting, and thinking about the young people?'

'I didn't give them a thought. I was thinking of us,' he had admitted.

'Yes' Daisy had murmured, ' "lovers" meetings.' She lifted her head and, reaching up, kissed him on the lips. It was as sweet as she remembered, and so was what followed.

'Come on, he'll be here tomorrow. Stop dreaming.' Violet's voice brought her back to the present with a start.

'Oh, Vi,' her voice was suddenly thick with emotion, 'I am so lucky, not only to have found James again but to have you as a sister—and such a lovely daughter.'

'That goes for both of us.' Violet sounded gruff. 'How about a cup of tea to celebrate—or something stronger?'

'Something stronger, I think.'

Laughing together, the sisters made their way back into the house.